PRAISE FOR AMINA AKHTAR

Almost Surely Dead

"Amina Akhtar's *Almost Surely Dead* is a witty, fresh psychological thriller that's part stalker thriller, part ghost story. This book took turns I never saw coming. I was up all night, tearing through the pages as the mysterious pieces came together, leading to an explosive conclusion."
—Mindy Kaling

"Twisty, chilling, and original, *Almost Surely Dead* is an absolutely addictive page-turner. I couldn't put it down."
—Meg Gardiner, #1 *New York Times* bestselling author

"A shocking act of violence opens the door to a terrifying mystery in this eerie, addictive thriller from Amina Akhtar."
—Chuck Wendig, bestselling author of *The Book of Accidents*

"I didn't think Amina Akhtar could get better, but she has—crafting a wholly unique and mesmerizing novel that is impossible to categorize or forget. Part thriller, part family saga, part supernatural horror, *Almost Surely Dead* will surprise you in the best way possible and leave you thinking about this magnificent book for a long time after you're done. A powerhouse."
—Alex Segura, bestselling author of *Secret Identity*

"Full of energy, suspense, and the frightening possibility of the supernatural, *Almost Surely Dead* is a spine-chilling thrill of a book that will grip you from the very first page and refuse to let go. A gripping gothic of the true crime podcasting era."
—S. C. Lalli, international bestselling author of *Are You Sara?*

"What's a girl to do when the universe seems to want you dead? The answer is nothing you'd expect—but everything you'd want from one of the most exciting thriller writers in the business. *Almost Surely Dead* is a sparkling, twisted gem of a book, a riotously funny and deeply unsettling examination of the ways in which we are—and in which we refuse to be—defined by our pasts. This is Akhtar's best work yet, and I loved every word."

—Elizabeth Little, bestselling author of *Dear Daughter*

"Amina Akhtar isn't a writer; she's a word magician, a wonderful comedian who juggles the darkest themes and the ugly things that make us human, the young, smart, fashion-savvy auntie who knows where the bodies are buried and reminds you to call your mom. And she keeps getting better with every book. *Almost Surely Dead* is a witty, wildly entertaining novel that dips its toes in the supernatural while delivering social commentary, highlighting the realities of the Pakistani diaspora, and dancing with the ghosts and superstitions we all carry in our blood. Don't miss it."

—Gabino Iglesias, Bram Stoker Award–winning author of *The Devil Takes You Home*

"Akhtar coils constant paranoia, flash-forward dread, and family tragedy into an electric threat of a novel. This book will have you glancing over your shoulder. A unique thriller."

—Hailey Piper, Bram Stoker Award–winning author of *No Gods for Drowning*

"*Almost Surely Dead* is such a masterful slow burn of a mystery it'll singe your fingertips. Amina Akhtar creeps you out, keeps you guessing, and forces you to the edge of your seat, constructing a story that, in the end, is as surprising as it is deeply human."

—Rob Hart, author of *Paradox Hotel*

Kismet

"An amusing takedown of influencer culture."

—*Kirkus Reviews*

"Readers will be curious to see what this talented author does next."

—*Publishers Weekly*

"Akhtar turns her sharp wit on the wellness community and its dark secrets in a thriller [that is] equal parts vicious and funny."

—*USA Today*

"Akhtar brings to her second novel . . . a gimlet-eyed view of Sedona, Arizona's wellness pretensions and a wicked way with one-liners . . . the surprises Akhtar has in store upend assumptions about trauma, healing, and the motivations of those who helicopter into lands they claim to hold sacred."

—*Los Angeles Times*

"New age empowerment goes awry quickly as psychic slips into psycho in *Kismet*, Amina Akhtar's second novel, a Hitchcockian horror thriller set in the red canyons of Sedona, Arizona."

—*Mystery Scene Magazine*

"Twisty, sardonic."

—Oprah Daily

"The alluring world of wellness gets a fatal awakening in Amina Akhtar's darkly humorous thriller *Kismet*."

—PopSugar

"Addictive."

—*The Big Thrill*

"An impressive blend of mystery, thriller, and dark humor that will draw you in almost instantly and not let go until all is revealed in the final pages."

—Bookreporter

"[*Kismet*] skewers the wellness industry of Sedona (Amina Akhtar is now based in Arizona) and also includes a light supernatural touch that's perfectly integrated into the thriller arc as a whole."

—CrimeReads

"Amina Akhtar weaves a wickedly smart tale."

—*Desi News*

"With *Kismet*, Amina Akhtar invites us into the foxhole with Ronnie Khan, a New Yorker stationed in Sedona, just in time for Wellness World War. I loved this book—the claustrophobia of wide 'open' exclusive spaces. Amina teleports us to the passive-aggressive front lines in this dry landscape where caftans and corpses are equally foreboding. You want Ronnie to make a run for it, but she's a real hero—she wants to make a go for it. Lucky for us, she stays. *Kismet* is wicked and smart, a fly-on-the-wall humdinger where a light social gathering spikes your blood pressure. Amina deftly intertwines the earthly with the otherworldly. Read it now so you can be the one telling your friends about *Kismet*."

—Caroline Kepnes, *New York Times* bestselling author of *You*

"Wickedly smart and outrageously entertaining, *Kismet* grabs hold and doesn't let go until a final twist that will have even the savviest readers gasping. Just like the clever, scene-stealing ravens, Akhtar skewers those who deserve it with her trademark wit while also layering in emotional nuance as compelling as the captivating mystery. At once atmospheric, chilling, and thought provoking, *Kismet* will surely be this summer's must-read thriller."

—Brianna Labuskes, bestselling author of *A Familiar Sight*

ALMOST
SURELY
DEAD

OTHER TITLES BY AMINA AKHTAR

Kismet

#FashionVictim

ALMOST SURELY DEAD

Amina Akhtar

MINDY'S BOOK STUDIO

Text copyright © 2024 by Amina Akhtar

Published by Mindy's Book Studio, New York

www.apub.com

Amazon, the Amazon logo, and Mindy's Book Studio are trademarks of Amazon.com, Inc., or its affiliates.

ISBN-13: 9781662507571 (hardcover)
ISBN-13: 9781662507588 (paperback)
ISBN-13: 9781662507595 (digital)

Cover design by Mumtaz Mustafa
Cover image: © Getty Images/EyeEm/Ashvini Sihra / Getty

Printed in the United States of America
First edition

For my dad and his jinn stories

A NOTE FROM MINDY KALING

I love an off-kilter, creepy story that keeps everyone guessing, like *You* or *Get Out*, and Amina Akhtar's new novel, *Almost Surely Dead*, is just that. It's a twisty psychological thriller with themes from desi culture that bring a whole other dimension to the story.

Dunia Ahmed, a newly single, thirtysomething New York City pharmacist, is *almost* murdered when a stranger tries to push her onto the subway tracks. Dunia tries to move on from the fluke attack, but little things are starting to eat at her. Why did that man target her? Why did he have her photo in his pocket? And why does it feel like the job isn't done? Through flashbacks to Dunia's childhood growing up Pakistani American, we learn about desi folklore: What if it's not just a person after Dunia—what if it's something far more sinister?

Amina's writing is so witty and fresh. I was up all night, tearing through the pages as Dunia's life and story came together, leading to an explosive conclusion. I have never read anything quite like this, and I'm so excited to publish it as part of Mindy's Book Studio.

One

I always imagined my life would flash before my eyes when I died. Like a film. But instead I saw nothing. Just pure panic, and my brain went blank.

Wow, this is it? This is all my brain will give me? No saccharine Hallmark moments I never had?

You may think your thoughts will be different as you're dying. But they won't be, not really. Maybe you'll wish you'd had more fun, loved more. I wished this would all be over, and death said, *Sure, why not.* Death is funny like that.

My would-be killer had his arms around me, so tightly I couldn't move. If I tried to shift, he only held on harder. And he was inching forward, closer and closer to the subway tracks. He was going to throw me on them and watch me die.

I was going to become a New York horror story. The sort of tale politicians used to stomp on the less fortunate. Because here I was, feet from the tracks. And then once I landed, a train would take me out. I wondered if the news would show my body, all mangled. Or maybe they'd have the courtesy to leave that out and run a nice photo of me instead. I could imagine my mother's voice yelling at me for not looking prettier today, more together. I hadn't even put proper makeup on, and now I was going to die. She'd warned me that would happen someday. Some concealer wouldn't have killed me. But she was dead, so at least she wouldn't see my photo. Small favor.

I wanted to be brave and step into this moment, embrace it, but instead I screamed. I opened my mouth and let out as much sound as I could. Because maybe I didn't really want to die.

"Help me! Someone help me!" I yelled, my voice louder than I'd thought possible. His arms only tightened around me. He smelled of sweat, of not washing, his body odor the last thing I'd inhale. I wanted to hold my breath. I didn't know this man—my attacker.

That was a lie.

He was my subway boyfriend. The face I saw regularly on my commute. We'd acknowledge each other, a nod, a wry smile. Anything to make commuting in the packed 6 train a little easier. I'd seen him regularly for weeks. He was cute in that way that disheveled white men are. Charming looking, even. He often drew in a sketchbook while I pretended to read a novel.

I'd make up stories about him in my head. One day he'd ask me out. I was single now, and fantasies were the safest way to date.

But now he was trying to kill me. Yet another man who snapped and lashed out at a woman. Being attacked is a little like being in a car accident. There's that moment of panic as you try to figure out what's happening, why your car is airborne. Or, in this case, why I was being pulled backward.

That's followed by disbelief. *This can't be happening, not to me.* And then, reality sets in. All this cycles in milliseconds. It was in these quick moments our caveman ancestors used to save themselves.

Fight, come on! I yelled at myself for not doing more. I slapped his hands, dug my nails in as much as I could. I tried to twist sideways to break his grip. Nothing. My pretend boyfriend held on so tightly, he was probably bruising some organs, maybe some ribs. Did that matter if I was dead?

He pulled me even closer to the tracks, and my terror went into overload. I'd read about this happening to people, and now it was happening to me.

Useless thoughts filled my head. Would the train go over me? Or would the force pulverize my body, turning my physical self into mist? Would it be fast? Would I feel the train hit me? Hear it? Your sense of hearing is the last thing to go, so they say. I bet I'd hear the squealing brakes, maybe some screams. Maybe I'd scream too.

This was not how I wanted things to end. Not that I had thought about it that much, beyond wanting to end my life myself at times. But not like this.

Part of me wanted to give up, go limp. This was the end; why fight it? But a more primal part of me, my lizard-brain side, kicked in. I wanted to live. At least right now I did.

"Help me!" My voice came out smaller and raspy this time. I needed to be louder. I took a deep breath and screamed as loudly as I could. "Help! He's going to kill me!" I yelled and cried. I kicked and flailed and tried everything to get away from him and get people's attention.

Mere seconds had passed since he grabbed me. And yet, it felt like I had been in this moment forever, a time loop in purgatory where I'd have to relive my death over and over again. I squirmed and tried to break free, but he still had the vise grip around me. I tried doing a motorcycle kick they'd taught us in grade school. Kick the shin and scrape down. He didn't even grunt. It was as if he couldn't feel anything. No pain. He just held on tighter.

My yelling had worked. Several guys rushed over to help, and others screamed and shouted at the man. They surrounded us and kept him from moving any closer to the tracks. I saw phones up, filming us. Me. *God, please don't let this be on the news tonight.*

"Let go of her!"

"What the hell, man?" There was so much yelling now. It was louder than my own heartbeat, which pounded in my ears.

They pried his arms away, and I lurched forward, gasping. I put my hand out to brace my fall.

All New Yorkers have one giant, collective fear of being thrown on the subway tracks. That, and falling through a subway grate. But these two moments were when other New Yorkers would step in to help you. Every other time you were on your own.

My helpers had my attacker surrounded, holding his arms. The man stared at me before his face contorted into full loathing and he growled at me. At all of us, but really at me. Full-on growled, like he wasn't even human. And I was his prey, his target, his reason for fury. The charming smiles from our commutes no longer existed.

He looked so normal, even now. Just an average white guy in skinny jeans and Converse, possibly hitting his forties. Probably artsy, with hair that he didn't tame. Maybe he had kids and lived with his wife in Park Slope. Or he was an aging Bushwick hipster who lived in a refurbished loft. Our moments of kinship on commutes had become my favorite times of the day.

Why did he want me dead?

He stopped moving, stopped trying to free himself. He stood straight, his arms relaxing, as if a switch had been flipped and he was no longer dangerous. The arms holding him let go but hovered in case he tried anything. He stared at me, his face changing again. He looked sad, rueful, almost apologetic.

Everyone stood close by warily, waiting for the cops. By now another train was rumbling in the tunnel. He didn't look away from me, not even to see the train. I stared back at him, trying to figure out why he wanted me dead.

The rushing air made my skin crawl. Something was going to happen.

"I had no choice," my attacker said quietly, with that sad, strange smile on his face. No one moved. It looked like smoke was around him, but that wasn't possible. Nothing was burning.

And then he waved—a quick hand gesture—before jumping backward onto the tracks just as the train pulled into the station. His blue eyes held mine, and that moment would haunt me forever. His eyes seeing into me, as if he knew my every thought. As if he knew I should have died. That by killing me, he would be doing me a favor. And then his eyes, head, and body vanished under the train.

Everyone screamed. The squeal of the brakes was deafening. I covered my ears to drown it out. It was like every person in pain in the world was wailing and shrieking at once.

I blinked. Drops sprayed my face. It was blood, and I was covered in it. We all were. The men who had helped me, the subway platform, the train itself.

I stared at the chaos unfolding before me. The train conductor was crying, before throwing up in a trash can. He'd come to work today, and then he'd killed someone. His train had hit a man, and that's whose blood was on us now.

I didn't even know his name.

Two

HOST ONE: Hello, everyone. I am so excited to welcome you to your new obsession, a podcast we've been working on for over a year. I'm Amanda Roberts—

HOST TWO: And I'm Danielle McGuire. We are two journalists and true crime fanatics who fell deep into one case. It's had us transfixed!

AMANDA ROBERTS: That's right! We're talking about Dunia Ahmed, of course. You may recall she vanished a year and a half ago. But prior to her disappearance, she was almost murdered on the subway. And then so many bizarre things happened to her. Some background on her: Dunia was thirty-six, single, and a pharmacist. She lived on the Upper East Side of New York. Her fiancé had recently dumped her, and her mother had passed away. Dunia was of Pakistani descent. You've probably seen photos of her—absolutely gorgeous, dark hair and eyes. But what's always struck me was how normal she seemed. Like, how could someone like her become a victim?

DANIELLE MCGUIRE: Right? If it could happen to her, it can happen to any one of us. Which is why we're doing this podcast. Since Dunia disappeared, there's been no official trace of her. There have been unofficial reports of sightings of her—though no one has been able to confirm them, even with photos. Which made us ask: What happened to her? Where did she go? Is she even alive? Also, what the hell, Dunia? Tell us what happened to you!

AMANDA ROBERTS: We're determined to bring attention to her case and see if we can finally get to the bottom of things—for her family and for her. But also, we need you to get as obsessed as we are with Dunia. We're going to tell her story chronologically, from the beginning. Some parts of this story made the news, but a lot didn't. Not everyone is aware of the story, so be patient if we're going slow. We'll try to avoid spoilers, so if you know what's about to happen or who has been charged for various things, please don't ruin this for everyone else. We know one person was charged, but we have to be honest: There's way more going on here. We're sure of it.

DANIELLE MCGUIRE: And we'll hopefully get the police to take another look at things. That's our goal, at least. Because we think everyone who had a hand in this woman's disappearance should be held accountable.

AMANDA ROBERTS: How cool will it be if the police end up solving this because of us? It would be legendary, right?

DANIELLE MCGUIRE: Totally! We'll be so famous then! We could have our own Netflix show! The police are willing to talk to us, which is fabulous news. I want to introduce you all to someone who knew Dunia, who worked on her case. Detective Alvarez was the lead on this particular case from the beginning. Detective, welcome. What can you tell us about how this started?

DETECTIVE ALVAREZ: Thanks for having me. I have to state this is an open investigation, so I can only tell you so much. But we are hoping this podcast will help us find new leads.

AMANDA ROBERTS: Let's start when you first met Dunia.

DETECTIVE ALVAREZ: The subway incident. I hate those calls. The kinds where no matter what you do, you can't save someone. Bad things happen, anywhere, anytime.

AMANDA ROBERTS: Of course, it must be hard to work those cases. But Dunia's case was different, wasn't it?

DETECTIVE ALVAREZ: It was unique, yes. I didn't think so at the time. But looking back . . . I wish I knew then what I know now.

DANIELLE MCGUIRE: Did you think anything about her background was a factor here?

DETECTIVE ALVAREZ: Her background?

AMANDA ROBERTS: Dunia was Muslim, correct? Was there any investigation into that part of her life?

DETECTIVE ALVAREZ: Her religion wasn't relevant to the case.

DANIELLE MCGUIRE: But she had some beliefs in the supernatural that some people have suggested explain things, or at least her behavior.

DETECTIVE ALVAREZ: I investigate people, crimes, not ghost stories.

Three

"Is she okay?"

"She's in shock."

"Did she know him?"

"Where are the cops?"

People were talking over me, about me, but not to me. I was the victim; no one wanted to get too close. That kind of luck could rub off on people. Not that I blamed them. Someone put a blanket on me despite it being August and that I was sweating. I shrugged it off me. I wanted to get the hell away from everyone.

"Give her space," a woman ordered. I didn't know her, but I was thankful. I wanted to go home. I was mortified I'd made such a scene. All this fuss was over me.

Some paramedics checked me out, and minus some scratches from when I was pulled from him, I was okay. Physically. But that was all they cared about.

"You'll probably have some bruising." That was the least of my worries.

Police officers stood all around me, like they were guarding someone important. For whatever reason, that made me laugh. And soon I was crying from laughing so hard.

"Hey, are you okay?" It was the woman. She didn't look like a typical cop, but she had the authority of one. She had her dark, curly hair pulled back in a ponytail and wore a blazer. Her skin color was the same as mine. She was taller than me, five foot seven or so to my five foot two.

I nodded. "I'm sorry, this whole thing . . ."

"It's a lot. I'm Detective Alvarez. Mind if I ask you some questions?" She had a nice smile.

I nodded. "Okay."

"Did you know him? Your attacker?"

I paused. I did know him, didn't I? "Only from commuting. A familiar face day in and out. But we never spoke."

We had been on the uptown 6 train from Grand Central to my stop, Eighty-Sixth Street. He'd caught my eye, and I smiled because that was our thing. I should have known better. Never make eye contact with anyone on the train. It was basic New York Woman 101.

"Did he say anything prior to the attack?"

"No. And I had headphones on." She should talk to the other subway riders. But they'd cleared out or stayed on the train, oblivious to death being so close to them. It was just me and the witnesses—the guys who'd saved me and the ones who saw him die. The station was now closed to everyone else.

"What happened next?" she gently prodded.

"I got out at my stop and then felt hands around me." I heard the tremor in my voice, and I hated how shaken up I was. "And then he pulled me back and dragged me toward the tracks." I swallowed. I didn't want to cry in front of this woman. "And I froze. For a moment. I didn't know what to do."

"That's normal and understandable." She nodded her head. I knew what she was doing. She was trying to relate to me, to keep me calm. I appreciated the effort.

I wanted to tell her how I'd imagined him wanting to kiss me, or at least getting my number. How I was disappointed that he only wanted me dead. But that sounded pathetic even to me.

"And then I yelled for help, and those guys came over and got him off me. And then . . . he just stood there. And he smiled at me, and it was so strange. It was almost apologetic? Like he was sorry for what he had done?"

"Did he say anything?"

My eyes widened. "It was something like 'I had no choice.' I have no idea what that means." She nodded. "He stared at me as the . . . as the train"—my voice caught—"as the train hit him. He just stared at me." There was smoke, I wanted to tell her. But I was certain I'd imagined that.

The detective put her hand on my shoulder but didn't comfort me otherwise.

"This was very helpful. The officers said your name was Ahmed?"

"Dunia Ahmed." I spelled it for her and gave her my contact info.

"Is there anyone in your life who would want to hurt you?" I didn't mean to, but I twitched when she asked that.

"My ex," I whispered. "He came to my work—near my work today. He's been trying to talk, but I'm not interested." I gave his name and number to her. Did I really think David could do this? I wasn't sure. His behavior had become so erratic. Not just texts and emails but following me around, showing up at my apartment at all hours. "But he would never hurt me," I added hastily. She glanced at me before continuing to write things down. I'd bet she'd heard that before.

"I may reach out to update you on this, if that's okay."

"Of course." I pointed with my chin. "Can I thank those guys?"

The detective nodded and motioned for someone to bring them over to me.

My eyes were tearing up again. *Dammit, keep it together.* The men didn't know each other, but somehow, they were going to be friends for life. I was sure of it.

"Thank you. I don't know what else to say. You saved my life."

They had blood spray on them still, and on their clothes. We all did. They'd be in therapy for this, but then probably be lauded as heroes by the news. I, on the other hand, was a victim now.

A police officer gave me a ride home to Eighty-Ninth Street, even though it wasn't far. I just wanted to take a shower and never, ever get on the subway again.

After locking my dead bolt and putting the chain on, I ran to my bathroom and heaved. There wasn't much in my stomach except coffee and bile, but it came up. I couldn't stop shaking and crying. That man had almost killed me. He wanted me dead. And now, he was nothing but blood spray and a mangled body. My stomach roiled from what had happened.

I looked up into the mirror as I washed my face, and my eyes didn't look right. They were wild, feral looking. Like I wasn't myself. The stray blood spots had to go. I rubbed my face until my tan skin turned red.

I had almost died. Was this close to it. And yet, by the grace of those guys, I wasn't. I didn't chalk this up to a guardian angel because I didn't believe in that sort of thing. If angels and demons were real, then my life wouldn't be a total mess right now. My parents wouldn't be dead. My fiancé wouldn't be an ex.

I turned the shower on as hot as I could and crouched down in my tub, letting the blood wash away. I closed my eyes. All I could see were his eyes. They were so clear, so blue, and so heartbreakingly sad. I knew I'd see them in my dreams forever. I used to look forward to seeing his eyes after work.

I didn't understand what had happened. Or who he was. Or what had triggered this. But mostly, why me?

I sat there for a bit, until my knees screamed as I stood. Then I let the too-hot water hit my face, slightly scalding me. Maybe it would burn my face off, and no one would ever come near me again. The thought made me giggle, in a deranged sort of way.

I got out of the shower, put on my robe, combed out my hair, and poured myself a glass of wine. I wasn't much of a drinker, but I needed something to calm my nerves. Every time I closed my eyes, I saw him smile at me, wave, and then kill himself.

Death shouldn't unnerve me this much; I was used to people dying around me. But this time it was different, and I couldn't shake how it made me feel: like I hadn't escaped, I'd only postponed things.

Four

Dunia, age five

I liked the doll in front of me. She was pretty. Her hair wasn't like mine, it was light, and she was smiling. It looked like my Barbie doll, but with cake. Ammi loved making doll cakes. My cakes were always pink and white. And the dress was full of frosting and flowers.

"I love it!"

Ammi smiled. She looked like a movie star with her hair up. She had on a shalwar kameez. She was more beautiful than my cake. Abu used to say it was love at first sight for them.

I clapped my hands while my parents sang "Happy Birthday" to me. They made it sound silly. "Happy burrr-dayyyy tooh youuuuu!" I looked at Baba, and he smiled at us. Everyone loved birthdays.

I held my breath and closed my eyes and wished that I'd be the best Dunia in the world; that way Ammi would love me like she loved Nadia, my big sister. I'd be so good, she wouldn't be able to not love me. And her face wouldn't look so sad all the time. Then I blew out the candles. The smoke drifted up in the air. The cake was vanilla, my favorite. I ate one whole piece and wanted more, but Ammi stopped me with a shake of her head.

It was just my family, my parents, my big sister. And Baba, my favorite of them all. We'd run around and chase each other. Abu would chase me while Baba, my uncle, looked on and laughed in delight.

My cake didn't have my name on it. Instead, my mother had written "My World." Because my name meant *world* in Urdu. Abu made her do that, because I was his world, not hers. We smiled and laughed when Abu said, "Say cheese!" Photos were very important to Ammi. She liked to show them off.

Happy birthday to My World.

I was wearing a red velvet dress that Ammi made for me. It had soft bows, and I liked touching them. She made our party dresses when she had time, and I loved them. It was a moment when I could pretend everything was okay. That I was loved like Nadia was.

I opened presents and ran around and fell down, scraping my knees. Abu picked me up and, to cheer me, gave me some pink icing. He always smelled good. I closed my eyes and took a deep breath.

"Beti, no crying on your birthday," he said. "If you stop, I'll tell you your favorite story at bedtime."

I nodded, wiping my eyes. "The princess and the jinn?"

"Okay. But don't tell your mother." He winked at me. Later that night he sat on my bed. Nadia got to stay up later than me because she was a big girl. We shared a room. "There was a jinn."

"What was his name?"

"Jamal."

"Like Ayesha Auntie's son?" I hated Jamal.

"Yes, like him. He is not a jinn," Abu added before I could ask. I wasn't so sure. Jamal was pretty evil. "Jamal one day saw the most beautiful woman, the princess."

"What was her name?"

"Dunia," he joked.

"No! I don't want the jinn to take Dunia. Name her something else."

"Okay, what about Sabiha."

I thought about it. I didn't know any Sabihas. "Okay, that's a good name."

"May I continue? So, Jamal saw the beautiful Sabiha. She had beautiful long black hair that looked like silk, and her voice was so melodious, she could make the birds stop singing and listen to her instead. And one day the jinn heard her sing while she was in the garden."

"Do jinn like music?"

"Very much. And art and poetry. Jamal the Jinn heard Sabiha sing, and he fell madly in love with her. Without even seeing her. So he went to her father, the king. And told him he would give the king anything in the world in exchange for his daughter. The king refused."

"Why?"

"Because his daughter wasn't something to trade away. And the jinn left. But he came back the next day, disguised as a prince. But the king knew he was a jinn and sent him away. He came back the next day dressed as a rich businessman. And again, the king sent him away.

"The jinn was angry, because he wanted Sabiha all to himself. And he was insulted the king kept saying no. So one night, he snuck into the garden and tricked her into asking him to take her away."

"Why did she want to go away?"

"She didn't. But the jinn said he could make sure she stayed in her garden forever and asked if she'd like that. She did. And once she said yes—even though she didn't know what she'd agreed to—he stole her away."

"Did she try to escape?"

"No, because jinn can create a make-believe world for their captives. Sabiha never realized she'd been taken and instead thought she was still in her garden, singing to the birds. So while she was in her garden, all of her family and friends grew old and died."

"How do they do that? Make you believe?" What if I were in my make-believe world right now? What if a jinn had already taken me?

"Magic. That's one of their talents."

"So, if I get taken, I won't know?"

"That's right. That way, you stay with the jinn. But you won't be taken. I promise. We have you protected. And if you don't go willingly, they can't take you. But they might trick you, so be careful."

"Why do they trick us?"

He shrugged. "Those are the rules for them. They have to make you want to stay with them and agree to it. Otherwise, no dice. But, and this is key, they can hurt people who don't agree. So we'll avoid them, and no one gets hurt!"

My eyes widened. They'd hurt me? "How do I avoid them?" I was panicking at the thought of a jinn coming into my room.

"Well, your mother does the secret kalma, right? That keeps you safe. No jinn can get near you. Okay?"

"Okay. If a jinn asked to marry me, would you say no?"

"Of course I would! You belong with us."

He kissed me good night, and I tried to sleep. I kept thinking about the jinn. Well, I didn't have a singing voice like Princess Sabiha, so I'd be okay. I hoped.

Abu left my door open, because I didn't like it closed. And I could hear him and Ammi fighting.

"Why do you tell her these stories? You know how she is."

"It's just a little fun," my dad said.

"No, she'll have scary dreams and then sleepwalk." Ammi was mad. She didn't like that I sleepwalked. I didn't, either, but I couldn't stop it.

"She'll be fine."

"She won't! You put these ideas in her head. And then she acts . . . the way she does. I'm tired of it. No more scary stories." They always fought because of me.

"They're just stories," Abu said.

"Are they? Rahmi started with the same stories. Look where she is now." Rahmi was Ammi's sister. Rahmi Khala was the family pagal. That meant crazy. She'd been sent to a hospital in Lahore, and we no longer saw her when we visited Pakistan.

I pulled the pillow over my head to cover my ears after I heard that. The last thing you wanted was to be called a pagal.

I wanted to yell that I was fine! But I kept my mouth shut and closed my eyes and thought to myself, "I won't sleepwalk. I won't sleepwalk." Over and over until I was sure my brain absorbed it. That way, it wouldn't let me get up. That had to work, right? Then Abu could keep telling me stories and Ammi wouldn't be so mad. Everyone would be happy.

"I am not a pagal," I whispered furiously.

Five

I woke up thinking of my dad. He died when I was little. My protector, my best friend. Maybe that was why the attention of the subway man made me misinterpret the situation. Daddy issues happened to the best of us.

My dad was always on my mind, mainly because I was blamed for his death. I know, heavy. But now in my waking hours, he was replaced with the subway guy. Those blue eyes flashed in my head, and that was all I could see. I blinked the image away.

My phone was blowing up when I finally got out of bed. My picture was apparently on the front page of the *NY Post*, and everyone I'd ever met felt the need to send me pictures of it that morning. "Subway Sicko Attacks Woman!" read the headline in big letters. I looked stunned. Shocked. My eyes were opened too wide, my dark circles making me look ill. My face had droplets of blood on it.

I could almost hear my aunties telling me why this was my fault. They were like the furies in my head, tutting at everything I did and said and wore.

"Please don't let any aunties see this," I whispered to my apartment, as if God were real and listening to me.

I didn't want to see my photo. Any of it. This was my nightmare.

I texted Kendra that I was okay and that I was hiding but loved her.

"I'm coming over." There was no arguing with her. I knew that and was relieved my best friend was coming. I showered again because I couldn't be too clean. I washed off imaginary blood from my face and hands. I scrubbed until my skin felt raw. And then I went to pick up bagels across the street. I felt like every person was staring at me.

Just get your coffee and food and go. You got this. I took the bag from the cashier, my hand shaking. The cover of the paper was next to the register.

"That's you?" the cashier asked. I'd been coming here since I moved into this apartment, four years ago.

"No, not me." I shook my head. "That poor woman." I ran out before any follow-up questions could be asked.

———

"Are you okay?!" Those were the first words out of Kendra's mouth at my door.

"I'm fine! I promise. I got us bagels." I wasn't fine. But I didn't want to dump this on Kendra. She had enough on her plate.

She hugged me tight, and I smelled her perfume, which was an intoxicating scent of cedar and leather. She always smelled great. I hoped she did a perfume line next. Kendra had her own beauty line that she launched after pharmacy school—where we met.

"I'm so grateful you're okay. Oh my God. That's scary." She sat on my sofa, and I poured the coffee into mugs. "Tell me everything—if you're up for it."

I wasn't, but I would. I told her what happened, how he grabbed me.

"Wait, was this the guy you'd been flirting with on the subway?"

"Flirting is stretching it. We mostly smiled. I'd never spoken to him."

"God, why are men so messed up?"

"I wish I knew." I laughed to show that I was okay. That this one violent act hadn't traumatized me in any permanent way. That I wasn't still terrified to go on the subway even though I was. I was a survivor, and I'd get through this. "I was at the end of the train and walking, and I felt hands go around my waist and yank me back."

Kendra gasped, her hand fluttering near her mouth. She was wearing a nude lipstick, and it made me want to find my own nude color, which was an ongoing exercise in futility. Everything was too beige or too pink for me. Her skin tone was darker than mine and not as yellow. I never liked my color. I was either too pale or too dark, depending on who was criticizing me. And the circles under my eyes defied every bit of concealer I layered on. But Kendra was stunning and had perfect skin. She was the one who got me to learn to love how I looked, despite years of aunties telling me I wasn't good enough.

"Oh my God. This is scarier than I realized."

"He started dragging me toward the tracks, so I screamed bloody murder, and some random guys helped me."

"And then he jumped?" Her brown eyes pierced into me. I'd tell her all of it, because she was family to me. Better than my actual kin.

I nodded. "He stopped struggling, so they moved their hands off him, and then he looked at me. It was so weird. He sorta smiled at me. And said something like he had to do it. And then he jumped in front of the next train, and blood went everywhere."

"Holy shit."

"Yeah, huh." I didn't succeed in pulling off the brave act I was doing. She saw through me. My voice had cracked, and I blinked away tears.

Kendra reached for my hand, and I left it where it was. Normally, I wasn't a toucher. Not for any particular reason—it's just that I grew up in a house full of nontouchers. No daily hugs; it wasn't what we did. At least not with me. I don't think anyone hugged me after my dad died until I moved away from my family.

"Are you okay? Like, really okay?"

"I am. I'm shaken up. But it's New York, right? We always read that this sort of thing can happen. And I lost one of my AirPods! I have to buy a whole new pair!" I joked, hoping to lighten the mood.

"That's the most messed up thing I've ever heard." She stared at me, and I had to look away. Kendra always had a knack for seeing right through me. In pharmacy school, she knew when I was struggling and would offer study sessions. She was the sort to get good scores, but she worked her ass off.

"Everyone expects a Black person to fail, so I'm going to ace this," she would say, and she *would* ace it. Kendra's entire plan was laid out, and she knew then what she wanted: her own beauty line. She worked at various skin care companies after graduating and had recently launched Joy Skincare, named after her mother. Kendra always said skin care brought her joy, and she wanted to share that with the world. She'd done it after being tired of using what she called white-women skin care and makeup. She was a visionary. I, on the other hand, was in pharmacy school because I never knew what else to do with myself. I had been rejected from every medical school I applied to, much to my mother's dismay. Become a pharmacist or live with my mother forever. And anything was better than being home with the silent accusations that hung in the air.

"It was not what I had in mind for a Friday night." I laughed, but it turned into a yawn. "And I ran into David. Or rather, he stalked me at the Starbucks by work earlier yesterday, before the subway." I told her how he'd grabbed my arm and a woman had intervened. My ex was always determined to be a part of my life.

"Do you think he's involved in this?"

"I don't know. I don't think David could be involved. Just a freak thing, right?" If David was involved, why would that man jump and kill himself? Wouldn't he have just told the police everything instead? "But I gave the cops his info just in case." That interaction with David seemed years away. He'd grabbed my arm; another woman helped me. How many bystanders would save me in a single day?

"I'm glad you're safe. Let's do nothing today."

"Can you do that?" I asked. Kendra was the busiest person I knew. She had appointments and lunches and meetings with investors, even on weekends.

"I can and will. Oh, I brought you some samples." She grinned. A beauty day was exactly what the doctor ordered. I went through the bag eagerly. "There's a new bronzer shade that is going to look stunning on you!"

"How's work going?" I wanted to talk about anything else but me and my brush with death.

"It's okay!" She frowned for just a second.

"Spill it, what's wrong?"

"Just new investor woes. I have this woman who wants me to go public with the company, and she's got great connections, but I don't know. I'm worried it's too much too soon, you know?"

"Do you have to do what she wants?"

"I'm not sure I'm ready. Maybe I'm just scared?" Kendra grimaced, and I reached for her hand to comfort her this time.

"You are ready, Joy is ready. But let me know how I can help."

"You can help by trying out this eye cream for me!"

———

My phone was ringing, and I stared at it, hoping it would stop. It did, only to ring again. My sister, Nadia, was persistent. If I didn't answer, she'd call me until my phone died. We had a complicated relationship, to put it mildly.

I sighed. "Hi, Nadi."

"When were you going to tell me you almost died?"

"It just happened yesterday, so—"

"Dunia, this is not okay."

I didn't bother saying it wasn't my fault, that this happened because of some crazy man. Because once your family thinks you're the source of all things wrong, you can never convince them otherwise.

"You have to be more careful. Maybe New York is just too much for you."

That was the pitch. Get me to move to Texas. Be a nanny to her kids. Be under her watchful eyes, just like I had been my entire life. Do whatever she said and only what she said.

"I'm just glad Ammi isn't alive to see your life unfold like this," she continued.

"I'm fine, I'm alive, and I gotta go." I hung up.

This was when she'd run to my mom and complain, but Mom was dead now. And I wasn't sad about it. I should have been, but wasn't.

I was a difficult child, I knew that. After Abu died, my mom couldn't even look at me. As if I were the one who made his heart stop beating. But she blamed me for it. And I believed her. My entire life I believed her. And so did Nadia.

I wasn't about to let my sister take that role in my life now.

"Abu, why did you marry into a crazy family?" I asked my empty apartment. I didn't think he was listening. I didn't think that was possible. But it made me smile to say it.

Six

Dunia, age five

"Do not touch my things." Nadia said it with a mean face. I never touched her stuff. I knew better. She was not a nice big sister. She'd take my toys, and when I cried, she laughed at me and called me a baby. Ammi only encouraged her.

"She's your big sister. You need to listen to her. Obey her."

When Ammi would say that, Nadia would stick her tongue out at me. I wished I didn't have a sister. But still, I obeyed. I listened. Because good girls did what their elders told them to.

Abu said that I only got one sister in this life and that I had to find ways to get along. But we didn't. Nadia would hit me, and no one stopped her. Except Baba, now and again. He once told me he didn't like Nadia but that I couldn't tell anyone that.

"She doesn't like to play," he complained. But I did, so we played all day, and whenever Nadia would come near us, he'd go to his own room.

Abu would bring me little gifts home from work. He would make drawings for me to cheer me up. He knew I was trying so hard to be a good girl.

My favorite drawing was above my bed in the room I shared with Nadia. It was a picture from one of his stories: the beautiful garden the princess lived in. But one day, I ran to my room to hide from

Ammi, who was in a bad mood again. And my drawing was in pieces on my bed.

"Did you rip my picture?" I asked Nadia.

"Yes."

No sorry, no nothing.

I didn't say anything because she'd tell Ammi. But in my head I thought, "I hate you and wish you were dead."

I never told anyone I felt that way about her, not even Abu-ji. I didn't want him to hate me too. At least I had him, and Baba. When Abu came to tuck me in and tell me stories (even when Ammi said not to), he asked where his drawing was.

I didn't meet his eye. "I don't know."

"Tell me, it's okay."

"Nadia ripped it up," I whispered. Being a tattle was bad.

Abu just nodded and then asked which story I wanted tonight.

"Abu-ji, tell me about the churail." The witch. I loved this story even though it scared me.

"Okay, don't tell your mother." He pretended he didn't want to tell me, but he did. "There was a churail outside our home in Lahore. She had wild hair, and her fingers were crooked."

"Why were her fingers crooked?" I held my hands up and bent my fingers.

"Because she was a jinn, and some jinn don't look all the way human. Some do. She didn't."

"Do some jinn look normal?"

"Some do, but don't worry, there are none here in America." He said it *Amreeka*.

"Okay, good," I said.

"But the churail wanted to come in, and she banged on the door every night for two weeks."

"Did she come inside?"

"No, you can't let them in."

I nodded. Of course you couldn't let them inside. "What happened?"

"She left, but not before promising one of our own would be haunted forever." That was the part that really scared me, but I didn't tell Abu that.

My eyes were wide. "And were they?"

"No! Nothing happened." He laughed.

"Oh. I'm glad. Is she still out there?"

"No, she's long gone, don't worry."

I was worried. If she wanted me, she'd be able to come into the window. I made sure Abu closed and locked it for me.

"Now good night." Abu kissed my forehead and left my door open. Nadia's bedtime was later than mine, so she'd come in to sleep at some point.

I heard Ammi whispering furiously at him.

"Why do you tell her these things? You know she'll get upset."

"She loves the stories."

"You have to stop. I can't deal with how she is because of these stupid tales. No more!"

I felt bad that now I'd gotten Abu in trouble too. And then sad because I loved the stories. Loved them more than almost anything. And Ammi wanted to take them away from me.

Seven

Transcript: *The Disappearance of Dunia Ahmed* podcast

AMANDA ROBERTS: Detective, can you tell us what you know about the sub-way attacker?

DETECTIVE ALVAREZ: His name was Skylar Jones. He was thirty-nine years old. Not married, had an on-again-off-again girlfriend who—at the time—we couldn't locate. We're operating under the theory that he was paid to stalk Dunia. He had cash deposits in his bank account, but we have not been able to trace them beyond that.

DANIELLE MCGUIRE: Is your theory that Dunia's ex hired this guy?

DETECTIVE ALVAREZ: It's a top theory. We don't know who hired him, but we have circumstantial evidence that it may have been someone Dunia had been involved with—

AMANDA ROBERTS: Her ex. So this David guy, what do we know about him?

DETECTIVE ALVAREZ: David Anderson dated Dunia for three years. They split not long before the subway incident happened. She had tried to get a TRO against him, and it was tied up in paperwork.

DANIELLE MCGUIRE: And this is why women don't report things. What delayed the restraining order?

DETECTIVE ALVAREZ: To be honest, just a paperwork mix-up. It happens.

AMANDA ROBERTS: And then women die.

DANIELLE MCGUIRE: So, okay, we have this crazy ex who is stalking Dunia. We have an assassin who was paid, but we don't know by whom. And we have a missing woman. I have to ask: Why hasn't David been arrested?

DETECTIVE ALVAREZ: Speculating is one thing. But in a court of law you have to prove guilt. And we don't have that evidence. I hope we will get it after this podcast airs, but otherwise, this is a cold case. We've interrogated Mr. Anderson numerous times, and we can't find a definitive link to Skylar Jones. It doesn't mean it's not there, just that we haven't found it yet.

AMANDA ROBERTS: Do you think Dunia is alive still?

DETECTIVE ALVAREZ: No, I don't.

DANIELLE MCGUIRE: Maybe she would be alive if she'd been able to get that restraining order.

Eight

I'm wearing a red-and-gold shaadi dress. One my mother picked out. It's fitted so tightly onto me, and I haven't eaten a proper meal in weeks, but it looks stunning. My arms are covered in gold jewelry and mehndi, and I'm ready. This is it. I'm about to be married.

My mom is smiling at me. She's so happy. So proud of me—for once. Even though I'm marrying a gora, a white man. I know I'm supposed to keep my head down, but this is a hybrid wedding. You know, part desi, part American. I glance up at David and smile.

"Babe, you ready?" He grins. "Babe, let's do this."

Babe. Something doesn't feel right with that. *Babe.* But I smile, ready to step forward and say I do, I take this white man to be my husband—

I woke up with a start, my heart racing and my sheets damp with sweat. I wiped the drool off my face. I was in my bed, in my apartment. I wasn't about to get married. That wasn't happening. I also wasn't about to make my mother happy. There was no more feeling happy for her.

It figured my nightmare would be about getting married, not almost dying.

The urge to pick up the phone and call my mom and apologize was so strong, I felt a pain in my chest, like I couldn't breathe. It was as if guilt from generations had been piled onto me, so that her disappointment in me was the only thing that sustained me. Gave me life. I was born to be a failure.

She had always lamented that it was because of my name. Abu named me. Most Pakistani-diaspora names for girls were like Zahra or Ayesha or Amina. But Dunia? That was because I was my dad's world. Ammi hated that.

"Who will marry a girl with a name like that?" she'd complain to him. I was five; why even worry about such things? But she did.

The sleepwalking didn't help either. I was one of those weird kids that would wander the house in my sleep. It drove Ammi insane. She hated it. Abu always told her I'd grow out of it, but I didn't. I still woke up outside my bed. It took some getting used to. Ammi always said that I was going to be the family pagal, replacing her sister, my Rahmi Khala, who—last I heard—was locked away in a hospital somewhere. That was my destiny.

But once I got engaged, it was as if I had become her perfect child. She started doting on me in ways she never had before. Wanting to FaceTime with me and help me pick out shaadi clothes. This all sent me into fits of panic. I think I preferred being ignored. I knew how to navigate that.

I can't say I missed my mom. Not exactly. I loved her, of course. But I couldn't tell you if she felt the same. It was complicated. She loved Nadia, though. So at least I witnessed her being an amazing mother to someone. Me? I was the leftover, the forgotten. I was the child who should have had the grace to die along with my father.

I was relieved she was already dead when David dumped me. Because that phone call would have been worse than anything else I'd endured. Finally going to therapy had helped me understand her. That she was trying to be helpful in her way. But it didn't matter; her words would always crush me. (Nadia filled that role for me when I informed her the wedding was off.)

In a way her dying had deprived me of being able to answer back. Not that I ever would. How do you grieve someone who hated you? I wasn't sure how to, but I was trying.

My alarm blared. Work called. Prescriptions waited for no one, especially not on a Monday.

———

"You had a question on your prescription?" I smiled and tried to look as friendly as possible. We had to, or we'd get negative reviews. Pharmacists were the unloved drug dealers of the world. Maybe if I sold weed, I'd have happier customers.

"Yeah, can I just take it when I want?"

I glanced at the customer and then the sertraline (Zoloft) prescription. "Uh, no, this is a daily medication. If you want an acute medication, you can ask your doctor about Xanax or other similar ones."

My job wasn't exactly the one I'd wanted or dreamed about. But the truth was I'd never dreamed about work. Why would I? I didn't care what I did so long as I had money and supported myself. And I did. Being a pharmacist was lucrative. Boring and annoying, and my days were full of irate patients, but I got paid. And I'd gotten into pharmacy school, which was the only thing about my life at that point that my mother approved of. Granted, it was in New York State, far from her. But that was a bonus as far as I was concerned. (My failed attempts to get into medical school were held over my head for years.)

Most of the questions patients had for me could be googled. But I answered them. Because that's what you did.

Back at my perch filling meds, and the pharm tech—Michael— tapped me on the shoulder.

"There's someone here to see you."

I groaned quietly. Please don't be David. Or the police. So far, no one had mentioned my little incident from Friday. That whole almost-dying thing. Maybe they hadn't seen the news. But I preferred no one talk to me about it. Just pretend it didn't happen and move along. I was good at pretending.

I put a mask on. A metaphorical one, not an actual mask. We'd been told to stop wearing ours despite various viruses having their way with the general population for years now. No, my mask hid me, hid my feelings. My mask was my survival.

"Can I help you?" I asked the South Asian man standing in front of me. He looked to be my age, medium height. Attractive. Did I know him? He looked familiar. He smiled at me.

"Dunia? Do you remember me? I'm Zabir, Arif's cousin."

"Ohhhh." He was Nadia's husband's cousin. "We met at the wedding?"

"Right! I saw you and thought that was you back there just now. I wanted to say hi."

"Well, hi!" I didn't know what else to say. I barely remembered the wedding. I'd had the flu during the entire thing but had to do all the things expected of me regardless, including giving a speech about how amazing my sister was. (My mom helped write that.)

"I—this is awkward—but can we grab a coffee soon? I'd love to reconnect." He looked eager for me to say yes.

My face was burning. Was he asking me out at work? This had to be a family thing, though? Like he was just making nice because we were now kin? Or something?

"Uh, sure." I scribbled down my number. "Great seeing you!" *Please leave, and please no one ask me about him.* I waved as he took the paper and grinned at me.

"I'll call you."

"Great!"

My face felt like it was frozen in a smile. Michael bumped my side.

"Who is that? And tell me everything." I shrugged, slightly mortified as he said that. "Oh, someone left this at the other window for you." He held up a thick linen envelope. My name was written in a beautiful calligraphy. I opened it.

I've found you, it read. What the hell?

"Well, that's not odd." I laughed nervously. Michael laughed with me.

"I found you—at work!" he joked. I put the note in my bag. Maybe it had something to do with my near death; maybe it was nothing.

Nine

Transcript: *The Disappearance of Dunia Ahmed* podcast

AMANDA ROBERTS: Dunia seekers, we have a thrilling surprise today. Please welcome Kendra Wright, Dunia's best friend. If anyone knew Dunia, it was Kendra. Thank you for speaking with us. We're really excited to dive into this mystery but also to get to know Dunia.

KENDRA WRIGHT: Well, you guys were pretty persistent.

AMANDA ROBERTS: How long had you and Dunia been friends?

KENDRA WRIGHT: *Have*, not *had*. She's not dead. She's missing. So please speak about her in present tense.

DANIELLE MCGUIRE: [*throat clears*] Yes, of course. How long *have* you two been friends?

KENDRA WRIGHT: About eight years. She's always been the sweetest person. And so funny. I don't know why this is happening to her. I don't know who'd take her. My family loves her. She's just the kindest person I've ever met.

AMANDA ROBERTS: Where did you two meet?

KENDRA WRIGHT: Pharmacy school. She was such a huge help to me then. She kept me sane when I felt overloaded. It was us against the world, or exams.

DANIELLE MCGUIRE: She started pharmacy school a bit late, didn't she?

KENDRA WRIGHT: At twenty-nine. She was hoping for medical school, but this worked out instead.

DANIELLE MCGUIRE: Can you tell us a little about your friendship?

KENDRA WRIGHT: Sure. I mean, Dunia has always been the nicest person. She'd lost her mom before all this began, and it really hit her hard.

AMANDA ROBERTS: In what ways?

KENDRA WRIGHT: At the funeral, Dunia had to perform the rites—for religious reasons. And she struggled with it. She was supposed to wash her mom's body and anoint her in oil. Dunia couldn't handle doing that. And I think the guilt of not being able to do it ate at her.

DANIELLE MCGUIRE: That's intense. Did she leave the funeral without doing it?

KENDRA WRIGHT: I did it for her, along with her sister.

AMANDA ROBERTS: Wow. I don't know if I'd do that for my friend, but that's amazing. Do you have any idea where Dunia is?

KENDRA WRIGHT: None. I mean, I feel responsible for so much of this because of—

AMANDA ROBERTS: Wait, no spoilers! We are going in chronological order of events. So let's let listeners meet Dunia through you first.

KENDRA WRIGHT: Spoilers? This isn't a TV show, this is my best friend's life.

DANIELLE MCGUIRE: And we are going to talk about why you feel responsible soon, I promise. Trust us, we only want the truth to come out. But first we need our listeners to know who Dunia is. You've had no contact with her? None? If the cops went through your phone records, they'd find nothing?

KENDRA WRIGHT: I know she's alive out there somewhere. If she's listening, I want her to know I'm sorry and that I miss her and we all just want her home again.

AMANDA ROBERTS: That's beautiful. Isn't that beautiful? And listeners, we have something beautiful for you. We partnered with a private eye to help you with all your searching and info needs. Just use the promo code Dunia15. You'll be so happy you did.

Ten

I woke up standing in my living room. I blinked, staring around me in the dark, the light from First Avenue filling my apartment. I was sleepwalking again. It always took a while for the veil of confusion to lift after sleepwalking. It was as if my dreams were still playing out, only I was awake. Or at least out of bed and walking. I hated sleepwalking. I hated never knowing what I was going to do. It was the main reason I never slept without pjs. Imagine waking up somewhere else, buck naked? No thanks. It was bad enough when I'd wake up in the living room with an irate David yelling at me to knock it off.

I had done this as a kid—it's normal for children to sleepwalk—but after Ammi died, it started up again. Nightly walks, doing strange things, waking up with random bruises. It didn't take therapy to know that I had unresolved issues with her.

After a while, I couldn't have David sleep over. Now I couldn't fathom having anyone over while I slept. I couldn't explain why, but sleepwalking filled me with shame. Normal adults did not sleepwalk. How could I get it to stop? I put holiday bells on the doorknob of my front door in case I opened it in my sleep. I cleared the space around my bed so I wouldn't fall down and break my neck.

I stumbled into the bathroom, and the circles under my eyes made me look particularly raccoon-like. *Just shower, go to work. Have coffee.* I could do this. I took off my clothes and let the shower heat up. That's when I noticed four bruises around my arm, above my elbow. Like a hand. They must have been from that creep on the subway. I wanted to wash them off me. I wanted no trace of him. I wanted to forget he existed, that he tried to kill me. It hadn't even been a full week yet, and I was pretending I was fine. No trauma here; I was unscathed! (Lies.) I had nearly died, and these bruises reminded me of that. I wanted to wipe the image of his blue eyes from my brain.

I closed my own eyes and envisioned taking the subway. Walking into the same station where I almost died. I could see it all, and it made me sick. I puked right in the shower, the water washing my mess off me. It was already Thursday, and I'd taken the subway zero times this week. Not with the threat of dying hanging over me. But taking an Uber twice daily was costing me a fortune.

Maybe I needed something for my anxiety? The mere thought filled me with shame. I could practically hear my aunties call me a pagal, a crazy person. That the only reason I'd need medication was because I'd lost my mind. I wished I could drown their voices out, but they owned prime real estate in my brain.

I didn't make it to the subway. I took one step outside of my apartment and walked the other way to the corner on First Avenue. I'd take a cab. It was the only option. I'd spend twenty-five bucks to get to work, but I'd be alive. Broke, but alive.

Work was a blessing, to be honest. I was too busy counting pills and calling doctors and giving various vaccines to think about almost dying. My coworkers watched me warily; no one wanted to ask me how I was, in case I was too honest with them. It was the elephant in the room, and I was happy to leave old Dumbo in the corner, ignored.

"Dunia? There's a detective here to see you?" Michael said, his eyes wide. I got up and saw the detective from the subway that night. My stomach dropped seeing her. I felt panicked, though I couldn't say why. Like she was here to arrest me. I closed my eyes briefly, and the events from last week washed over my lids. Her comforting me, asking me questions. His eyes staring into mine as he died. The sound of the train as it rushed into the station, the feel of the blood spraying us all. The screams.

I snapped my eyes open and pasted a smile on my face.

"Detective—sorry, I didn't catch your name," I said as I held my hand out to shake hers.

"Alvarez." She wore jeans and an ugly blazer. "I wanted to talk to you more about the incident that happened." *The incident.* Of course, that's what it was now. Not a life-and-death moment but an incident. A New York experience.

"Sure, let's go to the break room." Couldn't she have just called me? I led her to the back, down a corridor where the public restrooms were. I hoped no one was in the break room. Thankfully, it was empty.

I motioned for her to sit on the not-so-comfortable chairs.

"Ms. Ahmed, how are you doing today?" Alvarez smiled.

"I'm okay. Is there some news?" I sounded anxious.

"We have a bit more information on the man who tried to assault you." Detective Alvarez was staring at the bruises on my arm. "Those from him?" I was wearing scrubs. They were insanely comfortable and an approved look for work. But the sleeves were short.

I nodded and shut the door. "I think so, or one of the guys who helped me. It all happened so fast, you know." I covered my arm with my hand. "Would you like coffee or water?"

"I'm good." Alvarez smiled.

I sat opposite her.

"Dunia—okay if I call you that?—I wanted to go over what happened and see if you could think of any more details." She smiled as if we were friends. I could see how she'd get people to confess. Make them feel at ease. But I had nothing to confess. "You're certain you've never seen the man who attacked you before? Anywhere?"

"Just on the subway. I figured we shared a commute because he was always on the train when I got on." I didn't mention he was my pretend boyfriend.

"We found this in his things." Alvarez pulled a clear plastic bag out of her tote. Inside was a photo of me.

"What?" I grabbed the bag. The picture was of me, my face. But I hadn't taken it. "I don't know this photo. It's not one from my social media accounts." That roller-coaster feeling in my stomach was back. Why did he have this picture? How did he get it? Was it on him when he died? I didn't remember him ever snapping photos of me.

Alvarez cleared her throat. "He had a whole wall of pictures of you in his apartment."

My face burned while my heart started beating too fast. "A wall? Was he stalking me?" My voice had gone up a couple of octaves. *Please don't let me cry. Not in front of the police.*

"Looks like it."

Alvarez put one photo after another on the table, each one in a bag so no one would get prints on them. They were all of me in various public places: subways, walking on the street, eating at a café, even entering my apartment building. And so many from here, my job. Which meant he'd stalked me at work. There was something horrifying about seeing my life laid out like that. One snapshot after another, and I had been blissfully unaware he'd taken these. At any moment he could have chosen to attack me. How could I have been so unaware?

"Whoa." The understatement of the year. My hand shook as I picked up one bag after another. I looked happy, busy, annoyed in the photos—and completely clueless that death was lurking so close to me.

"You never noticed a man taking your picture?" she asked.

"Everyone has a smartphone. Why would I notice him?" I stared at the photos. "These were all the last couple weeks. I can't place the rest." That was about as useful as I could get. "That was with Kendra, my best friend. We went to dinner." I felt my eyes tear up, and I glanced away, embarrassed. *Hold it together.*

"How can you tell when they were taken?" Alvarez asked. I knew she was doing her job, but her questions were beginning to annoy me.

"My clothes, mostly. And where I was in the photos. Who I was with." I whispered my reply, my voice unsteady. This man had stalked me. Actually stalked me. And then tried to murder me. Why me? Why was my life turning into a Lifetime movie?

"His name was Skylar Jones," Alvarez said. She waited to see if it rang a bell.

I shook my head. "I'll check my social accounts. But his name doesn't sound familiar at all." Skylar Jones. A name to go with the blue eyes.

"Can you tell us if he was a customer?" she continued.

"I can't, not without checking with the legal department. It would help if you had a court order." I sighed. "I want to help, but my hands are tied there." Privacy laws weren't there to protect pharmacists; they were for the patients.

"You mentioned an ex-boyfriend was bothering you?"

I paused. "My ex-fiancé and I split recently. A few months ago. He dumped me." I laughed hollowly. "He's the only one I can think of. He's been persistent in reaching out to me, showing up at work, at my apartment, calling at all hours. I don't know if he's capable of doing anything like that. To be honest, I feel like I don't know him at all anymore." My face felt hot. Nothing like talking about the biggest failings of your life to the police.

Alvarez nodded and took the photos back. "We're following every lead, but this wasn't random. You were targeted, and we need to know why. We'll reach out to your ex.

"There's more," Alvarez continued. She pulled out photocopies of a journal. "He had a journal." I grabbed the sheets.

"'I can't stop, she's all I can think about. I'm not me. HELP ME! HE's stolen my life.'" I read aloud. "What the hell?"

"I don't think Mr. Jones was in his right mind."

"No, wow, this is creepy." I shivered.

"I want you to read through these in case they jog anything for you. They're disturbing, but it would help us." She wanted me to read the rantings of a killer. I wanted to say no, but it was ingrained in me to say yes to authority. That's how I was raised. Do what people ask, and don't rock the boat. "Here's my card. Call me if you think of anything. Okay? Anything, no matter how small, can help with a lead." Alvarez smiled again, and I wanted to like her, but she was the police. I was a brown woman living in the US. Trusting the police was a luxury I couldn't afford.

"Wait! This is probably nothing. But I got a strange piece of mail recently. No postmark, so hand delivered here. Could it be related? It said something strange about finding me."

"Can you drop it by the precinct? And can you put it in a plastic bag for me?" Alvarez asked. I kept feeling like I was the criminal. Like I had done something wrong by being attacked. Another woman being hysterical.

"Of course. I'll bring it by." I wanted to sound positive. But something told me this whole thing was only getting started. And that the late Skylar Jones wasn't going to be my only problem.

I walked her out and dreaded having to go back and see my coworkers' faces.

"Duhnia, it wasn't time for your break." My manager—Mandy—stood watching the detectives leave. She always said my name wrong: *Duhnia* (which meant "cilantro") versus *Doohnia*. Her hands were on her hips. She looked like an angry chicken when she stood like that, her head bobbing as she clucked at me. She liked to find reasons to make me feel like shit.

"Sorry, the police came to speak to me."

Her lips stretched into a smile of sorts. "Well, just make sure to tell them to come outside of work hours next time."

"Sure thing!" I replied; my fake cheeriness was like a mask. Like a blanket that would keep all my emotions inside. It was the only way to move ahead. I had to pretend I was fine. Just like I had as a child.

Eleven

Transcript: *The Disappearance of Dunia Ahmed* **podcast**

AMANDA ROBERTS: Detective Alvarez, what were your impressions of Dunia? What was she like?

DETECTIVE ALVAREZ: She was normal. Your average thirty-some-odd-year-old woman in New York. She had friends, a career; she seemed to be enjoying her life. In my brief interactions with her, she came off as a smart young woman who was dealing with a lot.

DANIELLE MCGUIRE: Do you think she did something to instigate things?

DETECTIVE ALVAREZ: No, and I'd be careful about victim blaming. In stalking cases—which this very much was—the victim hasn't done anything wrong. Sometimes small things we do can get twisted by perpetrators.

AMANDA ROBERTS: Right, of course. Now, what happened when you zeroed in on the late Skylar Jones?

DETECTIVE ALVAREZ: When we searched his apartment, it had been cleared out. No fingerprints, no DNA anywhere. Someone went to a lot of trouble to make sure we couldn't find them. The only things left were Skylar's clothes and the photo wall he had of surveillance pictures.

AMANDA ROBERTS: Of Dunia.

DETECTIVE ALVAREZ: Correct. And her friends. It appeared Mr. Jones had stalked her for a while. She was his target, but we didn't know why.

DANIELLE MCGUIRE: Was it the missing girlfriend? Had she cleaned up?

DETECTIVE ALVAREZ: I can only speculate, but it would appear so. Someone didn't want us to link them to Skylar, and we needed to figure out who that person was.

Twelve

Dunia, age five

"This is called a casserole." Ammi said it proudly. She set the dish on the table. It looked like a beige mess of noodles and chicken and sauce. I didn't want to eat that. I liked our khana, the aloo ghosht and daal she usually made.

"It looks funny," I said, wrinkling my nose.

"Just try it," she said, pouring some on my plate. She gave me the look that said *Stop talking*. She gave me that look a lot.

I put a small forkful in my mouth. I didn't like it. "I like our khana better." I pouted.

"We all do, but let's try this dish, okay?" Abu said. He covered his in green chutney. "Your mother worked hard on this."

"Carol gave me the recipe," Ammi said. Carol lived next door and sometimes watched me when Ammi needed a nap. I liked Carol; she was nice. But she couldn't cook.

After I'd pushed my food around for a few minutes, Ammi got mad and made me finish my milk and go to bed. "If you won't eat, you don't get any food."

I didn't argue. I didn't want that food anyway.

From my room I could hear my parents fighting. They always fought because of me. I hated it. They never fought over Nadia. What was so bad about me? I was trying to be good.

Today, I hadn't done anything that would upset my mom. But she still yelled at me.

Later, Abu came in to tuck me in.

"I'm sorry I didn't eat dinner," I said.

"Your mother is just tired, don't worry. Maybe you can go to Carol's tomorrow."

I liked that idea.

The next morning I walked up to my mom and hugged her and said sorry for dinner. "I'm sorry I'm not being good," I said. After my preschool class, Carol was waiting for me.

"Your mom had to run errands," she said. It was a lie. I knew adults lied to be nice sometimes. Carol's hair was red, and she wore really bright-colored dresses.

"Okay." I held her hand as we walked to her house, and she made me a peanut butter and jelly sandwich. Then she combed and braided my hair. It felt nice. Ammi never braided my hair.

"Auntie Carol? Why does my mom not like me?" I asked.

"Your mother loves you! Sometimes grown-ups get stressed out, and we seem angry. But we're not. You're the most lovable girl ever!" And she hugged me. I wanted to stay with Carol forever.

When Ammi came to get me, she had tea with Carol first. They were talking about me.

"It's very hard being a mother," Carol said. "But Dunia can tell you're upset with her. She's very sensitive."

I didn't hear what Ammi said, but I knew I'd be in trouble. I had told personal things to someone not in our family. That was bad.

Ammi didn't hold my hand as we walked next door to our small house. She didn't look at me or tell me to wash up. I did it anyway and then stayed in my room, where I wouldn't get yelled at.

"Dunia! Come here!"

Oh no, I'd done something. I walked out to see all the forks and spoons on the floor and the leftover casserole in the garbage.

"Did you do this?" Ammi asked.

I shook my head no. I hadn't done it.

"You bathameez. Pick it all up and put it in the dishwasher. Now." She pinched the top of her nose, which meant she had a headache now. I did as I was told. But I hadn't put anything on the floor or thrown food away. Not that she'd ever believe me.

Thirteen

Skylar Jones was not a social media mutual with anyone I knew. No Twitter, Instagram, or Facebook friends in common. I thought he would be linked to David and then I'd have my answer to all this. Because as scary as being attacked was, not knowing why made it even more terrifying.

If I knew why that man wanted me dead, then I'd know if anyone else did. That was my fear: that the reason this happened wasn't done, wasn't resolved, and I'd have to look over my shoulder for the rest of my life.

Shake it off. That's what I kept telling myself. People had bad things happen to them all the time and get on with life. I could too. I hoped. But knowing the why of things would get me there.

In the back of my head I kept thinking it had to be David who set this up. David, who I thought I'd spend the rest of my life with—not happily, but still!—had to be it. Who else would want to hurt me? David dumped me for being "weird" after my mom died, and then he couldn't stop stalking me. I wasn't weird; I didn't know how to grieve a woman who seemed to despise me my entire life.

I was so desperate to earn my mother's approval—anyone's approval, really—that I stayed in a relationship with someone like him. Petty. Jealous. Controlling. Like I'd exchanged my family for a man who behaved just like them.

Therapy had done wonders for me. So much so that I was relieved when David broke up with me. It would be easier this way, no mess. He couldn't be mad if he was the one who initiated.

My phone buzzed while I sat drinking coffee, trying to find how Skylar knew me. I didn't know him.

I'm downstairs, my phone read. It was David. Think of the devil and he appeared. I ignored him and made sure my door was bolted. The doorman knew not to let him up. I wasn't about to spend my Saturday morning with my ex.

Let me up.

Stop being such a bitch.

This is why you'll end up alone.

No good would come from interacting with him. And now I was trapped in my apartment. I called down to the front desk—thankful yet again that I'd managed to score a doorman building—and made it clear to call the police if he didn't leave.

The next text was too vulgar to repeat. I sure knew how to pick them.

My phone wouldn't stop vibrating. I could turn it off, but I wanted to be able to call the police if needed. They wouldn't do shit, but maybe they would scare him off. They had before.

The noise was driving me nuts.

I grabbed my phone. "Leave me alone!" I yelled into it.

"Uh, sorry? Dunia? This is Zabir. Is this a bad time?"

I froze. It wasn't David calling. It was Nadia's cousin-in-law. "Oh, sorry. I thought you were someone else."

"I see, sorry to startle you. Should I call back?"

"Uh, no, no, it's fine. How are you?"

"Well, I was hoping I could entice you to meet me for a coffee? Nothing crazy, just to catch up."

Catch up, as if we were old friends. I barely remembered meeting him at the wedding almost a decade ago. I didn't know how to get out of this without pissing off my sister.

"Um, sure, coffee." I could do coffee, right?

"Free today, or is that too presumptuous?"

I wanted to say no. I wanted to say I was trapped in my apartment, but if David had left I could sneak out. I could be free and have coffee. Isn't that what one did? My choice of activities was to riffle through Skylar's journal or have coffee, and Zabir seemed the less painful option, to be honest.

"I can meet you in a couple hours, if that's okay?"

"Perfect."

I could feel the future regret already blooming. This was going to be a mistake. But I was always bad at saying no to familial obligations. I texted Kendra in a panic, and she calmed me down.

"It's just coffee. You don't have to marry him. Or do you? Kidding!"

She was right: it was just coffee. I needed to be normal, do normal things. Normal people went for coffee.

———

We were meeting at Cafe Mogador on Saint Marks Place. I was relieved to be away from my neighborhood, away from any memories of that day. I decided to take the bus down Second Avenue. I wore a black dress with a belt that made me look more in shape than I was. I hoped I wouldn't be sweating by the time I got there, but it was the end of August, so I was out of luck.

I waited for the bus. It was a weekend, so I didn't think it would be too crowded. But when it came, it was packed. And I felt that same familiar panic rise up. *If I get on this bus, will I die?*

"Ma'am? You swiping your card or what?" the driver asked. I was holding up the line.

"Sorry, I made a mistake," I stammered and pushed my way off the steps and onto the street. I couldn't do this.

Should I cancel and go home? I looked at my watch—I had twenty minutes to meet him. Canceling now would be unforgivable. I had to go. I found a cab and jumped in, relieved the driver had the AC blasting. I reapplied my lipstick and fixed my sweating as best I could.

When I stood outside the café, all I could think was that this was a trap. A ploy courtesy of my sister. I was being irrational. Nadia had never been that cruel to me. But I didn't trust her. I couldn't trust anyone in my family except my dad, and he was long gone.

"What's the worst that can happen?" I asked myself. And didn't have an answer, because I bet Zabir really just wanted coffee. "I can do this." And then I went inside, my breath deep in my belly to keep me from running.

"Dunia, hi." I turned. Zabir stood there smiling. He had a nice smile, genuine. I smiled back.

"Hi!"

"Sorry for the last-minute invite, but I figured why not, right?"

"Right. No, it was good, I was going to be stuck in my apartment all day."

He led me to a table he'd chosen, away from others. I was thankful for that. I didn't want to keep watching my back.

"Can I sit against the wall?" I asked. After my near-death moment, I couldn't be too careful.

"Of course!" He sat opposite me, and I felt my stomach do that nervous thing, and I hated it.

"This isn't a date," I said.

"Okay? It's not a date." He smiled again.

"I mean, I just wanted to be clear. Sorry, things have been off lately."

The waitress came, and I ordered a latte and a pastry while he went for tea and hummus.

"I can imagine. I have to be honest—I saw you in the papers and realized you were Nadia's sister. I wanted to make sure you were okay."

He looked at me expectantly. He wanted a story. *The* story. I was learning that whenever anyone found out I'd survived a subway attack, they wanted to hear all about it. I had to perform my trauma for their entertainment.

"Ohhh, okay. I'll tell you about it."

"You don't have to. I really wanted to just make sure you're fine. I remember having a great conversation with you at the wedding and Walima."

I didn't remember those conversations. What had we even talked about? "I had the flu the whole time, so it's a little foggy for me."

"Well, you played it off well. You were thinking of going to pharmacy school back then. I assume that panned out, since you're a pharmacist."

"Yes! Couldn't get into med school." Which he no doubt already knew. I was sure he already knew everything about me through the family grapevine. Gossip was a way of life in my family.

"Me neither." Zabir laughed. "So I became a professor instead."

"Oh, well then, hello, my fellow nondoctor." We both laughed.

"Did you take the subway down? Are you able to yet?"

I shook my head. "I tried to take the bus, but I couldn't do it. Being in an enclosed space with people, I don't know."

"Are you okay here?"

"Yeah, I just need to keep an eye out for danger." I sounded insane. "I'm sure it gets easier as time goes on."

"Hey, I'd be the same in your shoes." He held my eyes a little too long. I looked away. I needed to be careful how much I said to him. As far as I knew he was a family spy.

"So, what do you teach?"

"South Asian studies mostly."

"Oh, cool." A subject I knew nothing about. I avoided anything that had to do with our culture. I was a bad person. "So your parents must be super proud of you." It was a statement, not a question.

"Well, they were until my divorce." He grinned sheepishly. "Now I'm the black sheep."

I held up my latte. "Should we toast to that? From one black sheep to another?" He laughed and clinked mugs.

"It's just you and Nadia, right? I was sorry to hear about your mom."

"Yeah, just us. We're not that close. You know, long-distance siblings and all."

"I feel that. I'm not close with too many people in my family at the moment." He kept staring at me intently.

"Can I ask—why did you want to have coffee? Besides seeing if I'm okay."

Zabir sat back and shrugged. "Sometimes a familiar face in the city is the best thing in the world."

I didn't know what to say to that. For whatever reason, talking with him made me want to smile. I didn't think I was ready for that.

"So, pharmacist extraordinaire, are you married?"

"Me? No. I was engaged. To a gora. It fell through after my mom died."

"Oh shit, I'm sorry. I shouldn't have been so cavalier about it."

"No, no, it's fine. It was for the best. I realized we were too different. He was actually the person I thought I was yelling at this morning. He has a tendency to not leave me alone."

That made Zabir sit up straighter. "He bothering you?"

I shrugged. "I'm hoping he loses interest soon."

"So you've lost your mom, your ex is being a nuisance, and you nearly died on the subway. Did you piss off a witch or something?"

I froze for a second before realizing he was joking.

"I mean, I wish I knew. I'll burn all the sage!" We both laughed, and I felt more relaxed. At ease. Maybe having a friend like Zabir wouldn't be so bad. So what if he knew my family. It didn't mean he knew everything, right?

He got up to use the restroom, but his phone remained on the table. I shouldn't have looked, but a text popped up on the closed screen. A text from my sister.

Tell me how coffee went, I need to know everything.

Nothing good could come from meeting Zabir. I'd known it. He was doing this for Nadia. He was a spy sent from her to keep tabs on my life. I blinked, grabbed my purse, threw some money down, and walked out.

I was a complete idiot, thinking Zabir was a nice man interested in getting to know me. He was doing an errand. A familial obligation that would hopefully elevate him out of his current black sheep status. God, I was so stupid.

I heard my name being called, but I kept walking. I was done with men and their nonsense, in every sense. I had no interest in dealing with them. Let Nadia send her spies; I'd ignore them all.

I walked up Second Avenue all the way home. I was too angry to get in a cab, and the subway was a no go. Every step I took echoed in my head. "Stupid, stupid, stupid."

When I got to my apartment on Eighty-Ninth Street, I checked that no one was around, no one wanted to kill me. And then dashed inside and up the elevator, finally breathing once I could dead bolt my door.

My phone was buzzing. I ignored the texts from Zabir's number and instead texted Kendra what happened.

What??? I'm coming over.

———

Kendra stared at me.

"So you think your sis sent him to spy on you or something? Why would she need to?"

"I don't know. She's weird. My whole family is. Was. They're not like yours, all supportive and shit." I had done my best to never talk about my family with people. The whole airing-of-dirty-laundry thing was instilled in me. But over the years, Kendra had knocked some of

my walls down. She'd even met Nadia at Ammi's funeral. Kendra knew
we were estranged, just not why.

"Is it so wrong for her to know you're okay?"

"Yes. Just trust me. After my dad died, my mom blamed me for it."

"Weren't you just a kid?"

I shrugged. "It didn't matter. And Nadia followed her lead. I just
can't have that in my life right now."

"Hey, it's okay, I get it." She put her hand on my arm. "You have
chosen family now. I'm here to support you in any way."

Chosen family was often better than real kin. When I was little, I
hoped some other family would adopt me, because without my dad,
there was no point.

"Thank you." I hugged her. I was trying to get better at showing
affection. "Anyways, not seeing Zabir again."

"Did you tell him why?"

"No, I left." I made a face, and she laughed.

"Well, that's one way to do it."

I did feel bad for Zabir; he seemed nice. But then I got mad all over
again. We had been having a good time, and it was all a lie. I was sick
of lies. I was sick of family bullshit.

"Anyways, how's work?"

"Uggghhhh." She rolled her eyes. "No one told me having investors
was going to be such a drag."

"Oh noooo, what's going on?"

"I need to make them happy while staying true to me, you know?"
Joy Skincare was expanding, and Kendra had eyes on a major retailer.

"Anything I can do to help?"

"Nah, you already are. Wait. Actually, there might be. I have one
investor who keeps bugging me to hang out after work. And it would
be so much easier if you were there. I know it's a lot to ask, but . . ."

"Just tell me where and when, and I'll be there." It couldn't be any
worse than the whole Zabir debacle, right?

Fourteen

Transcript: *The Disappearance of Dunia Ahmed* **podcast**

AMANDA ROBERTS: Welcome back, everyone. We've been getting so many messages from folks who were riveted by Dunia's case when she went missing. I know you're all eager to know whodunit, but just wait. It'll be worth it! We want you to get to know Dunia as only her nearest and dearest knew her.

DANIELLE MCGUIRE: That's right, which is why we're so pleased to bring David Anderson to our podcast. David, as you may know, was Dunia's ex-fiancé. Welcome, David.

DAVID ANDERSON: Thank you. I'm excited to tell you my side of things. The press has just dragged my name through the mud. My life has been ruined by all of this.

AMANDA ROBERTS: Before we get into all of that, we'd like to know what Dunia was like when you first met.

DAVID ANDERSON: She was awesome! Dunia from before—

DANIELLE MCGUIRE: Before when?

DAVID ANDERSON: Before her mom died. That's when she changed. But before all that, she was my dream girl. She was fun, smart, kind, and hot. [*laughs*] She was everything I ever wanted in a woman.

AMANDA ROBERTS: Tell us about your first date.

DAVID ANDERSON: We met on an app. And the first date was, hmm, I think it was at this wine bar in the West Village. She looked beautiful. I'd always wanted to date someone like her—

DANIELLE MCGUIRE: Someone like her?

DAVID ANDERSON: You know, that exotic vibe. I've had a thing for Indian girls, but I never dated one. And Dunia was a light, like she glowed from the inside. Just being near her was enough to make me happier than I'd ever been. But the date, yeah, we had some wine and some cheese, and we talked for hours. It was, no joke, my dream date. I was so lame I brought her flowers. I just knew when I saw her profile that she was the one.

AMANDA ROBERTS: Awww, that's so romantic! You guys dated for three years or so?

DAVID ANDERSON: Yep. I wanted to propose right away, I won't lie. I was head over heels in love with her. She was stunning and so exotic! But she wanted to take things slowly. She hadn't had too many good relationships— which was good news for me because that meant she was single. But she was very skeptical of me at first. Not that I blamed her! [*laughs more*]

DANIELLE MCGUIRE: Dating in New York can be challenging, so I feel for her. I'm the same, I never let myself get too carried away by a man. How did you propose?

DAVID ANDERSON: I wanted to go all out and do some big spectacle, but she hated that sort of thing. No attention, no PDA. It was different— maybe because of her family? She didn't ever show love and affection if we were in public. But when we were home, she was amazing. Anyways, the proposal. Right. I kept it chill. I ordered her favorite food and wine and had dinner at my place, and I proposed. I would have loved to do it in a restaurant, but she once said she'd rather die than have one of those.

AMANDA ROBERTS: Intense! But that sounds lovely.

DAVID ANDERSON: It was. We were happy. I was happy. She made my life easy and fun. I . . . I thought this was it, you know? I wish I could go back and talk to that Dunia. She would have listened. But . . . I'm sorry, can I have a moment?

DANIELLE MCGUIRE: Of course. Let's all take a quick break.

Fifteen

An hour into my shift, and Michael the pharmacy tech called me over. "She says her prescription isn't right." I'd been on autopilot, filling every prescription that came in. Anything to avoid dealing with people.

I nodded, looking at what the doctor's office had sent over.

"Ma'am, I'm sorry about that. Let me see if I can help fix this." The prescription had been dispensed as the doctor had requested, but so often the docs got things wrong. Most of my day could be spent fixing their mistakes. "So it looks like the error is with your doctor's office. What is the dosage you should be getting?"

"Double that." She was angry, her lips thin.

"All right, let me just call them and sort this out. You can move to that window over there." *Be chipper.* I had to be as bubbly as I could be because bad reviews online could sink us. Corporate took those reviews very seriously.

I fixed the mistake—the doctor had written it wrong—and after ten minutes her new pills were ready.

"Sorry about that. Your doctor had to resend the scrip. Anything else I can do for you?"

"No." She paused and looked at me. "Weren't you that lady from the subway? The one who got pushed? I saw you on the news."

I froze. I had been dreading the moment someone at work would bring it up. Flames rose on my face. I stammered, "Uh, yes—yeah. That was me." Dammit, I didn't want to deal with this at work. This was why I didn't want any stories written about me. I'd declined speaking to any reporters; I wanted the story to die. As soon as the next sensational story hit, I'd be forgotten.

The woman just stared at me. And for a moment, one quick moment, I swore her eyes changed. Had shifted colors from brown to dark black.

She muttered something, but I didn't hear.

"Pardon?"

"You don't belong here," she hissed. I stepped back in shock. I blinked, and everything was normal: the woman was just standing there, waiting for me. She hadn't said anything to me about dying. Her eyes weren't black pools of nothing. I had hallucinated at three in the afternoon on a Tuesday.

"I said I'm glad you're okay." She smiled, a little moment of kindness.

"Thank you."

I took a break after she left. My brain was playing tricks on me, and I didn't like that one bit.

———

On my break, I googled Skylar Jones—again. I was the stalker now, determined to find out anything and everything about him. Each stupid update, tweet, and post was a clue to his deranged mind.

His social media posts were horrifyingly normal. Average white dude in New York. Nothing exciting, nothing that said he'd become a stalker and murderer. Or an attempted one. Wasn't that what everyone said about every white killer? "He seemed so normal." What did I expect? A picture of me with a target on it? (Yes.) Him holding a gun? (Perhaps.)

He read a lot, and he played guitar. Of course. He was probably that guy at parties who started performing when no one wanted him to.

If he had a girlfriend, he didn't show her face or name her. Just bizarre cryptic notes here and there about "B." And not one thing linking him to me at all. He was a random person who had tried to kill me. Which made me angrier than if I'd known him. He had no reason to want me dead. None. He was just some guy who woke up and decided to kill someone, and I happened to be there. Chance. Fate. Call it what you want; I called it hell. I couldn't make sense of something like that. It didn't fit into how I saw the world. Zero logic.

My phone buzzed, and I jumped. It was Kendra, confirming our dinner plans later. I'd almost forgotten. I was doing girls' night with her and that investor.

———

"Liz, this is Dunia Ahmed. Dunia, this is Liz Small." Kendra waved her hands like a magician, and we all three sat down to dinner.

Liz was gorgeous. She was athletic; her arms were toned like I could only dream of. I did my HIIT workouts and yoga, and my upper arms were still too fleshy. She had a bob that was a silver gray—it was stunning on her. She wasn't old enough for the hair, and that made it even cooler. She was wearing some cream-colored blouse that hung off her frame. She looked—to put it bluntly—rich. And happy.

"Duhnia! I have been bugging Kendra to let me meet you. All she does is talk about you," Liz gushed. Her words were kind, but there was a coldness in her eyes I couldn't place. Like she was assessing me. Taking stock. The way you would a new project or an apartment you wanted.

"Really?" I felt myself blush. "I'm not that exciting. And it's Doohnia." I always had to correct people, but that difference in vowel sounds mattered.

"Isn't that what I said? Do you have to do that a lot? That must be so annoying for you! What if you went by a nickname? Like, Doohn. Doohn! I like it!"

"I prefer Dunia, to be honest." I shifted uncomfortably. "*Duhhhnia* means 'cilantro.'" I grinned to show it wasn't serious.

"Well, I'm thrilled you convinced Kendra to finally have a girls' night. I'm a little obsessed with her." Liz winked as if Kendra weren't sitting right there.

"Me too. She's amazing."

"And so brilliant!" Liz focused her eyes on me. "I know you, though. Don't I? Don't tell me." I heard Kendra clear her throat and realized I was clutching the tablecloth tightly with one hand. "I've got it! Oh my God, you were in the papers! I never forget a face."

Her eyes roamed my entire face as if she could learn all my mysteries from my skin.

"Dunia had an, uh, incident on the subway," Kendra said, jumping in to save me.

"A guy tried to push you onto the tracks? Am I right? See, I really never forget a face," she repeated.

"Uh, yeah. It was, what, almost two weeks ago. It feels like yesterday and forever ago at the same time." I laughed.

"That's a trauma response, the time thing. It happens to all of us." Us? Before I could ask what she meant, she was peppering me with questions. She wasn't aggressive, not exactly. She was American. A white American. They were allowed to be loud, boisterous, and nosy. Those were all things my mother never let me be, even though she wanted me to assimilate. I had to be quiet, do what I was told, and never cause a scene. Liz was the type of person you described as a force. And right now, all her force was directed at me. "What was the guy who tried to kill you like? Was he nuts? Was it terrifying?"

I nodded and began the story. I knew the deal. If you had a newsworthy tale, you had to share it on demand. Liz gasped and grabbed my arm throughout. I winced as she gripped my fading bruises.

"And the police said he had photos of me. Like, one on him, others in his apartment."

59

"So, wait, he targeted you?" Kendra forked some tuna appetizer into her mouth. We were at one of those restaurants with white subway tile that had become ubiquitous in Manhattan. Always with some silly name, like Monty's or the Polka-Dotted Zebra.

"Yeah, and I can't tell how he got them. We have no one in common. No one at all. The cops think he was stalking me."

"And you didn't notice?" Kendra asked.

"No. Did you? Because I was with you in some of the photos." I sounded bitchy. But I was tired of that question. No, I hadn't noticed him. Did anyone notice every person who has their phone out near them? Anyone could be stalking any of us, and we wouldn't even know.

Kendra's eyes widened. "Oh God. That's scary."

"I wonder what set him off? He must have had a normal life before, and then . . . ," Liz said.

"Was he a customer? Like at work? Had you ever seen him before? There has to be something, right?"

I shrugged. "I don't know. I can't look up records like that without reason, and even if he was, I can't tell the cops."

"So what?" Liz said. "Break the rules. You almost died." She looked angry. Not at me, but for me. "You should know more about him."

"You're right, I should. It's been challenging to get the police to tell me more. They did give me a copy of his journal, though—"

"Whoa. What did it say?"

I shrugged. "I haven't read it yet. I'm a little scared to see what's in there." That was the truth. I thought I'd dive right in, but I kept staring at the pile like it contained the end of the world. What if there was a reason he'd come after me? What if I deserved to die?

"So creepy," Liz affirmed, nodding. I glanced at Kendra and back at Liz. I could see how it would be challenging to say no to this woman. It made me feel good that Kendra wanted me to help her with this. With Liz. "I'd be happy to come over and help you read them. I can just sit there, but you shouldn't do it alone."

"Maybe?" That wasn't a bad idea. "I just wish I knew why he did it. Because I don't know how to stop it from happening again." I felt my face warm as I said that. That was my big fear right now, that it would happen again.

"I'd want to know too! Kendra and I are here for you." Liz said it like she was my new best friend. I glanced at Kendra, who shrugged. "You know what you need? Something to make you feel strong and safe. Like, okay, this is totally not the same thing, but after a bad breakup and family drama, I got a talisman necklace. And I swear I felt better. It was in my head, but it works!"

"Oh, maybe! What did you get?" She showed me a gold circular coin with some Greek goddess on it.

"It's Hecate, because she's a badass."

I didn't know how a necklace was going to make me feel better, but I appreciated the thought.

"We are here for you. But right now, I could use some more wine," Kendra said, breaking the tension.

"Ditto, but only one more glass. Work night and all."

"Let's toast to no more psychos trying to kill you," Liz said. Kendra and I stared at her in shock before I burst out laughing.

"That is the best toast ever. Yes, let's toast to that."

Kendra thankfully launched into her latest product that she was developing—a foundation that also fought wrinkles—and I was relieved. I'd much rather talk about her than my subway attack.

"Tell Dunia about your new lip care!" Liz said, her eyes wide. "You're going to love it. Kendra is a genius!"

"It's a lip oil that stays put. Just wait until you see what's next!" Kendra smiled.

"We should do a girls' weekend soon," Liz said. "Just to get you away from all this. What do you think? We could go up to the Catskills or something. I have a house up there!"

"Sounds super fun!" I said, and Kendra nodded.

When I got home, Kendra texted me a giant thank-you. I had done something for her, for once. Usually it was her taking care of me. Liz texted us both, making my first group chat. She said she "loooooved" us both so much. I replied back with a heart emoji.

———

Police stations looked less exciting in real life than on TV. Just a boring office where they could lock you up if you broke the law or annoyed them. I was there to see Detective Alvarez. I had the note that was left at work with me. Bagged, as requested. I waited on an uncomfortable seat as people milled about. Some came in wearing handcuffs, others, crying. This was not a nice place to be.

"Dunia?" Alvarez stood in front of me. I wondered what her first name was. She had never told me.

"Hi, I'm sorry to bother you. I brought this." I held up the bag.

"Great, I was just thinking about that. Follow me."

She led me to a room that was probably where people confessed to her. Told her all their sins, begged her to not lock them up.

She took the baggie from me. I cleared my throat.

"I was thinking of those photos of me. If we didn't have anyone in common, do you think someone gave him those photos? Like, a hit? Or maybe he was just stalking me?" *Did my ex do this? Did he set me up? Am I going to die?*

"It's a possibility."

"Have you been able to get any records to see if he was at my pharmacy?"

"We're working on it."

"I need to know how I knew him. I need to know why he did this. Can you please help me find out?" I hated the way my voice sounded like I was begging. But I needed this. She had to help me.

"We are looking into that, I swear. We're talking to everyone he knew. So far, no one knows you, has no connection to you. The only person we haven't located yet is his ex-girlfriend Bea."

I nodded, but my frustration was obvious.

"Skylar targeted you. I don't know if that means anyone else is." At least she was being honest.

"I guess I'm being paranoid that there are more threats out there."

"That's perfectly normal. Have you reached out to victim services?"

I shook my head. "Not yet. I just . . . I need to know why. Why did he do this? Why did he try to kill me? Why me?"

"We may never know exactly why, and that's something you're going to have to live with. Therapy can help with this. I highly recommend it."

"But there has to be a reason."

She looked at me with a mix of pity and understanding. I guessed this was what victims dealt with. The unanswered questions. The feeling like your world was just pulled out from under you.

Alvarez nodded. "I'm not going to tell you not to worry, because anything can happen in this city. Just be aware of your surroundings. Maybe vary up your routes home. And definitely consider not wandering around alone."

"Okay."

"Do you have a doorman building? You're up in the Eighties, right?" I nodded. "Tell them to not let anyone in to see you without confirming their ID."

"Anything else?"

"Try not to overworry. Just be aware. I promise we'll figure out if there's something more happening here." She tried to be reassuring, but how reassured would you have been?

I thanked her and left, glancing at every person who came too near me on the sidewalk. I needed to do something, or I'd be a nervous wreck the rest of my life. Maybe I should get a gun? I laughed at that, but part of me really wanted one. I wanted to feel safe again.

Sixteen

I am not a victim. I am a survivor. And I will fight like hell.

I was repeating that to myself as I got ready for work. *I am a survivor. I will fuck you up.*

Was it working? I had no idea, but I needed to get myself in a better mindset and fast. I was sick of being poor Dunia. I needed something to help me feel better. Maybe Liz was right and I needed a talisman of sorts. A necklace. It sounded stupid, but having something remind me I was safe—I was a badass; I was not going to die—was necessary.

I remembered my dad telling me when he was little, he had bad dreams. And his grandmother piled necklaces onto him, and they went away. And then he placed his blue tasbeeh around my neck. It was what Americans would call a rosary, made with blue evil eye beads.

I had that necklace still. I'd kept it all these years. David had gotten annoyed by it because he wasn't into that "mumbo jumbo religious stuff." I kept it in a small wooden box. It was one of the few things I had from my dad, and I wanted to keep it safe.

The box was on my bookshelf. I opened it, and—it was gone. My dad's tasbeeh was missing. This couldn't be right. No one else knew about it. I frantically started searching for it, anywhere it could have fallen. It was too important to forget about. I yanked books off the shelf, opened any box that was near, and nothing. It was gone.

I sat down in defeat. My one thing from my father, and it was gone. I wanted to cry, to sob, to let it all out. But I couldn't. I had to go to work.

All day I thought about that necklace. I wanted to get home as quickly as I could. I was going to find it. It was probably somewhere stupid, somewhere I put it for safekeeping and forgot about.

I practically ran home after work. I was out of breath and exhausted, but I had to find it. I knew it sounded lame, but it was my dad's, and he was everything to me.

I tore my apartment apart, and after hours of making so much noise my neighbor knocked on my door, I found it. It was behind my dresser and in pieces.

"Oh God." Beads were falling off the string. This was a disaster. When had this happened? And how? The string it was on looked cut, not frayed. Had someone done this? Had David?

That asshole. I texted him that too. **Did you break my necklace? You psycho.** And then blocked him. I'd read it was better to not block stalkers, so you had proof against them, but I was so mad. Who did that? Who destroyed something with such sentimental value?

"I'm going to restring this, and it'll be like new," I said out loud, so I had to do it. I gathered every bead I could find and placed them in the wooden box. At least I had it, or most of it. And I would never forgive David for this betrayal.

I wanted to tell my dad I was sorry about this, that I'd failed him yet again. But he couldn't hear me, so what was the use?

———

Sooo great meeting you the other night! I meant what I said about helping you deal with that scary journal. Lemme know if you want company? Liz texted. This would be good, right? I clearly needed the help. I hadn't even touched the pages Detective Alvarez had given me. They felt evil in some way. Like just having them kept Skylar around. I had to do this and get it over with.

YES!! I'd love that. Maybe this weekend? I needed time to put my apartment back together after my frantic search.

Perfect! Wanna see if Kendra can join?

I could just picture us having brunch while discussing the psychotic ramblings of a man who wanted me dead. Did mimosas go better with that, or Bloody Marys?

Come Saturday afternoon and Liz was at my door.

"I brought some wine," she said, holding the bottle up. "I figured we could use it."

"Thank you for helping me with this."

"I'm thrilled you're letting me!"

She flung her purse down and kicked off her shoes. "No Kendra?"

"She's out of town." Her factory was on the West Coast, and at some point, she was going to move operations fully to California.

"Oh right! I forgot. Duh. Wow, what a cute space this is!"

I had laid out the pages on the coffee table. I poured the wine, and we sat on the sofa. We didn't touch the papers for a while.

"How was your week?" Liz asked. "Wait, cheers to new friends!"

"Cheers! It was okay. I mean, no one tried to kill me, so that's good."

She snorted. "You almost made me spill my wine!"

"Ha, sorry." My phone rang, and it was Nadia. I muted it. "My sister. We, uh, aren't close."

"Ugh, family is rough. I just got back in with mine. They hated my ex and were going to cut me off. But he and I are through, and I'm back working in the family business—investing their money." She rolled her eyes. "At least I can invest in cool companies with the cash, right?"

"Yeah, that's good! Sorry they hated your ex. My family tolerated mine, but after we broke up, my sister told me she was glad." After Nadia blamed me for the break, she said it was good I hadn't brought an outsider into our family.

"Oh noooo! When did you break up?"

"Uh, like a few months ago? My mom died, and he didn't like how I grieved."

"You're kidding?"

"No, and get this. He didn't like this necklace that was my dad's, and I found it broken the other day. Like, who does that? My dad died when I was little." I needed someone else to be outraged for me.

"Holy cow. What a jerk. I'm so sorry."

"And he's stalking me, which totally isn't helping my sanity."

"We should kill him," she joked. "Just get rid of him."

"Ha! Yes. Let's kill everyone who annoys us!"

We laughed and drank enough wine to fortify us for the task ahead. "Shall we just split the pile up?" I suggested. "And anything about me we can keep together."

"Sounds good. What are we looking for?"

"Beats me. The police wanted me to look at it all, see if anything rang bells. They don't know much about the guy."

Liz grabbed my hand. "You can do this. You're a brave woman. A survivor."

"I'm really glad we met. I know we barely know each other, but I've been struggling with all of this. So thank you for helping me." It was the absolute truth.

"That's what friends do!"

We opened the papers together. There were some drawings. He apparently sketched people on the subway during their commutes. But seeing as how he tried to kill me on my commute, the images were a little creepy. This man was watching everyone. I wondered briefly if his sketches would fetch money now that he was dead. And a would-be killer.

"He was a good artist," I said. Liz agreed, and we kept flipping through pages.

He scribbled things next to everything he drew. Minor things, about the day, about what music he listened to, what the person reminded him of. The notes and drawings seemed harmless, but then the drawings got darker. *Spring day. Warm out. Shoes were red. Bea said she loved me.* These soon gave way to *Evil evil evil, must stop* and *Find her.* Instead of people's faces, he started drawing something black, something that looked like smoke. Smoke, like I'd seen that day he died. Maybe I hadn't imagined it.

"Whoa."

"What is it?"

"See this smoke thing? I swear that day it happened, right before he jumped onto the tracks, there was this dark smoke all around him. But nothing was burning."

"That's weird," Liz said.

"Very."

"Oh, and the Bea he mentions—that's who the police think is his girlfriend, but they haven't found her," I explained.

"They can't find her? They're the police," Liz said. "How can they not find one person?"

"I don't know. I think it's odd that she hasn't come forward. I mean, if my boyfriend or ex did what hers did, I'd be at the police station. But that's just me."

"Maybe she doesn't know. I mean, it's possible. She could be traveling or at a retreat or something."

"Maybe? God, what a horrible thing to come home to, then." I shuddered.

Skylar had some self-portraits, which started out fine. But then he scratched out his own eyes in every drawing. And the smoke monster was behind him, or with him. Creepy. He had drawings of some woman, but her face was blank. He had made a note about his girlfriend. "I found a way to support us. Money is coming!"

"I wonder if I was the money—they found cash deposits in his account, but the police haven't traced where it came from."

"This is so creepy."

After the strange and scary illustrations came mine. And seeing myself unaware of being watched—even as a drawing—was stomach turning. There I was, on the subway, minding my business. I never noticed him drawing me. Following me. He had seven drawings of me. Just me. And they were good illustrations! If he hadn't tried to kill me, I would maybe be flattered. But then he scribbled my eyes out in a few and added scary notes.

She's the one.

She didn't notice me.

Her, why is it her??

Look at me!! Why won't she look at me??

He won't leave me alone. I can't stop this. I can't save her.

She has to die. But if I kill her, I'm dead.

I did this for Bea, I have to keep going.

I know what this is. I found someone who can help.

I'll never be free! Never!

His last note was scrawled in some liquid that had spilled everywhere. I wondered if it was blood.

Reading his handwriting made me feel sick. Anxious. Like any minute he was going to jump out at me and try to kill me again. I couldn't look at the pages anymore. None of my questions were answered. Instead, I had more. Didn't he have friends or family to help him? Why hadn't any of his people known he was unraveling? Why didn't they step in to help him? And who was the "he" Skylar mentioned? Was it David? Had David threatened to kill him?

Liz gently pulled my hand away from my mouth. I hadn't realized I was covering it.

"You okay?" she asked.

"No. How did I not know he was following me? How could I have been so oblivious?"

"It seems like you had a lot happening in your life around then. Don't be so hard on yourself. And he was really not okay mentally. I mean, look at his ramblings."

"I know, but I just, what if it happens again? What if this isn't over?"

"It has to be. He's dead." Her voice was harsh. "Sorry, but I hate him for what he did. Or tried to do."

I nodded but didn't say more. Liz poured more wine even though I protested.

"I'm a lightweight! I don't drink much."

"Listen, if this isn't worth drinking over, what is?"

She had a point.

"Let's toast to you," I said. "To Liz, my new friend who is amazing, and thank you so much." We clinked glasses, and then I pumped her for information. "You know everything about me already, so tell me about you. Are you dating anyone?"

Liz made a face. "Not since my breakup—which was five months back."

"I'm sorry. Why is dating so hard?"

"We're total catches! Look at us. We're gorgeous, we're successful, we're fun. And we're sitting on your sofa reading a madman's journal on a Saturday evening."

I couldn't help but laugh. "It's not the most exciting way to spend the weekend."

"No, but I'm glad we got to hang out."

She told me about her ex, how he left her for another woman. How she caught him cheating. "It was awful, I thought he was it. And my family all knew, they'd seen it coming. I can't even be mad at them for trying to save me from him. They figured he was after my trust fund."

"I'm sorry," I said. "You know, I haven't told anyone this. But David cheated on me. That was what broke us apart. He thought I was too distant, and so he slept with someone else." I could hear the bitterness in my voice. "So, to hell with cheaters."

"To hell with them!"

Seventeen

Transcript: *The Disappearance of Dunia Ahmed* podcast

AMANDA ROBERTS: I want to welcome back David Anderson to the podcast. David, you were telling us about your relationship with Dunia. What was your favorite moment with her?

DAVID ANDERSON: Favorite? Wow, that's tough. There are so many! I'd have to say those weekend mornings when we could be lazy and just hang out and go to brunch and not do anything all day. I loved days like that because they were hard to come by.

DANIELLE MCGUIRE: What happened to make the relationship change?

DAVID ANDERSON: She became a different person once her mom got sick. Really anxious and, I don't know, cold? If my mom died, I'd be emotional. She was fully shut down.

AMANDA ROBERTS: What do you mean?

DAVID ANDERSON: If I mentioned her mom, she'd just freeze up. No emotion, nothing. Your mom's going to die, and nothing? It showed me a side of her that was scary. Just cold and unfeeling.

DANIELLE MCGUIRE: They had—from what we've heard and read in her journal—a tough relationship.

DAVID ANDERSON: Yeah, I guess. She never talked about it. She avoided anything about her childhood. And then she started doing things that felt unsafe.

AMANDA ROBERTS: Unsafe for whom?

DAVID ANDERSON: Me. She sleepwalked. She didn't do it until her mom died. And then every night she was wandering around while I was asleep. But sometimes I'd wake up and she'd been talking to someone who wasn't there. Or just staring at something I couldn't see.

DANIELLE MCGUIRE: That's unusual, but I don't know if I'd say dangerous.

DAVID ANDERSON: There was an incident. One night I woke up to her in the kitchen, holding a knife. The stove was on. It was just too much. I already couldn't sleep over during the week because she kept me up all night. But after the knife, I didn't feel safe.

AMANDA ROBERTS: That's understandable. What happened next?

DAVID ANDERSON: I told her she had to get help for this or we wouldn't be able to continue. I hate ultimatums, but I had no choice. I needed her to get help.

DANIELLE MCGUIRE: And did she?

DAVID ANDERSON: No. At least not while we were together. I tried to talk to her after we broke up, but she wanted nothing to do with me. I was so worried about her, but I felt helpless. Did she say anything about me in her journal?

AMANDA ROBERTS: We'll get to that. But wow, Dunia seemed troubled. This would be too much for me if I were dating her. But weren't you curious about why she was so cold about her mom dying?

DAVID ANDERSON: . . . I guess? I mean, I didn't really dig into it.

Eighteen

Dunia, age five

I'd woken up from a bad dream again. I had them a lot. Abu was in my room, making me drink water.

"You're okay, just a dream."

"It was scary," I said, trying to not cry. I was a big girl; I had to be brave. Nadia was still asleep. I wished I could sleep like her.

"It's okay, bad dreams happen," Abu said, smiling. "You know, when I was your age I had bad dreams all the time. Do you know what my ammi did?"

I shook my head.

"She gave me a necklace. A talisman. And do you know what happened? The bad dreams stopped."

"Can I have a necklace like that?"

"Yes. Hold on." He ran out of the room and came back holding a small wooden box. "This is from Mecca. You know where that is?" I nodded. "It's what my ammi gave me." He opened the box and held a tasbeeh made from pretty blue beads. I'd seen Ammi use her tasbeeh for prayer. "Just put this on, and you won't have bad dreams."

"Promise?"

"Well, we'll try our best to make it work." He winked. He put it on me, and I lay back. I was feeling better. I held the beads in my hands.

"Thank you, Abu-ji."

"Now go to sleep before Nadia wakes up."

He left after giving me a good night kiss, and I held on to the beads around my neck. I closed my eyes and prayed they'd work. No more nightmares. No more scary things. Just happy sleep dreaming about kittens.

I heard my mother's voice. She was mad. My eyes popped open.

"Why did you do that? It's shirk." I didn't know what that word meant.

"It's a tasbeeh, it's fine."

"You need to stop telling her these stories and the ways of your family. They're not right. She just needs to pray more."

"She's fine, she's just imaginative. Come on, let's not argue."

I didn't know why she didn't like me having the necklace, but I swore I'd hold on to it forever. It would keep me safe; Abu said so.

Nineteen

After work and another day of hoofing it home. Days of wandering Manhattan all ran together. Thankfully the weather was still nice. I didn't know what I was going to do come winter. I'd have to get over my fear by then.

Today was my mother's birthday. I should have flown to Texas to visit her grave, but I wasn't that kind of daughter. Let Nadia handle that, I was trying to figure out my own murder mystery.

I was somewhere in the East Sixties when I stopped in my tracks. A woman wearing a pantsuit like Ammi would wear. Matching top and bottom, three-fourth sleeves, colorful and bright.

Before she died, I'd gone to see her. She still wore her two-piece matching shirt and pants; her hair was nearly gone. She was so thin, so frail. She told me she had one thing she needed me to do.

"Dunia," she had said. "I want you to be safe. And to be happy."

"I am safe and happy." I braced for a lecture on how I wasn't living right and then felt guilty for thinking unkind thoughts about my dying mother.

She gripped my hand. "Say the secret kalma."

That was a prayer she would say at night when we were little. She'd say it and then clap three times and blow air on me. Phook marring, it was called. She said it would keep all the scary things away when I was little. But it didn't. She was the scary thing in my life, and the prayer never kept her away.

"I will," I lied. I didn't even know how to say it.

"Promise me you'll say it." I promised, but I didn't remember the prayer. And she seemed too exhausted to tell me, so I said yes, and she let it go.

"I tried my best to keep you safe," she said. "I tried so hard."

"You did, Ammi. You kept me safe. Don't worry about me, okay?"

"Beti, all I can do is worry. You don't know what could happen after I'm gone."

I blinked. I was back on the street, walking home. Had I zoned out? The secret kalma. I never had remembered it. Not saying it—after I had promised a dying woman I would—was another failure on my part.

No one ever tells you how to get through grief, how to not let it take over your life. Because it does. Every part of your life is hit. And sometimes, just when you think you're turning a corner, months after your loved one died, you get hit by something new all over again. It doesn't stop. You just have to learn how to live with it, until the pain of them not being in your life anymore becomes a dull ache. What really got me, though, were the conflicting emotions. I loved her, I hated her, I wanted her approval, I wanted to do everything I could to piss her off. Even dead, my mother ruled over my life.

I wiped my face with a tissue and kept going. I couldn't help crying now and again and hated myself for it. I was so deep in thought that I was oblivious to what was happening around me. That was my mistake.

I didn't fully notice the car that was creeping along with me. It was just a slow car, nothing to worry about.

The light changed, and I crossed the street. I heard a car rev and some screeching, and then before I could register anything, I was on the ground; a man was next to me.

"Ooof!" I gasped as pain from the fall filled every part of me.

"Are you okay?" the man asked, his face alarmed, his pants now torn from shoving me and subsequently falling himself.

"What happened?"

"That car just tried to hit you!" He pointed to a speeding car, too far for me to even see who was in it.

"I got a picture of the license plate!" a woman said as people helped us both up. I had yet again been saved by complete strangers. Never let anyone tell you New Yorkers are mean. They aren't. They help—when other New Yorkers want you dead.

"I—thank you. Are you okay?" I asked the man who had saved my life.

"I'm fine, but that looked deliberate. I was watching that car follow you for half a block. You have someone after you?"

"We should call the police," the woman said.

Everyone was talking, and I couldn't get my brain to focus. What had happened? Why did I feel so embarrassed? I was mortified and wanted to slink away. But I didn't know how to escape this group of people who wanted to make sure I was fine. I felt pure panic.

"Dunia?"

I turned my head. "Zabir? What are you doing here?" He was standing there, out of breath, looking at me. I was even more confused now. What was going on?

"You're bleeding," he said. I looked down, and my elbow was scraped.

"Oh. Guess I got off lucky if that's all it is."

"Are you okay? I heard that car peel out of here and saw you. Did it try to hit you?" he asked. I didn't know if it was shock or stress or whatever, but I couldn't find myself able to answer anything, especially not questions from Zabir. My bystanders answered for me.

The police came quickly—the Upper East Side was like that. You know, wealthier, whiter than other parts of the city, so the response times were fast. The bystanders all gave statements, and someone gave me a tissue for my arm. I declined having the paramedics called. I wasn't that injured.

"You need to call Detective Alvarez," I told the police. "She's going to want to know about this."

I got the contact info of the man who saved me. I wanted to do something nice to say thank you. I was going to have to set up a savior fund for everyone who kept me alive. It felt like I'd been standing around with this crowd gawking at me for hours. My phone—which had cracked from the fall but still worked—said it had been only thirty minutes.

I didn't know who was in the car—the police asked. I hadn't seen the driver. I wish I had. I wanted to know who'd tried to kill me this time. But it was another mystery the police probably wouldn't solve.

The entire time they were asking questions, Zabir stood next to me. Finally, they said I could go home.

"You sure you don't want to get checked out?" one officer asked.

I shook my head. "I'm fine, I just need to get home. Thank you."

"I'll get her home. I'm a family friend," Zabir said. The officer looked at me, and I nodded. May as well get this over with; my day had already gone to hell.

Zabir got a cab somehow—close to impossible at rush hour, but he did it—and gently helped me into the back.

"Eighty-Ninth and First," I said, sitting back.

"Are you okay? What just happened?"

"I almost got hit by a car." I let out a laugh; it sounded flat and lifeless. He was about to ask me more when I held up a hand. "Can we wait till we get to my place? Please." I didn't want this cabdriver to see me fall apart, which I was very close to doing.

By the time we got to Eighty-Ninth Street, my elbow was throbbing. Maybe I should have had it looked at. But my only thought at the time was to get home. Home was safety. No one was trying to kill me there.

I let Zabir come up with me, and he stopped to pick up an envelope at my door. My name was written in pretty calligraphy on the front. I knew what that was and chose to ignore it. One crisis at a time here, folks.

He got me an ice pack from my fridge while I sat on the sofa, dazed.

"Here, this may help. You sure you don't want to go to the hospital?"

"I'm fine." It came out angry. "Are you going to tell Nadia about this?" He looked confused.

"She's your sister. Shouldn't she know?"

I stared at him. "No. She shouldn't. But do what you want. Wait, why were you there?"

"I was at the Met, checking out an exhibit, and wandered down. It was lucky I ran into you. I saw it happen from half a block away and ran over."

Lucky. I was never that lucky. "Or you tried to kill me and wanted to see if it worked." It came out without me meaning to say it. My filter had left, and now my mouth was saying whatever came to mind.

"You think I tried to kill you?" He said the words slowly.

"Well, you're spying on me, aren't you? Maybe you followed me?"

"I'm not spying on you!" The shock on his face seemed real, but I didn't know him enough to tell. He could be the world's best liar; I had no idea. I didn't know him enough.

"What do you call coming to see me because Nadia asked you to?"

"I'd say that her interests and mine aligned. But that's not what happened."

"What the hell does that mean?"

"It means I asked her about you when I saw the paper, and I asked if it was cool if I checked on you. Your sister didn't ask me to do anything, and she said you'd be upset if I even mentioned her name."

"Oh." I didn't know what to say. Was he lying? I couldn't get past him being there right as I was almost killed.

"Maybe we should talk about this later? You nearly just died."

"It's a thing I do," I joked. He didn't laugh.

"I'm serious. Why don't you let me grab you some dinner, and you clean up your arm. And then we can talk."

I let him help me up and went to the bathroom, where I gently washed my scraped arm. The wound was going to leave a big scar. I heard Zabir talking to someone. I bet it was Nadia. I knew he was full of shit. I threw the bathroom door open to see Detective Alvarez in my living room.

"Oh." Why did I keep saying that?

"Dunia, are you all right?" Detective Alvarez asked. "I got the info from the uniforms on the scene. Are you up for telling me what happened?"

"Sure, uh, have a seat." I didn't have many places to sit—this was a New York apartment, after all. She sat on one end of the sofa; I was on the other, while Zabir hovered.

"Did you see the driver?"

"No, nothing. But someone got the license plate. It should be in the statement."

"Have you noticed anything unusual recently? Anyone around who shouldn't be?"

"Just my ex. He's been calling, the usual. And, well, him." I nodded at Zabir.

"Zabir Mirza," he said, giving his name. "I'm a family friend. I walked by as it all happened but only caught the aftermath."

Alvarez nodded. "We have a BOLO out for the car, so let's see if anything comes from it." She glanced at my bloody arm. "Maybe you should stay home for a while. Your accidents are adding up."

"I have to work."

"I understand, but keep your guard up."

"Surely it was an accident?" I said. I hoped it was.

"It could be, but with your recent attack I want to be sure. I will get to the bottom of this."

"Will you? Because it's been a month since I nearly died, and we don't know why he did it. And now another possible attack? Sorry if I'm doubting you, but I need to know what the hell is going on."

Alvarez just stared at me for a moment. I think we were both in shock that I'd been that up front with her.

"I know where you're coming from. Investigations take time. Just know that your case has my undivided attention, okay? And we hit a snag investigating Skylar Jones's apartment. It's been cleared out by someone, not the landlord, so besides the photos and journal, we don't have much."

I didn't know how to respond. *Sorry you can't figure out why this stranger wanted to kill me?*

I watched her leave. I forgot to give her the new note that had been left. I hadn't even opened it.

Twenty

Transcript: *The Disappearance of Dunia Ahmed* podcast

AMANDA ROBERTS: We don't have a guest for today's episode, but we have something better.

    DANIELLE MCGUIRE: We have Dunia's journal. And let me tell you, it's like she's here with us.

    AMANDA ROBERTS: Right? It's the saddest thing. She was in so much turmoil over her mom dying. But also, they were not close. Like, listen to this: "I miss Ammi. Even if she hated me. Even though I was never good enough, I wish she were here. At least so she could tell me why she hated me." Wow. Her mom sounded intense. Like, imagine making your daughter think you hated her?

    DANIELLE MCGUIRE: So sad. That poor woman. She wrote more about her mom. There's a whole thing about how her mom wouldn't let her get any sun because she was too dark. I know there's a cultural thing there, but that's just so mean. And a mom figure named Carol that I think was her neighbor at some point? Her dad had passed when she was little, and Carol stepped in to help.

    AMANDA ROBERTS: She also wrote a lot about David: "David's mad at me for something I did, but I was asleep. It shouldn't be held against me if I can't remember what I did! I wish I could stop being such a freak." She was hurting.

DANIELLE MCGUIRE: So much. On a side note, isn't David so sweet? I was expecting to hate him, but I couldn't.

AMANDA ROBERTS: Right? And you listeners clearly feel the same, because we got so many requests to meet him. We'll pass your messages on to him, but we aren't a dating site. But maybe we should start one for our true crime–obsessed listeners!

DANIELLE MCGUIRE: Oh my God, that would be amazing: *Dying to Date!*

AMANDA ROBERTS: This is going to happen, so follow us on all our socials for more info.

Twenty-One

Zabir had been staring at me since the detective left. "Spit it out," I said. "Whatever you're thinking, just say it."

"I'm trying to figure out what's going on, and why you're so casual about almost dying." He sat where the detective had.

"Casual?" I let out a laugh that was partially a sob. "No, I'm trying to not lose my shit. I have no idea what's going on, so if you figure it out, let me know."

He nodded. "You didn't have to run out on me that day. You could have asked me about Nadia."

I shrugged. "I saw her text. I get it, you're the black sheep because you got divorced. How better to get back into everyone's good graces than by spying on her crazy sister?"

"That's not what happened. I told you, I asked if I could check up on you. I don't know, the subway thing, that's intense. All of this is."

"So Nadia isn't spying on me?"

"Not with my help. I won't tell her about today if you don't want me to. But I would like to know why you're so against her. She loves you."

"Ha!" The sound was harsh even to my ears. "It's not love, it's control. And I'm not interested. Look, thank you for helping me get home, but I'd like to be alone and pull myself together." I didn't mean to be rude, but I needed to think. And I couldn't deal with anyone else's feelings right now.

He looked disappointed. I was good at disappointing family, so he'd fit right in with them.

"Sure, but is it okay if I check in on you again? Not spying, I swear. I'm just worried about you."

"You don't even know me?"

"Well, I still worry. And I promise, whatever happens, I won't tell your sister how you are unless you want me to." I stared at him. Was he telling the truth? I had no idea, but I nodded.

"I'm going to hold you to that."

———

True to his word, Zabir didn't mention anything to Nadia. Or at least she didn't text or call me in a panic, yelling at me for almost dying again. I didn't trust him, but at least he wasn't as bad as I thought. Did this mean I owed him an apology? I wasn't sure. To be honest, the only person I trusted right now was Kendra, and by extension, Liz.

Once Kendra got back in town, we all had dinner at her apartment on the Upper West Side. I was thankful she didn't make me go out in public. It was hard to navigate trying to get over trauma while also being a fun and supportive friend.

"I have a present for you!" Liz said, holding out a gift bag.

"For me? But I didn't get you anything?"

"Just open it."

Kendra watched as I pulled out a small box. Inside was a gold necklace similar to Liz's.

"It's Persephone, goddess of the underworld. Because you almost died. Now you have a talisman of your own, and no one can ruin it like what's-his-name did to yours."

"What am I missing?" Kendra asked.

"Oh, David ruined a necklace that belonged to my dad. Liz, thank you! This is so thoughtful!" She helped me put it on. "Now we need to get Kendra one."

"Way ahead of you!" Liz said, and pulled a box out of her purse. "I figured we are goddesses, so let's adorn ourselves properly. Yours is Aphrodite, because of beauty and also for luck to get into their store." Aphrodite was the largest beauty retailer in the world. And Kendra had her sights set on them.

Kendra put hers on, and we took group selfies. Liz dubbed us the Goddess Girls. "I like it! Maybe I can do a goddess line of makeup. All gold and bronze."

"This is why you're a genius. Take my money, please!" Liz laughed. "I had these made with your initials on the back."

The Goddess Girls. These were the people I belonged with. Not with David, not dead on the subway tracks, but here in Kendra's apartment.

"Hey, you here?" Kendra asked. I had zoned out.

"Sorry, I had something weird happen. Well, a couple things. Wouldn't mind getting your take?" They both nodded; Liz leaned forward to hear.

"So I was walking home from work the other day because I can't do the train yet, and I was almost hit by a car. And in the crowd around me, who do I see? Zabir."

"Wait, what? You were almost hit by a car?" Kendra said, her face and voice full of alarm. "Are you okay?"

"Who's Zabir? And what?" Liz asked.

"He's my sister's husband's cousin, and we had coffee recently. I swore he was doing it because Nadia wanted to keep tabs on me."

"Back up. You were almost hit by a car??" Kendra said again. "I need to know more. Were you hurt?"

I held up my scraped elbow. "Just a scratch. It was so bizarre. After the police took our statements, Zabir got me home, and he swears that he didn't spy on me, that he wanted to see me and it had nothing to do with my sister."

"Do you believe him?" Kendra asked.

"I have no idea."

"Can I ask—why do you not like your sister?" Liz asked.

"Long story short, my mom blamed me for my dad dying, and Nadia sort of followed in her footsteps."

"D's dad had a heart attack, so it's totally messed up."

"Whoa, and I thought my family was bad."

"So, now what do I do with Zabir? I mean, he keeps texting, checking in. I don't think he told Nadia about the hit-and-run."

"Is he cute?" Liz asked. "What, you were thinking it too!"

"I was. Is he?" Kendra added.

"Kinda, yeah. Actually, very? He's divorced and a professor. But I could never date someone related to Nadia."

"By marriage, it doesn't count!" Kendra laughed.

"Anyways, I have no idea what's happening in my life. And I keep feeling like at any moment someone is going to jump out and murder me. How do I get this feeling to stop?"

"Honestly, time."

"Yeah, Kendra's right. Time, good friends, maybe therapy, and lots of wine," Liz added.

"Wine I can help with," Kendra said, refilling our glasses. "And just take it day by day. You're doing pretty great, all things considered."

"Wow, I love the friendship you two have," Liz said, her voice wistful. "I lost a lot of my friends with the whole brouhaha over my ex. They took sides."

"I'm sorry." I put my hand on her arm. "They sound shitty. You have us now."

"Damn right I do!"

Twenty-Two

Transcript: *The Disappearance of Dunia Ahmed* **podcast**

AMANDA ROBERTS: This is an exciting episode because it's a twofer! We had so much new Dunia info to cram in that we have an interview with her sister and with Detective Alvarez. Let's start with her sister, because if anyone can shed light on Dunia and her family life, it's her. Please welcome Nadia Chaudry.

NADIA CHAUDRY: And thank you for having me on. I hope that this podcast helps us get closure on things.

DANIELLE MCGUIRE: We have a copy of Dunia's diary—

NADIA CHAUDRY: You're saying it wrong. It's Doohnia, not Duhn-ia.

DANIELLE MCGUIRE: I don't hear a difference? Anyways, we have her journal, and she talks a lot about her childhood. She made it seem very . . . traumatic.

NADIA CHAUDRY: It was. Dunia was always such a fragile person. Even when she was little, we all knew we had to protect her.

AMANDA ROBERTS: Protect her from what?

NADIA CHAUDRY: Herself, mostly. You know about the sleepwalking, right? She did it all the time. She'd sometimes leave the house, and the police would come. I think at one point CPS came because people kept finding Dunia out at night alone.

AMANDA ROBERTS: Can we talk about your father?

NADIA CHAUDRY: Sure. Abu was amazing. He loved us, but Dunia was the apple of his eye. When he died, Dunia took it so badly. We all did, but she was there when it happened.

DANIELLE MCGUIRE: It was a heart attack, right?

NADIA CHAUDRY: Pulmonary embolism. There was nothing Dunia could have done. In fact, she did what she could—she ran to the neighbor for help. But it was too late.

AMANDA ROBERTS: Dunia's writings indicate that she felt you and your mother blamed her for her father's death. Can you give us some insight on that?

NADIA CHAUDRY: I don't know if *blame* is the right word. Abu's stress level was high because of her. Our parents fought a lot because of her. So naturally, people thought none of it would have happened had Dunia not been . . . Dunia.

AMANDA ROBERTS: Do you blame her?

NADIA CHAUDRY: No. I may have when I was younger and didn't know better. I didn't realize how troubled my sister was back then. I didn't understand everything.

DANIELLE MCGUIRE: What didn't you understand?

NADIA CHAUDRY: We have a history of mental illness in my family. And unfortunately, Dunia wasn't able to avoid it. She heard voices, talked to people that no one saw. My mom thought she was haunted. I don't know if she was ill or haunted. I'll be honest with you. I'm a believer, and I've tried to reconcile what I saw with logic, and I come up not knowing for sure what happened. And—well, she did some things that really terrified my mom.

AMANDA ROBERTS: Like what, if you don't mind us asking?

NADIA CHAUDRY: We shared a room—this was before Abu died—and Dunia tried to smother me with a pillow while I slept. She said she was sleepwalking, but it was so scary. My mom had her moved to the guest room that was also my dad's office. And she put a lock on my door. I think a lot of what Dunia experienced was us trying to keep everyone safe.

AMANDA ROBERTS: Whoa. We didn't have any idea. That's so freaky.

NADIA CHAUDRY: Like I said, she was very fragile and troubled, and while I'm not surprised she's disappeared, I wish she'd have left us a note or something.

DANIELLE MCGUIRE: You think your sister is dead, then?

NADIA CHAUDRY: That would be the kindest outcome for her, so yes.

AMANDA ROBERTS: Dunia seekers, we will have more from Nadia later in the season. But let's do a recap: Dunia was maybe nuts, she hated her mother, and she attracted death. Like, the grim reaper had her name on speed dial.

DANIELLE MCGUIRE: Yep! That poor woman was a walking magnet for crime. People just wanted her dead!

AMANDA ROBERTS: It's so bizarre, right? Detective Alvarez is joining us again to tell us all about the would-be hit-and-run that nearly took Dunia out. Welcome back.

DETECTIVE ALVAREZ: Thanks for having me again. The hit-and-run occurred early September as Dunia was walking home.

AMANDA ROBERTS: She was walking from Grand Central to Eighty-Ninth and First Avenue because she was traumatized from nearly being killed on the subway. For listeners not in New York, that's a lot of blocks. More than forty.

DETECTIVE ALVAREZ: That's correct. She was unable to take the subway, so she walked. As she approached East Sixty-First Street and Third Avenue, a red early-2000s Corolla-type sedan sped up and turned. We traced the license, and it came up stolen. A bystander witnessed this and threw Dunia out of the way. No one was seriously injured, but the car took off.

DANIELLE MCGUIRE: Do you know who was driving it?

DETECTIVE ALVAREZ: At the time, no. We learned after the fact—

AMANDA ROBERTS: Hold up, no spoilers! Now, I heard that there was someone at the scene that Dunia knew and who will become key in all of this: Professor Zabir Mirza.

DETECTIVE ALVAREZ: Right, he was a family friend who happened to be walking by. He didn't see the car or driver, just heard it and ran to see what was happening.

AMANDA ROBERTS: That's rather convenient. Did you look into his story?

DETECTIVE ALVAREZ: We did. He went to a Met exhibit and was walking around after. We have security footage of him at the museum. But his presence certainly raised questions about what he intended for Dunia.

DANIELLE MCGUIRE: How so?

DETECTIVE ALVAREZ: As I was going through his statement, his name rang a bell. It had come up on a phone-record search we did on Skylar Jones.

AMANDA ROBERTS: Whoa, so Skylar had called or had contact with Zabir?

DETECTIVE ALVAREZ: Precisely.

DANIELLE MCGUIRE: Oh my God. And Dunia had no idea!

DETECTIVE ALVAREZ: Not until I informed her. I think she was growing close with Mr. Mirza, so it was a shock to her. He was a family friend, but I suspected they were dating. Now, I don't have proof he had anything to do with her subway attack, but it was such a bizarre coincidence that it couldn't be dismissed.

AMANDA ROBERTS: Did he ever explain why he had contact with Skylar Jones?

DETECTIVE ALVAREZ: A bit. Was it to my satisfaction? No. He claimed he was helping Skylar with a haunting? That Mr. Jones had called him out of the blue for help. It was all too suspicious to me. Because after the subway incident, Zabir entered Dunia's life.

AMANDA ROBERTS: What a coincidence. So suspect. Did you consider him involved in the case?

DETECTIVE ALVAREZ: Absolutely. I warned Dunia to avoid him. She couldn't take chances. She didn't know what his intentions were. And he wasn't the most forthcoming with us, which only added to my suspicions.

DANIELLE MCGUIRE: Ladies, you have to be careful who you date! You need to run background checks. It's the only way. We have a private eye we work with if you need to order one. There's a ninety-nine-dollar special on our website right now.

Twenty-Three

Zabir kept checking in on me. Which I didn't mind as much as I thought I would. In fact, if I were being honest, I started to look forward to his texts. Did I still suspect he was telling Nadia every bit of info? Absolutely.

Still alive? he texted after work one day. I had just walked into my apartment.

Since this am, yes. Barely, long day. That was an understatement. The computers had gone down at work, and it had taken hours before we could fill any prescriptions. People were understandably pissed.

Good. Want to have dinner with me?

I froze. Dinner was something more than texting. Dinner meant a date, maybe.

Um, when?

Tomorrow night? Somewhere near you.

I wanted to say yes. And no. Instead, I shrieked and tossed my phone across my apartment because I was suddenly a teenage girl again.

I ran to retrieve my thrown phone and texted Liz, asking what I should do.

Say yes!!

Be like Liz. I could be like her. I accepted the date and then screamed into my pillow. I guess I did like Zabir after all. Or maybe it was the idea of a man interested in me again. David wrecked my self-esteem enough that I didn't see myself as a viable relationship option. But perhaps that was wrong?

What if all this were some nefarious plot to get me to spill my secrets?

"Okay, now you sound paranoid," I said to myself. "Nutjob."

I had a date, and I had no idea what to wear. Or how to act. Or what Zabir really wanted. I texted Liz some more. I needed backup on this.

I'm coming over, we'll pick looks! Being friends with Liz was like having the girlfriend you'd always wanted. I had never had friends like her or Kendra growing up. I couldn't wait for her to help me figure out an outfit for my nondate date.

"Why do you have holiday bells on your door?" Liz asked. She came over quickly—her apartment was downtown but a quick Uber ride up. I was amazed she even had time for this—Kendra was swamped at work.

"Oh, uh, this is embarrassing, but I sleepwalk, and I figure they'd keep me from leaving my apartment." I was staring into my closet, trying to will the perfect dinner look to appear.

"You're kidding!" She stared at me with fascination. "You're so weird in the best way. What do you do?"

My face felt like it was burning. I hated feeling like such a freak. "Uh, just walk around mostly."

"Do you leave your apartment?"

"No, but I used to when I was little. Leave the house, I mean. But that's what the bells are for. Just in case. Ugh, I have nothing to wear!"

"You should film it."

"My date?"

"No, film yourself sleepwalking. Put cameras up and film whatever you do at night. Just to see. I mean, it's a good way to keep an eye on yourself, right?"

In all my years I'd never once considered putting a camera up to watch me sleep. It felt so horror-movie-ish. What if I saw something terrifying on camera? What if I was the thing that was terrifying?

"I don't know," I demurred. I had to think about it.

"I'll help you set them up! It'll be fun, come on." And she started searching for cameras online despite my protestations against the idea. But there was no saying no to Liz, not really. I think that was what made her good at what she did. Investing in and growing companies took someone like her.

I had pulled three outfit possibilities out of the closet and brought them to the living room. "I don't want him to think this is a date."

"But it is a date."

"I have no idea. I can't figure out what he wants."

"Maybe he just wants you. You said he was single, right?"

"Divorced, yeah."

"I need to see a picture of him. ASAP."

She started searching his social media and pulled up his Facebook. It didn't seem updated much, but a photo was there.

"Oh, he's cute! Okay, look, if he's not a big weirdo, then you have to date him. You deserve a little fun. You've gone through hell. Time to enjoy life now."

I wasn't about to date anybody. Not now. I needed to focus on me. Which is what I said to her, and to which she rolled her eyes.

"Please, one of us should be getting laid."

"Well, you can have his number and hook up, then." I didn't mean it, but this topic was too uncomfortable for me. I wasn't ready, and I had no idea what Zabir's intentions were. Was I just letting my anxiety get the best of me? Probably.

"What's this?" Liz had put her phone down, her attention now on the latest note that had been left at my door. She reminded me of a kid sometimes, constantly looking around and picking things up. I hadn't even opened the note yet.

"Oh. Nothing." I grabbed it from her hands.

"That doesn't sound like nothing. Spill?"

I sighed. "I've started getting these weird notes left for me at work and here, and I need to give it to the detective."

"Since the subway? Open it. You have to. I need to see it." Her voice was commanding; I couldn't say no. I sliced open the envelope, and the card inside read, *I'm coming for you.* "What the hell? I can't believe you didn't tell us about these. How many have you gotten?"

"Just a couple, and to be honest, I've had so much going on, I forgot. Don't tell Kendra. I don't want to worry her. She's so busy."

"A secret? Okay, lips are sealed." She made a lip-locking gesture, her eyes excited at the idea of hiding info. "Now, let's find you a sexy outfit that also says 'This might not be a date date, but please ogle me.'"

"A tall order," I joked.

She ignored the clothes I had taken out and dug deep into my closet, pulling out a black dress I hadn't worn in ages. "This. It has to be this."

"No, that's too . . ."

"Sexy? Hot? Absolutely stunning? Go try this on. I want to see it on you."

There was no saying no. At all. I pulled the dress over my head in the bathroom, lamenting my unshaven legs. "Don't look at the hair, I'll deal with it," I warned as I walked out. The dress fit my chest well—and flared out at the waist. It looked good, but wasn't it too much for dinner?

Liz's face said it all. "You must wear that. And then call me after to see how it goes. A date! My girl has a date! What shoes are you wearing?"

"Are you always like this?" I asked.

"Insanely supportive of my friends? Yes."

"Good, because so am I, and next we need to find someone for you."

"Working on it, and it's TBA. I'm not saying more." She grinned before diving through my shoes. She, of course, found the perfect pair to wear.

———

I want to say I wasn't nervous all day. That the next day I didn't drop an entire bottle of pills all over the floor at work as I was counting them. I had butterflies that made me want to vomit. I hated this part of dating. Or whatever this nondate was. I hated the anticipation, the hope. Hope was what crushed me.

I ran home from work as quickly as I could. It was challenging on any day to walk the forty-plus blocks. But add in dodging anyone who got too close to me and watching every car, and I was damn near exhausted by the time I got home.

I knew I should cancel. I should. Tell him I wasn't up for this. But I wouldn't. If nothing else, I needed to know what his interest in me was. I still didn't trust him, but did I trust anyone? (Kendra and Liz, and that was it. A short list.)

"Ugh, why am I even doing this?" My empty apartment didn't answer me.

Zabir wanted to meet at this Italian spot not far from me, a ten-minute walk at most. He'd offered to pick me up first, but I'd declined. I didn't want him over; I wasn't sure why. But I was trying to trust my instincts, and they said to meet him there.

Instincts. I had no idea if mine were good or bad, but whatever they were, they had to keep me alive.

Zabir was already waiting outside the restaurant by the time I walked over. "I hope I'm not late?" I said.

"Not at all! You look amazing." I wore the dress Liz had said to wear. I felt like a sausage stuffed into my Spanx. Anything to look good, I guess.

"Uh, thanks, so do you." He was in dark jeans and a nice shirt, and that counted as dressy for men.

I was grateful for the wine when it came to our table, and even more thrilled to see him drink. I was never sure if other desis would have alcohol. It was a litmus test of sorts. If they had wine, then maybe they weren't too religious and about to tell me to pray more. I had no issue with anyone being religious, just as long as me not being religious also wasn't a problem. Which it often was. So many years of being told to pray more, that I was a shaytan, a devil, swirled in my head.

"I'm glad you said yes. I wanted to see how you were after—"

"Almost dying? I'm still here, so that's good, right?"

"Do you always make jokes about nearly dying?"

I shrugged. "Beats being traumatized, which I also am. Deflection is good! Now can we talk about anything else, please? I'm trying to get my life back to normal as much as I can."

His lip quirked. God, he was cute, though. His temples had streaks of gray that made him look distinguished. On me, it looked old. I needed to focus. Find out what he wanted, don't get lured in. (Too late.)

"Well, I taught three classes this week—school started last week."

"Oh, right! South Asian studies. So does that mean history?"

"One of them is a history class about colonialism and Partition. One is about women's rights on the subcontinent. And one is about folklore."

"I have to be honest, I know nothing about any of that. I'm a bad desi." That was the truth. When my mom pushed me away, I stopped being interested in anything having to do with our background. If I wasn't good enough for her and her friends, then why should I care about the culture? I'd only recently wished I knew more, but there was no crash course for identity crises. If someone made one, they'd probably rake the money in.

"Ha, well, I'm happy to fill you in. So, can I ask you—what is the deal with you and Nadia? Too intrusive?"

I shook my head. "We had a very different upbringing from each other." When he didn't say anything, I kept talking. I told him about my dad and how my mother blamed me.

He looked shocked. "I can now understand why you avoid your sister."

"She never mentioned it?"

"I've only talked to her when I see Arif. Which is like once a year at most?"

"So not a family spy then. Cool, cool. I don't know much about our culture, and I hate that, but also, I kind of hate that my culture shunned me, if that makes sense. I wish I'd had Nadia's childhood, to be honest."

"I'm sorry. I see why you feel that way. But if you ever have questions about anything, I can try to answer them."

I wanted to ask everything. Why did the oddball kids get shit on so much? The ones who didn't fit in? Was every family like mine? Was it normal to act like I had? Instead I went with a very different question.

"Okay then, why'd you divorce? If I have to tell you my secrets, you have to tell me yours."

"Ugh, God." He covered his face with his hands but laughed. "Okay, so I got married at twenty-six, and she was someone my parents loved. Daughter of family friends. They'd always wanted us to get married. But then it turned out she didn't actually love me and had a girlfriend on the side. I wouldn't have minded covering for her if she'd let me know. As it was, I fell in love with her, and it wasn't reciprocated." I watched the candlelight flicker on his face. It made him look serious and, at times, sinister. A play of shadows.

"I'm sorry. Do you guys still talk?"

"Yeah, she's happy. She married her girlfriend. Her parents are trying to come to peace with it all. Which makes me happy. But it was hard to love someone who loved someone else. I wish our culture was a little more open on that front."

"I can imagine." Desi parents had a very firm concept of what they wanted their kids to be. And if you deviated from that, well, it wasn't fun.

"Anyways, it's my turn to be happy," he added.

I didn't want to touch that comment with a ten-foot pole. If he meant me, I wasn't ready for that. "I'm not sure what your interest in me is, but I'm not ready to date seriously."

There, I'd said it. At no point was I leading him on.

"Is this a date, then?" He grinned; my face flushed. "I am interested in you for so many reasons, and I'm happy starting as friends and seeing where things may or may not take us. How's that?"

"That is . . . not as scary. Okay, I can handle that."

The dinner was fun. It was nice to talk to someone who understood how I grew up. Who got how my family was, even if some things defied explanation and logic (my mother).

"At some point, I'd love to know more about your dad. When you talk about him, your face lights up," Zabir said over tiramisu.

"He was amazing. I wish he were here."

"He might be. Some people believe the spirits of the dead never leave us."

"Well, I'm not one of them. I'm a firm believer in the end is the end. Total atheist here. Or agnostic. I'm not sure which."

He sat back, appraising me. "You know, there might be more to our existence than what we see."

"And that's fine and dandy, but it doesn't affect my day-to-day, so I'm not worrying about it until I'm dead."

"That's fair. I like people who are open—both that something may exist, or it may not. We don't really know."

"Yeah, like if there's concrete evidence of an afterlife, I'll believe. But until then, I'm sticking with what I can see and feel. But also I'm not religious. Mainly my mom ignored that part of my upbringing, so I never knew it." More like she ignored me. She was fairly religious, but when it came to me, she didn't bother after a certain point.

"I'm more fascinated by the folklore and stories passed down generations," he added.

We talked for hours. And drank more wine. I was certainly tipsy by the end of the date. I hadn't meant to be. So when he asked to walk me home, I, of course, said yes. Safety in numbers and all that. The walk was a bit stressful in that I worried what he expected at the end of it. But I didn't need to be.

He walked me home, we said good night, and he asked if we could hang out some more. I agreed. No passionate crazy moment; it was all very nice. And just the speed I needed.

He texted on his way home. I had a lot of fun. Can't wait for our next date.

Liz was going to be so proud of me.

Twenty-Four

AMANDA ROBERTS: Okay, Dunia seekers, we have another amazing surprise for you. This took some negotiating and a lot of back-and-forth to get this person to agree to speak to us. It wasn't easy, but she's a great "get."

DANIELLE MCGUIRE: That's right! None other than Liz Small is joining us to talk all things Dunia!

AMANDA ROBERTS: The myth, the legend!

LIZ SMALL: Oh, stop! [*laughter*]

DANIELLE MCGUIRE: We're just so psyched you agreed to join us. As you know, we're a little obsessed with you and Dunia. We're going to unravel your friendship from the beginning—no spoilers, okay? When you first met Dunia—

LIZ SMALL: It was like love at first sight! She was so resilient. I know a thing or two about that. She was really holding it together. I was so impressed by her fortitude.

AMANDA ROBERTS: Now, in her journal, Dunia said she had to meet you to help Kendra. Can you explain how you knew them?

LIZ SMALL: I'm blessed to come from money, and part of my role in the family estate is to invest in companies. I invested in Joy Skincare, Kendra's brand. I didn't push to meet Dunia; I was looking for new girlfriends to hang with.

AMANDA ROBERTS: So you gave Kendra money and then suggested you meet her best friend?

LIZ SMALL: Kendra talked about her nonstop. Like, in every meeting or conversation. And once I met Dunia, I understood why. But also, I saw the story about her in the news. Kendra set up a girls' night, and Dunia happened to come. There was no forcing this friendship.

DANIELLE MCGUIRE: What were your initial thoughts when you met Dunia? Did you find her strange at all?

LIZ SMALL: No. She did seem a little unsure of herself. Like, she was shaken up, you know? Which makes sense. Having to survive that is intense.

AMANDA ROBERTS: Was she devout?

LIZ SMALL: Like, religious? No, not at all. She never mentioned anything about religion.

AMANDA ROBERTS: Interesting. Did she tell you she was being stalked?

LIZ SMALL: By her ex, yes. You know how those things go. Men can be so irrational. David would not leave her alone.

DANIELLE MCGUIRE: You and Dunia became close really fast.

LIZ SMALL: Honestly, I think it's because I understood what she was going through. She never told anyone, but her ex cheated on her, and I'd been through that. I had my own issues I was healing from.

AMANDA ROBERTS: Wait, David cheated on her? We did not know that. He seemed so nice.

LIZ SMALL: Men are good at deceiving.

DANIELLE MCGUIRE: Was Kendra jealous of your friendship?

LIZ SMALL: I think it's natural to be jealous. She and Dunia started having issues as things went on. Even stopped speaking for a bit. I hope I didn't cause that rift.

Twenty-Five

My head was foggy from the wine. I never drank that much. Not that I'd had a lot—but a few glasses over a few hours was more than enough to do me in. I'd shuffled out of bed to make much-needed coffee when there was a knock at my door.

"Surprise!" Liz was holding a paper bag. The doorman hadn't called up, so I was extra confused. She was wearing a cream-colored jogging suit that somehow looked incredibly good. How she managed to be so pulled together so early I would never know.

"How'd you get up here?"

"Oh, the doorman is so sweet, I told him it was a surprise."

"Awww. Well, come in. Want coffee? I'm only on my first cup. Nursing a wine hangover."

"I brought bagels and cameras, so yes."

"Cameras?" What cameras?

"For your sleepwalking, duh." She brushed by me and put everything on the coffee table. I didn't remember saying yes to the cameras. Had I?

"First, tell me all about the date. Every gorgeous detail, please."

"Coffee, need more coffee," I rasped.

She ignored me and pulled her bagel out of the bag. She waited, watching me expectantly.

"Fine. It was fun. We talked a lot about family and shit. He's really nice."

"And . . . ?"

"And what?"

"Did you make out?"

"No, we did not! He walked me home, asked for another date, and that was that."

She stared at my face and then laughed. "You're so red, you like him!"

"Ugh, it's too early for this." I grabbed coffee for us both. "Cream or sugar?"

"Oat milk if you have it." I didn't. I made a note to myself to keep oat milk on hand for Liz.

"It's fine, I'll drink it black."

"Sorry! I'll stock up for your next visit." I yawned. "Anyways, cameras? I didn't think it was a go?" A.k.a. I didn't remember saying yes.

"I figured if I made it easy for you, you'd go along with it." She smiled.

"Is that how you get things done? Impressive."

"What can I say, I'm a go-getter." She was, and there was going to be no arguing with her on this. Besides, how bad could having cameras be?

"Okay, well, go get the cameras up while I sit here and try to be human. Sound good?"

"I'll handle everything. Got a stepladder?"

While Liz worked away, angling a camera at my bed—which made me all kinds of uncomfortable—Kendra texted apologizing for being busy.

Never apologize for that! Have so much to tell you—Liz is here!

Liz is at your apt? Why?

Helping with cameras. Long story. When are you free?

Dinner this week? Just us?

Absolutely!

"Okay, what do you think of the angle?" Liz asked. "The camera will catch you getting out of bed and moving around. Where else do you need one?"

"Um, the living room. I wake up in here a lot. It's weird, I keep dreaming that something is here that shouldn't be, and I think I'm searching for it?"

"You're such a freak, I love it."

After she was done, she showed me how to get to the videos. They would email themselves to me, and so if I ever did anything in my sleep, I'd have a video ready to go.

"I don't know if I ever want to see it, to be honest. What do I owe you for the cameras?"

"Oh, don't worry about it. A gift from me." It was an expensive gift.

"You don't have to bribe me to be your friend, you know," I said quietly.

She raised a perfectly tweezed eyebrow before nodding. "I guess I'm used to people who want me to help them in some way. I don't even think about it anymore, to be honest."

"You can buy gifts all you want, but I don't need them. I just want you to hang out. Wanna watch some shitty reality TV with me?" That was the extent of my functioning.

"God, I thought you'd never ask! And then I need more details about last night!"

I rolled my eyes but was actually excited to share. I'd had a date! It had gone well! I gave her all the details, and she seemed to approve. My life was finally looking up.

———

Come Monday, Mandy pulled me into her office. She didn't look happy and avoided my gaze. This couldn't be good. Had I done something?

"Is everything okay?" I asked. I hated when I messed up at work. I also hated how much I needed approval from authority figures.

"We've had some complaints about you."

"About me?" What had I done? I racked my brain but couldn't come up with anything worthy of a complaint. Just patients mad their insurance companies weren't paying for stuff, or their doctors wouldn't prescribe what they wanted. None of that was in my control. I did my best to mitigate things for them.

"Look, I know you're dealing with a lot with the whole subway thing, but I need you to be focusing while here at work. We've had two negative customer reviews about you specifically."

"What did I do? So I know to fix my behavior."

"They said you were rude and that you filled the wrong medication."

"The only time I can recall anything being filled wrong, it was because the doctor prescribed it incorrectly. I fixed it."

"Dunia, please stop arguing with me—"

"I'm not, I'm trying to figure out when I made a mistake so I can do better."

She sighed and pushed a paper in front of me. "Sign this. It's your first warning. If you get more, you'll be placed on an improvement plan." An improvement plan. That was the road to being fired. I knew Mandy had been waiting for this moment. She didn't like me, never had. Her predecessor had hired me, and she wanted to get rid of me.

There was nothing I could do. I signed, apologized, and got back to work. I had messed up, and I didn't know how or when.

"You okay?" Michael asked.

I nodded but didn't speak. I focused on filling pill bottles and calling insurance companies and doctors' offices. I had to do better.

The last thing I needed was to lose my job on top of everything else. But I felt like the biggest loser that day. Dunia, who couldn't even do her job right. Pathetic. My joyful weekend was long forgotten by the time lunch rolled around. I wanted to just hide. Which I did, after work. Zabir texted, but I told him I'd had a rough day at work and would talk to him later. I didn't want people to know I was such a screwup. Was I taking this too hard? Yes, but I hated doing a bad job.

———

The highlight of my week was dinner with Kendra. We met for sushi, and she gave me the biggest hug.

"You okay?" I asked.

"I am, I just needed some Dunia love."

"Well, let me give you a better hug, then." And I squeezed her as hard as I could.

"Better!"

"So, what's happening?"

"Just expansion woes. Liz has made some huge introductions for me, and I'm trying to ramp up production so I can meet expectations. It's a lot. I love it, but it's a lot."

"I'm sorry. Can I help in any way?"

"You already are. Liz is just . . . a force. You know?"

"Oh, yeah, I do." I told her about the cameras and how Liz decided I needed them. Kendra looked worried.

"I didn't know the sleepwalking had gotten that bad."

"It's fine, she just thinks it'd be fun to see it. I disagree, but it's Liz."

Her mouth quirked. "She's great at turning no into yes, and that's why she's with us. I mean, she's opened so many doors. I just have to . . . get it all done."

"And you will! She also picked out my outfit for my date—oh my God, I didn't even tell you." I covered my mouth. I couldn't believe I hadn't told Kendra about my date.

"What? When? With who?"

"With Zabir. We had dinner on Friday."

She counted on her hands. "Six. It's been six days since that date, and you didn't tell me. Six days."

I told her about all of it, the dinner, the conversation, the cute way he texted me daily to make sure I hadn't been murdered.

"Well, I need to meet him. And soon. Has Liz met him already?"

"What? No! I wouldn't do that." I felt so guilty now. I hadn't meant to freeze her out. Kendra's work was so important that I didn't want to add things for her. But I'd screwed up. I reached for her hand. "You are my best friend. Always. Liz is just fun to hang with."

"I insist on meeting him so I can suss him out myself. And then we'll talk about how you'll make this up to me."

"How about dinner's on me?"

"It's a start."

I didn't tell her about work. I was too mortified. An emotion I was getting far too used to feeling.

"How are you otherwise? After your almost accident?"

"I'm trying to be more aware of my surroundings, I guess."

"Any updates from the police? On anything?"

I shook my head. "Well, someone cleared out Skylar's apartment, so the police don't have too much info besides his stalker photo wall and journals. It's so frustrating. I just want to know who was behind this and why." I felt the mood shift. I didn't want dinner to be a pity party. "But tell me about the new launches. What's going on?"

Kendra grinned. "I don't want to get too excited yet, but something huge is happening. Just wait till it's finalized because I'm being superstitious."

I knocked on the wooden table three times. "I'm ready whenever you can tell me."

———

When I got home, there was another letter against my door. I was getting sick of these. I should have asked Liz to put up a camera here. I opened it. *He can't save you.*

"Thanks, cryptic stalker," I muttered. Another note to give to the police.

That night I sleepwalked again. I woke up facing my living room windows, overlooking First Avenue. I was thankful yet again that my windows only opened partway. Imagine being able to get out in my sleep, twenty-nine floors up. I watched the videos out of a sick curiosity. There I was standing in the living room, and then by my bed. And I couldn't be sure, but there was a blurry spot almost out of frame. Maybe a camera defect? I'd have to ask Liz.

Twenty-Six

Dunia, age five

"No, I want her in a dress. A nice dress." Ammi wanted family photos, which meant putting on our nicest clothes and going to Sears. Abu suggested a cute little shalwar kameez. Ammi shook her head. "They should look Amrikan."

This was a thing with her. Us looking Amrikan. Like we belonged. I think Carol had even taken Ammi shopping to show her what to get us.

"But they look so cute in their kupra!" Abu protested. But it was no use. It was what she wanted.

"They need to fit in here. For as long as we live here." Ammi hoped we'd move to Pakistan, a place she knew well. A place she wasn't an outsider. She fought with Abu to move back.

She combed my hair, hard. And then accidentally burned me with a curling iron. I started crying.

"Stop crying!" she snapped. Then she paused. "Sorry, beti. I'm just trying to get us ready. Does it hurt?" She looked upset. I wished she was able to tell us what was bothering her, but I was scared she'd say it was me. I was what bothered her. That her friends thought I was a pagal and didn't want me around.

I wiped my eyes.

"Good girl, you're being brave." She smiled at me. It was moments like this that I loved. Me and her. And no yelling, nothing but us together.

She finished fixing my hair and was satisfied with how I looked. We went and took the photos, and once Ammi had the prints, she showed them off proudly.

"Oh, you know, you really should think of putting makeup on Dunia," Ayesha Auntie tutted. She was Ammi's best friend and Jamal's mom.

"Makeup? At her age?"

"Just to make her less dark for the photos."

"Oh." Ammi nodded. My darker skin was a problem that needed fixing. I listened to all this.

My skin was an issue. I could fix that. I went into Ammi's room and sat down in front of her dresser. Her makeup was there. I could make myself pale. I could make them love me. I poured out her foundation and put it all over my face. I was white now!

I walked out to show her my work.

"Look, Ammi!" I said excitedly.

She and Ayesha Auntie gasped. "What did you do?" Ammi asked.

"I made my skin look like yours!" I said proudly.

"Oh-ho!" Ayesha Auntie said, shaking her head. But she was laughing.

"Let's go wash your face."

"No! I want to look like you."

"Okay, but not like this. Come."

Ammi roughly wiped the makeup off me. She wasn't happy with me. I had tried and failed yet again to make her proud of me.

Ayesha Auntie laughed from the doorway. "At least she knows her skin is bad. That's good. Easier to work with."

Twenty-Seven

"I can't believe you don't know how to cook." Zabir laughed. He was kidding, I hoped. "My mother had my sister in the kitchen when she was four. I had to beg her to teach me." He was over for dinner. I really didn't cook, I was terrible at it, so he picked up some Chinese takeout, complete with dumplings.

"She taught Nadia, but she didn't want me to get hurt, I guess. I mostly learned the basics of microwave cooking from my neighbor Carol." I felt guilty at even telling him these secrets, as innocuous as they were. "You won't tell Nadia I told you this, right?"

He looked surprised. "No, of course not. I swear."

"Okay. I know I'm being paranoid, it's just she and I had very different experiences, so you know how it is."

"The golden child versus the black sheep. We all have those stories." He smiled wryly. "Even me."

"What's your family like?" I asked. I needed to stop sharing about myself and get more dirt on him. He glanced down for a moment, his long lashes distracting me.

"They're coming to terms with my divorce, so that's good. I used to think they were so suffocating with their rules and traditions, but then I realized as I got older that they were doing their best. I mean, our parents were younger than us when they had us. It's crazy to think of that. They're humans; they had the same issues we do."

I nodded, though I wasn't sure I could say the same about my family. I wanted to lighten the mood. "Imagine if two black sheep get married?" I laughed loudly. Zabir just peered at me with those intense, inquisitive eyes. "I was joking, I'm not proposing to you."

"Too bad, I'm a catch."

"And I'm not?"

Talking with him was so surprisingly easy. Even though our families were very different—his wasn't that religious; they didn't have the imam on speed dial, like my mom did—their customs and lives were like mine. Minus the whole ostracizing-a-child-for-things-beyond-her-control thing. The more desis I met, the more I learned just how peculiar my family was in comparison. Maybe we weren't the norm? Maybe my childhood had been extra messed up.

"My family isn't fond of my courses, though," he said.

"Why? What's wrong with history?"

"It's the folklore class. I teach about the scarier elements. You know, shaytan and jinn. Some people are really scared of them," he said.

I blanched. *Shaytan* was what my mother called me when I was little and she thought I wasn't listening.

"Are you okay?" he asked.

"Oh, yes, sorry. I don't believe in that stuff. Can't be scared of something that isn't real." I felt my face warming again. I wasn't ready to share these things with him or anyone. Besides, things that went bump in the night almost always had an easy, logical explanation. Pipes, bad wiring, carbon monoxide poisoning. Very few ghost experiences were actually ghosts. If any.

"You don't think they're real?" he asked, pausing dipping his dumpling in sauce. "Because I do." Was he teasing me again? I had a hard time discerning.

"Stop it, you do not!"

"I do. I teach about it, in fact—in my folklore class."

He couldn't be serious, right? "You're joking."

"There are so many tales about jinn that I think they have to be real. And I've seen one." I dropped my chopsticks.

"Why don't you come to my lecture? It's tomorrow evening at six thirty. You should be out of work by then, right?"

"Oh. Um, I can. Wait, am I going to see a bunch of coeds who are hot for teacher?"

"Why, jealous? And nah, I grade too harshly for anyone to have a crush."

The banter and flirting were thrilling. Even if it was about the monsters my dad told me about as a child. And I liked the idea of seeing him in his element. Professor Zabir, kind of hot.

"Okay, I'll come. Can I bring a friend?"

"The more the merrier."

There was more I wanted to say to him. I wanted to tell him my mom's fear became an obsession. And that over time, it drove a wedge between us that we'd never heal. All because she was scared of some silly stories. I wasn't sure how I felt about going to a lecture where the monsters from childhood were considered real. But I didn't know how to tell him that. It was too soon. I also wanted to say I was enjoying myself, but I felt silly.

"What's wrong? You look unhappy?" he asked.

"It's just . . . there's more to my childhood, and I'm not ready to tell you all of it. And I don't know how I'll feel about a jinn lecture. Let's say maybe I'll come, but if I don't, don't be mad?"

He reached for my hand. "You do whatever makes you feel comfortable. I promise I won't take it the wrong way."

He was in every sense the opposite of my ex. Where Zabir was kind and thoughtful, David was charming and a little cruel—which he covered with jokes. It was unnerving to all of a sudden be with someone who cared about my feelings. It made me dizzy.

"Okay, so maybe. A good, solid maybe." I grinned, and we moved on to easier, more fun topics. Like the fact that he needed to go clothing shopping soon and hated the mere idea of it. I offered to go with. Not that I was an expert, but it was more fun with friends, right?

"I'm absolutely taking you up on that." His smile was so genuine, it made my heart skip a beat. "You okay?"

"Yes. Uh, I'm just enjoying myself, and I'm not sure I'm used to that."

"Well, you should get used to it. Because you might be stuck with me. I'm gonna keep my eye on you," he teased. My face stayed burning for the rest of the evening. He kissed my cheek before leaving.

I, of course, invited both Kendra and Liz to the lecture the next night. If I were going to this, I needed backup. Maybe someone to hold my hand.

The next evening, I walked downtown and met Liz outside the Brown Building by Washington Square Park. "I don't get it, why are you so scared of what he's going to talk about?" Liz asked as we waited for Kendra. Zabir's class was going to start shortly.

"I had a very superstitious family, and they sort of took things to extremes." *Please don't ask more,* I silently begged.

"Oh. Yikes. Well, hopefully this will be more fun than scary. There's our girl!" She waved Kendra over, and we went inside, going up to the sixth floor. The room was a large lecture hall, and we sat in the back, where no one would notice us.

Class started, and Liz grabbed my hand. What if Zabir was awful? What if he was brilliant and I was awful in comparison? Kendra grabbed my other hand. Thank God for good girlfriends.

"Welcome back, class! Last lecture we talked about the different folklore topics, but today, we're going to dive into my favorite one: the jinn."

Liz mistook my discomfort for nervousness. "He's so cute," she whispered loudly.

"Let's talk about the different types of jinn," Zabir continued. He went through and listed names I didn't know about: the Marids, Ifrits,

Ghuls. "Where do we know that last one from? It's where we get the word *ghoul* in English."

Despite my fears, I was rapt. This was more interesting than any class I'd taken, ever. He was rattling off more names for different types of jinn. This was so different from the stories my dad told me. Those were more macabre fairy tales; this was a full classification of jinn. There were stronger jinn that could shape-shift and look like humans or animals, and weaker ones who didn't do much except lick your feet at night. (I was never sticking my feet out from under my blanket again.) Some would go near humans; others wouldn't. He talked about how they were created from smokeless fire, unlike angels (made from light) and humans (clay).

"Sometimes, witnesses report seeing walking black smoke when they see a jinn." That stuck in my head. Skylar's journal had a smoke-looking thing.

I felt a pang, listening to Zabir. There was so much about my own culture I didn't know. That I'd run from. Or that my mother had pushed me away from. She hated all things jinn, and the only times she and Abu would fight was when he told me those stories and I acted out. And then when I was old enough to make my own choices, I ran from everything. I wanted to be far away from people who thought I was crazy. I wanted a fresh start with no one expecting anything from me.

"Can we meet him?" Liz asked after the lecture ended. "Are you okay with that, or . . . ?"

"Yeah, actually, that would be nice."

We waited ten minutes and then walked over to Zabir once the students had finished talking to him.

"Dunia, you made it!" He hugged me. He smelled incredible, and despite myself I inhaled deeply.

"That was amazing! You're such a great professor." I was gushing.

"It helps that the source material is fascinating." He turned to Liz and Kendra. "Hi, I'm Zabir."

"I'm Liz! That was so interesting!"

"Kendra, nice to meet you."

"I hope you don't mind," I added. "I needed backup for this."

"Not at all! You guys hungry?"

"You read my mind." Liz laughed. "Maybe you're a supernatural force."

"Maybe I am." Zabir winked at us. I felt my stomach flip, and Kendra grabbed my hand to steady me.

"I like him," she whispered as we walked to a Sardinian wine bar Zabir knew about. That meant everything. A seal of approval. Kendra never liked David and only put up with him for me.

"He gives me butterflies."

"That's good! You deserve good things."

The night turned into Kendra and Liz grilling Zabir and him handling it with humor. I just watched in both horror and fascination, mixed with delight that everyone was getting along.

"Married? Divorced?"

"Kids? What about your family?"

"What are your intentions with Dunia exactly?"

The last question made me choke on my wine. "My intentions—you okay?" I nodded. "Well, I'm hoping to get to know her so we can see how we like dating. And take it nice and slow. Maybe get her to spill some of her secrets." He glanced at me as he said it, though his smile belied his seriousness.

"You do have a lot of secrets, D," Liz added. "Like, the sleepwalking alone."

"You sleepwalk?" Zabir asked, his eyes excited.

"Uh, yeah. That's why there are cameras up in my apartment."

"I put them up!" Liz chimed in.

"I thought you were either doing an OnlyFans or really into security."

"What?" The laughter was contagious. "No, I just get up and run around my apartment." That was an understatement. I had done things, but those secrets needed to stay with me.

"You could make a killing with feet videos," Liz chimed in. I groaned.

"So you really sleepwalk?"

I nodded. "Since I was a kid. But wait, how many classes are you teaching each semester?" I knew the answer, I just wanted to change the subject. I wasn't ready to tell all to anyone yet, even if they were handsome and sweet.

My subject change was successful! And we all started sharing school stories.

"I met D in pharmacy school, and I knew then she was going to be a bestie for life," Kendra said.

"Wait, Dunia, what was Kendra like?" Liz asked.

"Oh, driven, brilliant, knew exactly what she wanted and didn't let anyone stop her—kind of like how she is now. I just tagged along for the ride."

"You're selling yourself short! Dunia helped me with classes. We helped each other, really. It was nice having someone else to work with."

I didn't know what Zabir thought of my friends, but he seemed to be having a good time.

After Liz and Kendra left, it was just me and Zabir. And despite having been out with him before, I felt nervous to be alone with him.

"Thanks for coming to the lecture. It was nice to see a friendly face."

"It was so interesting. Not at all the stuff I was taught."

"One day you'll have to spill all and tell me about it. Walk you to a cab?"

"Please."

He held my hand as we wandered east so I could take a cab straight up Third Avenue.

"I'm glad you weren't scared by the jinn." He leaned to kiss my cheek and put me in a cab. I waved as we drove off.

I sat there grinning like an idiot for the entire ride. But a good evening could do that to you! I appreciated how slowly he was going. Kendra and Liz were both blowing up my phone, raving about Zabir. I was so engrossed in my texts that when I got out of the cab and walked into my lobby, I didn't notice who I'd walked right past: David.

He grabbed my arm. I screamed and dropped my already cracked phone. The doorman jumped up.

"Is there a problem?"

"No, tell him it's fine. We're friends." David smiled. I used to think that smile was so handsome, but it seemed wrong now. Distorted. Like it was hiding something.

"It's not fine. Let go of me. You can't be here. You have to leave."

I picked up my phone—thankful it hadn't fully shattered—and walked into the elevator. David was shouting at me as the doors closed, but I didn't listen to whatever he wanted to say. I watched him as the elevator doors closed, and for a brief moment it looked like he was standing in front of smoke. That couldn't be right. I must have been tired, and Zabir's lecture was in my head.

Another note was waiting for me outside my door. I was more convinced than ever they were from David.

I was going to see if Detective Alvarez could help with a restraining order. I had done everything I was supposed to, and nothing happened. The justice system in a nutshell.

Twenty-Eight

Dunia, age five

"Look how cute they are together," my mother said, pointing to me and Jamal. We were swimming in our pool. I was only allowed to swim when one of my parents was watching, and I always had to wear the highest SPF Ammi could find. I heard her but dove underwater to pretend I didn't. I came up in time to hear Ayesha Auntie.

"No, Jamal is too good for her. Maybe okay for Nadia."

"Nadia is too old for him," Ammi said.

"And Dunia is a pagal." Ayesha Auntie laughed at that. Ammi's face darkened. She looked mad. "Look at how kala she's getting," Auntie tutted.

I wanted to practice my swim lessons. I wasn't the best swimmer, but I was learning. But swimming meant being in the sun. I had put sunblock on, so I didn't know what the problem was. Jamal was getting darker than me, and yet she said nothing.

"She'll never find a husband if she stays that dark."

A husband? Me? Gross! I was five. Boys were gross.

I dove under water again so I couldn't hear Auntie complain about me. There was nothing I could say or do to stop her from saying mean things. She was my elder and Ammi's friend. I had to just smile and be polite and listen to her and say, "Ji, Auntie."

I swam to the surface, but something pushed me down. A hand. Jamal's hand. He was holding my head underwater. He always played mean jokes on me like this. I shook my head so he'd move, but he wouldn't. He held on tighter. I couldn't get away. I tried to kick, but he wouldn't let go.

My lungs felt like they were going to burst. I wanted air, sweet, yummy air. Why wouldn't he let go?

I closed my eyes for a second. I was tired and just wanted this to stop. The next thing I knew, I was lying next to the pool, and Abu was patting my back as I coughed up water.

"What happened? What did you do??" Ayesha Auntie shrieked.

"What's wrong with you?" Abu yelled at Jamal. "You could have killed her!" He was furious.

"Jamal did nothing!" Ayesha Auntie protested.

"He held me underwater," I said, coughing. Nadia had been the one to dive in and get him to stop. She scowled at him.

"He did, I saw him." She may have not been the nicest sister, but she helped me with Jamal.

"She must have done something, because he would never do that," Ayesha Auntie said. But I hadn't done anything.

After that, I refused to ever be in the pool with Jamal again. He was a mean boy, and no one would stop him from hurting me. So I stayed in my room every time Jamal came over. When Jamal did come to our house, he wasn't allowed in the pool. We could only swim when Abu was around to watch us. So Ammi had us go to Ayesha Auntie's more.

I didn't like going because they had a dog. She was the only auntie I knew who had one. It was a white furry one named Baby.

We weren't allowed a pet. Ammi didn't want the hassle of having to take care of us and an animal. Most desi families we knew didn't like dogs. They thought they were dirty and didn't want them inside. I knew that was a lie, but I couldn't argue with my parents. So no dogs, no cats, no hamsters. Every time we prayed, I asked Allah for a kitten.

I never got one; I probably prayed wrong. Or maybe I was so bad I didn't deserve a pet.

"Can you just behave, for once?" Ammi asked when I cried about going to their house. "Be like Nadia." Her favorite thing to say. *Why can't you be like your sister? Nadia never acts out. Nadia never sleepwalks. Nadia isn't a shaytan.*

I was still crying when we got to their house.

It was so weird that a desi family had a dog. Most of the time, they had to keep Baby locked in a room because everyone was scared of her. But Ayesha Auntie let the dog out when we were there. Baby was a mean little dog. Jamal was meaner.

"Dunia, come here, play with her. She won't bite you." Jamal smirked. I should have known not to listen to him. But I went over and put my hand down, and Baby snapped at it.

I yelped.

"She's just playing. Here, let's feed her." He picked up some bread from a table that was outside. I didn't know to question why it was there. Or why he wanted me to help him with the dog.

He dropped a slice, and Baby went for it, eating it with a speed I'd never seen before. Jamal watched me and grinned. He dropped the next slice and told Baby to wait.

"Dunia, pick that up. I didn't mean to drop it," he said. I believed him.

And I did what he asked. I picked up the bread, and it was at that moment Baby's teeth sank into my arm.

There was blood everywhere. I didn't know what to do so I screamed. I screamed until my parents ran over and Abu picked me up.

"Abu!" I shrieked, while Jamal watched.

"Baby is just very serious about food," Auntie said, smiling at me. "Don't take her food away next time, okay?"

"Jamal said to."

"What?"

"Jamal told me to pick up the bread."

"No, no, beti, Jamal would never do such a thing. You know, dogs can tell when someone is a pagal."

"Why do you guys never listen to her? Jamal did tell her to pick up the bread." Nadia stood, her hands on her hips, yelling at my mother and Auntie Ayesha. I never thought she'd do that.

Abu took me for stitches at the ER; Ammi and Nadia stayed behind. As we left, I waved at Jamal's brother Adnan—he was the nice one. He looked so angry. He'd seen what Jamal had done. But Auntie Ayesha would never believe him.

I had to get twelve stitches on my arm. Ammi wouldn't look at my bandage, like the sight of it sickened her.

The dog didn't get put down. I know because I was forced to see it every time we went over for dinner. I didn't want Baby to die; I just wanted her kept away from me. Auntie Ayesha started putting her in a bedroom for me.

Adnan told me once that he played pranks on Jamal, so much so that his brother was terrified of the dark. He'd hide under his bed and shake it while Jamal slept. That's when the bed-wetting started. I loved it. Jamal deserved every bad thing ever.

I begged my mother to not make me hang out with Jamal. I told her he scared me. That he was mean.

"He's just being a boy. That's how they are. He probably likes you. Come on, be a good girl now."

Boys got to act out, but girls? No, we had to behave and be good and not imagine things that scared everyone. Only Baba agreed with me. He tried to reason with my parents, but it didn't help.

"Do you know what karma is?" Baba asked me. I shook my head. "It means that all the bad things Jamal does will come back to him. Don't worry about him, okay?"

"Okay, Baba."

When Jamal fell down the stairs a week later, I shrieked that it was karma.

"He deserved it!" I said, skipping around the house. My mother was horrified. Jamal had broken his leg. He was stuck on crutches. He should have died, but I didn't tell them that. I didn't say that's what Adnan was going for when he pushed him. I just cheered it all on.

Twenty-Nine

I had more of those creepy letters to drop off with the detective, so I stopped by on my way home from work the next day. I wanted to ask her about helping me with David. It wasn't her job, but maybe she could make things happen. I needed him to go away.

She led me to a room this time, and she took the letters I'd put in plastic bags.

"These were delivered where?"

"My apartment. They were outside my door."

"And the doorman didn't see anyone drop them off?"

I shook my head. "No, but my ex was in my lobby right before I found the most recent one last night. Can you help me with the restraining order? I don't know what's taking so long."

"I'll look into it. I have some new information I wanted to run by you. So glad you came by." She looked serious, but then, my cases were serious.

"About Skylar?"

"Yes. Sit, please."

I'd been hovering at the table. I sat and waited for whatever she was going to tell me. I braced myself.

"We found someone he had been in contact with before the attack. As in, quite a few calls back and forth."

I felt my stomach drop. She was going to tell me my ex had planned this and tried to kill me. I knew it. I took a deep breath.

"Skylar had reached out to Zabir Mirza," Alvarez said. "The man who was a witness at your hit-and-run."

I blinked. "I'm sorry, did you say Zabir?"

"Yes."

I could hear my heart pounding in my ears. What did Zabir have to do with this?

"He's a family friend," I stammered. "We've hung out a bit recently. He never mentioned Skylar or knowing him." It was like the world around me had crumbled, and I was standing on the edge about to plummet down. Zabir knew Skylar?

"Here are some phone records." She laid out the pages, showing me a number that Skylar called a lot the week before he tried to kill me. And that number had called him back. I pulled out my phone and compared the digits. It was Zabir's number. Zabir knew the man who tried to kill me. He'd spoken with him before the attack. And he hadn't said a word to me or the police. I felt sick.

"Is there a bathroom I can use?"

"Yes, down the hall to the right."

I ran. I was going to vomit, and I needed to get to the ladies' room. I steadied myself, washed my face in the sink, and tried my best not to look like the rug had just been completely pulled out from under me.

I slowly walked back to the room.

"You okay?"

"Just shocked. Zabir . . . he's my sister's husband's cousin. He reached out to me after the attack, and we've been hanging out. He never told me he knew Skylar." I didn't tell her we'd gone on dates, that for the first time in a while I liked someone. That he'd made me feel hopeful about things. Hope was what crushed you in the end.

Alvarez's face looked worried. "Dunia, listen to me. We don't know his motives or what is happening, but until we do, do not be alone with him. Please. We will pull him in for an interview. We've left him messages, but please, please keep yourself safe. It could be a harmless coincidence, but I don't believe in those."

I nodded, not sure I could speak. Was this why he wanted to hang out? Was he trying to finish the job? If so, why all the flirting? Why meet my friends? That was just mean. He was getting me to like him so he could, what, kill me? Was that the plan? Make this as painful as possible?

I cabbed it home, not trusting myself to make the walk. I texted Kendra and Liz that there was an emergency and I needed someone to come over if they could. Both showed up to my apartment an hour later.

"What's going on? You look terrible. What happened?" Kendra asked. "Let me get you some water."

I waited for them to sit down before I told them everything I'd learned.

"Wait, Zabir knew Skylar?" Liz asked, her face as shocked as mine.

"Apparently. There were phone records. It was his number. I don't know what's going on, but he's involved and—" The dam finally burst. I sobbed. I couldn't help it. Just when I thought I'd turned a corner and my life was getting back on track, the man I was sort of dating was somehow involved with my attacker.

"Does this mean he wanted you dead?" Kendra asked.

I shrugged, wiping my face with a tissue. "I have no idea. But the detective said to not be alone with Zabir until they have time to figure out what was happening."

"This is full-on terrorism," Liz declared. We stared at her for using such a loaded word. "What? I'm an ally, okay. But he's terrorizing you."

"Let's maybe calm our language until we know what's going on," Kendra said gently. "Listen, why don't you come stay with me this weekend?"

I shook my head. "No. He's not going to scare me out of my own apartment. I just—why me? Why are these crazy guys attracted to me?" What had I done that deserved this?

No one had an answer. But I knew what it was. The common denominator in all of this was me. It had to be something I'd done.

"Are you okay?" Kendra asked, taking my hand. I shook my head.

"Fuck him. Just fuck him!" Liz declared. I'd never seen her look so angry. "I'm sorry, but that's so messed up. I hate him."

"Me too," I said.

"Oh my God, what if he was the one in the car who tried to hit you?" Liz asked. "He showed up after it happened, right?"

I nodded. "He did, and he was out of breath, like he'd been running. Oh God, this is bad. Whoa." The idea that Zabir had wanted me dead was like throwing the heaviest weighted blanket on my head. Like I couldn't keep myself upright, it was too much.

My phone chimed. It was Zabir. I hadn't answered any of his texts.

"Want to block him?" Kendra asked.

"No, I need to be sure if he threatens me, I can take it to the cops. Don't worry, he won't catch me unaware again."

———

That night, I dreamed that my mother was here, in my apartment. She was drinking tea. And complaining. Her two favorite things to do.

"Never should have trusted that Zabir. Look how he is. It's why he's divorced."

"Thanks, Mom."

"You never listen to me."

What was it called when you dreamed up the same arguments and fights you had with your mother your entire life? To me, it was hell. She was dead, yet her arguments hadn't died with her.

When I woke up, I didn't even look at my phone. I didn't want to see or talk to anyone. It was a Saturday, so I could. I was going to hide. But first I'd let Kendra and Liz know so they didn't panic that I'd been murdered. That thought made me laugh. If you'd asked me months ago if that was a real fear, I'd think you were nuts. And yet, here we were.

Not dead, just hiding, staying in my apt all weekend. xx.

It seemed the safest way for me to live right now: not leaving my apartment. Sure, I'd become that crazy old lady in a housecoat and slippers who yelled at the young hooligans in the hallway, but I'd be alive. If I focused on staying alive, maybe the pain I felt from Zabir's betrayal wouldn't be too overwhelming.

I even ordered in bagels to be delivered from across the street. *Hello, world, 'tis I, Dunia the shut-in.* Okay, maybe I was losing my mind. But who wouldn't if they were me? I had been attacked at least once—not sure about the hit-and-run—and found out the man I was sort of dating was involved.

I'd like to say I managed to organize my life, come up with a plan of attack on Zabir, figure out why he wanted me dead—but I didn't. I watched Lifetime movies and shuddered at the thought of my life becoming one.

I was only interrupted in my wallowing and despair by Liz, who showed up at my door at seven that night.

"I brought wine, ice cream, and face masks."

"Oh, thank God."

We sat and watched movies where the woman was in danger, drank until we were tipsy. On commercial breaks, Liz went on tirades about Zabir.

"That schmuck. He fully is lying to you. God, and then he has the gall to be so charming. I hate him."

I nodded, too tired to do more.

Liz went home at midnight. I'd ignored my phone. I had five unread texts from Zabir.

"Not tonight," I muttered and went to bed. If only I'd stayed there.

I drank three glasses of wine, again, far more than I should have. Drinking too much made me sleepwalk. All night I ran around my apartment like a mouse in a maze. Searching for something, I had no idea what. That was the mystery of my dreams. By the time I cracked my eyes open in the morning, I was thoroughly exhausted.

I sat up and groaned, my head pounding. I'd have to tell Liz to cool it with the wine. My phone was already buzzing.

Are you okay? Did I upset you or something? Can you please talk to me? Zabir had texted. I wasn't ready for this.

I got up and searched for snacks. I needed to do a solid grocery run, get some healthy food. But then again, why be healthy if someone was going to murder me? My hangover logic made sense, and I threw my shoes and a bra on and went across the street for a much-needed bacon, egg, and cheese.

I was ravenous and wanted to get home as fast as I could. But I was waylaid by someone I absolutely didn't want to see: Zabir.

"You're alive," he said, standing outside my building.

"Disappointed?" I glared at him.

"What?" He looked legitimately confused.

It was now or never. *Just say it. Tell him you know.* "The police asked me why Skylar Jones was calling you. And why you called back. And they'd very much like to speak to you."

His face paled.

"Shit. I was going to tell you."

"What? Tell me what? That you knew the guy who almost killed me? Were you in on it with him? Did you try to kill me?"

"Dunia, no, that's not what happened! Please, let me explain."

"Explain it to the cops. I never want to see you again."

I walked inside, told the doorman to not let anyone up, and got to my apartment before I burst into tears. I'd lost my appetite.

Thirty

Transcript: *The Disappearance of Dunia Ahmed* **podcast**

AMANDA ROBERTS: Detective Alvarez, can we circle back to this Zabir Mirza character? Something about him isn't sitting right with us. He just happened to know the man who attacked Dunia? And then he himself entered Dunia's life after she almost died? Like, what did you think about all of this?

    DETECTIVE ALVAREZ: I thought he was hiding a lot of info. I still do. I don't believe in coincidence, not in a case like this. I think he had to be more involved than he's letting on.

    DANIELLE MCGUIRE: Do you think he conspired with Skylar to murder Dunia?

    DETECTIVE ALVAREZ: Yes, but I could never find the motive. There didn't seem to be one, no matter how much we dug. We tore Zabir's life apart. We questioned colleagues, students, his ex-wife, his family. We didn't leave any stone unturned.

    AMANDA ROBERTS: And nothing?

    DETECTIVE ALVAREZ: Nothing that I could definitively pin on him. He had an alibi for the subway attack, he had an alibi for the almost hit-and-run. But he knows far more than he's been letting on. He did supply us with transcripts and recordings of his calls and meeting with Skylar. But I have to wonder how much he's holding back.

    DANIELLE MCGUIRE: Do you think he knows where Dunia is?

    DETECTIVE ALVAREZ: Or where she's buried. Yes, yes, I do.

Thirty-One

I went on autopilot through my days. Get up, go to work, don't die, fill prescriptions, be polite, get home alive, ignore all texts and calls from Zabir. The only people I did talk to were Kendra and Liz.

Liz had made it her mission to get me through this, and several times that week she came by for dinner and wine. I declined the alcohol; I didn't want to sleepwalk on a school night.

I did show her the videos of me running around in my sleep from the weekend. The cameras emailed them. I hadn't wanted to watch, but I made myself.

In the videos, I moved around my apartment, stopping and staring into corners like I was trying to hunt for something. And then I moved to my closet and dug through it before going back to bed. It was so surreal to watch.

"Freaky!" She was both amused and amazed.

I rolled my eyes but laughed along with her. At least she wasn't in cahoots with my would-be murderer. Unlike some people I knew.

"Do you see that blurry spot there?" I pointed to the edge of the frame. "Is that the camera? Because I keep seeing it."

"Let me look."

My phone rang while Liz examined the cameras. It was my doorman. "Uh, Dunia, there's some man down here, and he won't leave."

"Who?"

In the background I could hear Zabir. "Tell her I'm coming up."

"Sir, you can't!"

"Stop me, then."

"I'll handle this," I said to the doorman, who I hoped wouldn't do anything to hurt himself. I could deal with Zabir. I had Liz, and anyone dumb enough to go up against her deserved what they got.

"Hey, Liz, feel like confronting Zabir? Because he's on his way up."

"What?!" She got down from the stepladder. "I will fight him." Her eyes blazed.

The knock on the door made me jump, but I calmed myself and let him in.

"Dunia, you have to talk to me. Please. I didn't have anything to do with that man trying to kill you. I never met him, I swear—"

"Why should we believe you?" Liz asked. Her voice was so cold.

He glanced at her and halfheartedly waved. "Because I didn't know him. He called me for help; we met at my office one time. I know, I lied about not meeting him before. But that was it. I have the voice mails. But once I saw the news about what happened and that he tried to kill you, I had to see if you were okay. That's why I came to your work."

"And that hit-and-run? You were there. Why? Were you trying to see if I was dead?" His face blanched at my accusations.

"No! I told you, I was walking from the Met. I'm sorry, I know how this looks, but I swear to you I didn't try to kill you. Or have anything to do with it."

Something else had occurred to me in all this. A jinn-studying professor wanted to hang out with me? Nadia had told him more than he had let on.

"I know my sister told you all about me. I know you probably wanted to see for yourself. What am I, some research project for you?"

"What? I don't know what you mean." He looked confused, but I didn't know what was an act and what wasn't. I couldn't trust this man.

"You need to leave before we call the police." His face fell. He looked so dejected. But this was his fault! I was just trying to stay alive.

"Here—I transcribed all our calls. You can read them and let me know what you think. And after, if you want to talk, you know where to find me." He shoved a large envelope into my hands and left.

"The balls on him," Liz muttered. "What did you mean about your sister?"

"Nothing."

I ripped open the envelope. There were pages of calls transcribed, including a voice mail from Skylar asking for help. *I googled you,* it read. *You can help me. This is something you know about. Please help me, I'm running out of hope.*

And then the calls back and forth. Nothing about me was mentioned, not my name, not my murder. Just Skylar saying something was after him and Zabir trying to figure out what. It gave me chills.

Liz read every page with me.

"It's like he was trying to help Skylar. Help him mentally."

"Maybe."

"Doesn't change anything. He should have told you all of this before, when he saw you at work. What kind of jackass tries to date you instead of being truthful. Promise me you'll never speak to him again." Liz looked so serious. "Promise me."

"I promise, he's out of my life. Let me call the detective, though, tell her what he dropped off. Just so she has copies." I left a message for Alvarez. I was sure she had the transcriptions, but just in case.

"Are you okay?" Liz asked.

I nodded. "Sure. I mean, the man I was dating was chatting with the man who tried to kill me. And then hid it from me, no big deal. I think it's time I swore off dating for a bit. No more men, just focusing on me."

"That's probably a good idea."

After Liz left, I couldn't help but go over the papers again. I read them closely. Skylar thought he was being haunted. And only Zabir could help. Which made no sense. Unless Skylar was under the impression a jinn was after him. Great, now my childhood monsters had become grown-up ones. A crazy man was haunted. It didn't explain why Zabir didn't tell me, why he'd held this back. Why didn't he go to the cops first thing?

None of this made sense. Not one bit. But I knew one thing: I wasn't going to make it easy for anyone to come after me. If anyone tried to attack me, I wasn't going down without a fight.

I had started searching for self-defense courses in August, when Skylar had tried to kill me. Now I was going to do more than search; I was going to go to one. I was going to learn to fight like hell. I'd make myself as much of a badass as I could. Cue up "Eye of the Tiger," because I was mad as hell.

———

The class I found was offered as a two-hour seminar for women at a jujitsu place in Lower Manhattan. Kendra offered to come with me, and I said yes, though every part of me wanted to not bug her. "I'd love that. I could use the support!"

But she ended up being tied up at work.

I was disappointed; I can't lie. I wanted her there with me. But I understood. Some things I had to do on my own. I couldn't lean on Kendra and Liz forever. I needed this class. I was vibrating with anxiety. I needed to find an outlet. So I went alone.

The instructor, a Black woman with the most amazing arms I'd ever seen (she was a boxer) was named Terry. She taught us how to get out of anyone grabbing you from behind, how to fight someone if they'd covered your eyes, and—what I found the most useful—how to yell when faced with an attacker. She had a man helping her; he attacked each of us in demonstrations. It was terrifying and brought up so much from that day on the subway platform. The first time her partner lunged at me, I froze. But by the fifth time, I was getting out of holds and pushing him hard.

"We're taught to be silent, but this is your life. You need to yell, scream, do whatever you can to get them to leave you alone," Terry said. I nodded along. Yes, I had to be loud. I had to get everyone's attention; it was the only way to stay alive.

She made us yell in her face. I winced at the idea. "You are not a victim. You may have been mugged, assaulted, beaten. But you are not a victim. If you believe you're a victim, you won't fight back. You are not a victim. You have agency and power. Your attacker wants to take that from you. We won't let them!" We all mumbled agreement.

"Yell at me, come on!" she urged. She stood inches in front of my face. "Come on, Dunia, yell at me."

I felt so stupid. But I opened my mouth and loudly said, "No!"

She rolled her eyes. Harsh, but fair. "That's all you got? Louder!"

"No!"

"LOUDER! Come on, you're about to die, and you're worried about being too loud?" I thought of that day on the subway platform. Of Skylar dragging me to the tracks, and having to yell for help. I did it then; I could do it now. I could fight. I took a deep breath.

"NOOOOOOO!" I roared, and Terry took a step back, surprise on her face.

"Didn't know you had it in you." She nodded. "Are you a victim?"

"I AM NOT A VICTIM!"

"Good. Everyone, be like Dunia. Be loud."

That felt better than any gold star I'd gotten in grade school. *Yeah, be like me, I'm not a victim!* I was, but now I was going to fight and yell! It seemed silly, but I felt invigorated. Like Terry understood me and why I was there. She knew how to say things to me to get me to grasp them.

"You know, there's nothing wrong with being a victim," Terry said as class wound down. "But don't let what happened stop you from fighting. Change your mentality. Yes, something awful happened, but you are now learning how to fight back. You are survivors. Don't forget that!"

I was a survivor, and no man was going to take that away from me. Not Skylar, not David, and not Zabir.

After class, I waited to thank Terry and find out about more lessons I could take.

"You did great. Good job."

"Thank you. This is the first time I've felt empowered since . . . I was attacked on the subway and almost thrown onto the tracks."

She nodded, her eyes wary. "You're not the first and won't be the last. I can help you. The number one thing is to fight as dirty and as loud as you can. This is your life; you have to do whatever it takes to keep it. We never like making scenes, but we have to if we want to survive."

She gave me a schedule of classes, and I promised I'd come try them. I hoped I would keep that promise. I liked how Terry made me feel. I liked not being a victim. And I really, really enjoyed yelling "NO!" I needed this for my own mental state.

I texted Kendra that she'd missed a great class and hoped she'd try out another one with me. I wasn't mad she bailed. She had to run her company. It was hard work being the boss. Sometimes, you had to pick work over your friends, even when they needed you.

———

I was invigorated, and had Zabir or David had the bad luck to be outside my building, I'd have clocked them. Okay, maybe not, but I'd have yelled really loudly. But the only thing waiting for me was another one of those creepy notes outside my apartment door. If I could yell at a stupid piece of paper and make it go away, I would have.

"I hate you." I said it out loud, but not so loud that my neighbors would hear. I picked it up by the corner and threw it on my coffee table.

I opened it.

You can't fight me.

"Wanna bet?" I asked, then felt stupid for talking to myself. I bagged it up for Alvarez. I hated those notes and the person who wrote them. Every time I got one, it was a reminder that this person could find me, no matter where I went. That I wasn't truly safe anywhere.

I was all set for a night in when Liz texted, asking to hang out. She was bored. But I was beat after my class and stayed in.

Maybe tomorrow? she asked.

I think that can work. Just nothing too crazy.

Zabir hadn't texted or reached out, but Alvarez had left a message. She wanted to talk to me. Added that to my to-do list for tomorrow.

———

"We spoke with Mr. Mirza," Alvarez said over the phone. I was on my break at work, and we'd played phone tag up until now. She explained they'd gone through all his evidence. "It appears Mr. Jones was having delusions of some ghost or demon haunting him. Based off his medical records, which we just got, he was on antipsychotics. I think it's safe to say he was unwell, and he decided Mr. Mirza somehow was the one person who could help him."

"So Zabir isn't involved? At all? It's just a coincidence that he got the calls?" I was skeptical, to put it mildly.

". . . Not that we can see, but I have to be honest, something doesn't sit right with me. I'm still investigating. If you can avoid him, that would be my recommendation."

"I will, thank you. Any update on those notes? I got another one."

"Not yet. They're at the crime lab. We have a bit of a backlog, so it may take a few weeks."

Thirty-Two

Transcript: *The Disappearance of Dunia Ahmed* **podcast**

AMANDA ROBERTS: Today we have on someone we've been dying to talk to: Professor Zabir Mirza. Zabir teaches South Asian history at NYU and was a friend of Dunia's. Welcome.

ZABIR MIRZA: Thanks for having me.

DANIELLE MCGUIRE: Just so listeners know, you're the cousin of Dunia's brother-in-law, right?

ZABIR MIRZA: Yes, that's right.

AMANDA ROBERTS: Why did you want to meet with Dunia? It was right as all of this was happening.

ZABIR MIRZA: To be honest, I saw her face on the cover of the papers and wanted to make sure she was okay.

DANIELLE MCGUIRE: We heard you knew her attacker. Did that factor in?

ZABIR MIRZA: . . . It did. For the record, I had no idea that Skylar Jones was going to try to kill Dunia. If I had, I'd have intervened or called the cops.

AMANDA ROBERTS: Why didn't you go to the cops after you saw the news and heard what he had done?

ZABIR MIRZA: I was trying to make sense of things. Look, Skylar came to me talking about hauntings and raving about something stalking him.

DANIELLE MCGUIRE: Why'd he come to you?

ZABIR MIRZA: One of the courses I teach is about South Asian folklore. He must have googled and found me. I didn't know him prior to any of this.

AMANDA ROBERTS: Let me get this straight. A random man calls you up and says he has a ghost, like the kind in your course, and then he tries to kill someone you're sorta related to? By marriage? That's a bit far fetched, don't you think.

ZABIR MIRZA: It's what happened.

AMANDA ROBERTS: Why didn't you tell Dunia this when you hung out with her?

ZABIR MIRZA: Because I thought Skylar was insane and didn't realize how much more to all of this there was. And to be honest, I wanted to see if Dunia had any inkling of what he had said to me. It was curiosity at first. And then I didn't know how to broach the subject with her. I regret it all immensely.

DANIELLE MCGUIRE: The police think you know where Dunia is. Is that true?

ZABIR MIRZA: No. If I did, I'd tell someone, anyone. I wish I'd been able to help her.

Thirty-Three

"Tell me all about your class," Liz said, tucking her perfectly pedicured toes under her. I wasn't up for being in public after helping patients all day. So she came over to my place. Her toenail polish reminded me I was in dire need of some beauty TLC, but I hated going to nail salons. Something about other people working on me made me feel uncomfortable.

"It was so good. You should go to one. She taught us all these moves, but what I found to be the most helpful was yelling."

"Yelling?"

"That day on the subway platform, I didn't want to make a scene. But I had to, because that's how people came to help me. We're taught to be quiet—women, you know?" I wasn't explaining it well at all.

"Ohhh, I get it. Be loud, fight, make a scene, that sort of thing."

"Yes! It was so cathartic."

"If anyone has things to yell about, it's you." She wasn't wrong. "Did Kendra enjoy the class?"

"Oh, she didn't go. She had some work thing."

Liz looked confused. "She did? I didn't know that. I would have gone with you!"

"I know, but I feel like I've been leaning on you guys a lot. I needed to put on my big-girl pants and do this by myself."

"I'm glad you did. Any word from Zabir?"

I shook my head. Just hearing his name made my heart race, and not in a good way. "I talked to the detective, and they went through all the calls. I guess it was one of those internet services, so it recorded them. And she said it sounded like Skylar was having delusions that a ghost or something was after him and thought Zabir could help, and they exchanged calls, and that was it."

I didn't add that I wondered if I'd messed up. If Zabir was innocent, had I made a mistake pushing him out of my life? But he'd held key information back—from both me and the police. An innocent person wouldn't do that.

"Look, all of this is weird as hell," Liz said. "I think it's good you're not seeing him until you know everything. What if more comes out? I just, I don't know. Better to be safe."

"You read my mind. I feel like maybe I overreacted, but also he really messed up!"

"If anything, you underreacted. I'm gonna pour more wine. Want any?"

I shook my head. "I don't want to drink much on a work night. I think drinking makes me sleepwalk."

"Oh God, I'm sorry, I had no idea. No booze for you, then!"

"Not till the weekend."

"What else makes you sleepwalk?"

"Stress, which, ha! No getting rid of that. Sleeping pills too. So I avoid them. But mostly if I drink more than a glass of wine, I'm probably going to do something."

"So cancel the Ambien party I had scheduled for us, got it."

I had been tempted to text Zabir and start a conversation about everything, but I deleted it every time I tried typing a message. I had so many questions I needed answers to. Like how well did he know Skylar? Did he learn who the mysterious girlfriend was? Did Skylar tell him he had to stalk and kill me? Nothing felt right. And like Liz said, I didn't know the full story yet. I didn't know why he hid this all from me. I had to find out. If nothing else, I'd get closure. But just not tonight. I wasn't ready to talk to him, not quite yet.

"Oh, wait, did you hear the good news?" Liz asked; her eyes sparkled.

Good news? Now that was sorely needed. "No! Tell me!"

"Kendra got into Aphrodite!" The largest beauty retailer in the world was about to stock my friend's beauty line. And I had to hear about it from Liz.

"Oh my God, that's amazing! That would explain why she's so busy."

"Yeah, it's going to be a lot of work, but I'm so proud of her."

"We should do something for her."

"Absolutely."

"Hey, do you think I should dye my hair darker?" Liz asked, holding a lock of her silver-blonde hair. "Then we'd all be brunettes!"

"I like that you stand out. Your color suits you."

"Okay, fine, but maybe I'll go pink or something. Or is that too midlife crisis?"

We shifted our talk to beauty and relaxed for the rest of the day. No creepy notes, no stalkers, no lying dates, just us. It was exactly what I needed.

———

We managed to secure a night with Kendra. It was nearly impossible to get her to leave work early, so we were doing a late dinner on Friday night. Nine o'clock. I maybe had a small meal before because I couldn't wait that long.

"Kendra!" I hugged her when I saw her. Her eyes looked tired, like she hadn't slept. Her makeup, though, was flawless. I had a gift for her. It was a text she'd sent me years ago in pharmacy school about launching her own line and getting into big retailers. I'd had it framed. "For you."

"What, oh wow, this is so sweet! I can't believe you kept that text!"

"I knew it would come in handy one day. You manifested that. You made it happen. I'm so proud of you."

"Don't make me cry, because I just did my makeup." She laughed. "I can't wait to tell you about the launch—you have to come!"

"Wild horses couldn't keep me from going, or whatever that saying is." We ordered some drinks while we waited for Liz. I got a wine spritzer so I could pace my drinks.

"Spritzer?" Kendra wrinkled her nose.

"I can't drink too much, or I sleepwalk."

"No! I had no idea. Hey, how are you with the whole Zabir thing?"

"I'll fill you in once Liz gets here."

Liz was twenty minutes late, which wasn't the biggest deal. But when she walked in, she looked wild. Her hair was a mess, her eyes were large, and she looked like she was going to murder someone.

"What happened?" we both asked.

"I need a drink, stat." She ordered wine and nearly drank the whole glass in one go. "I cannot believe what just happened. Oh my God. Dunia, I was outside my apartment waiting for my Uber, and guess who I ran into? Zabir."

"What? What did he want?" Kendra grabbed my hand.

"He wanted me to talk to you, and I told him no. And you'll be so proud of me. I hit him."

"You hit him?" I had to have heard her wrong.

"I did. I hit him so hard. I hope he has a bruise. That's what he gets for fucking with my friend." There was a fire in Liz's eyes. I had never seen this side of Liz, and judging by Kendra's face, neither had she.

"So, what happened after you hit him?" she asked.

"He ran off like the baby he is. I'm so glad you saw his true colors before you got in too deep." Liz ordered another drink. "Sorry, I just need a moment to compose myself." She went to the bathroom to freshen up.

"Whoa," Kendra said when we were alone. "That was something."

"Yeah, I don't know how to feel about it." Maybe it was good she had done that?

"I can't help but think if either of us had done that, we'd be in jail," Kendra noted.

"So fast. We'd never get away with it."

We stopped talking when Liz came back, looking far more like herself.

"Sorry about that. Anyways, Kendra, congratulations again. You're about to be such a star!" Liz said as she drank her second glass.

"Let's see if our table is ready?" I suggested. I wanted food in her before she drank more. She wasn't drunk, but she was growing louder and more agitated from her run-in.

"Good call!" Kendra added. "And girl, I couldn't have done it without your connections, so thank you!"

"Damn right!" Liz said loudly. Kendra and I exchanged nervous glances.

"Liz, you okay? You seem a little upset? Was it just Zabir or . . . ?"

"Of course it was him. I can't believe he'd treat a friend like that. Honestly, I'd die for you guys. Full-on die."

"No one is dying, we're just going to eat," Kendra joked, trying to defuse things. To say dinner was awkward was an understatement. Yes, we'd all had our drunk moments, but never quite like this. Liz was close to making a scene every few minutes.

Another bottle of wine was ordered. Liz was drinking for all of us. Kendra and I stuck with water at that point. We didn't say anything, though. Liz was having an off night.

"I wish you'd seen his face when I hit him!" She snorted.

"Did you slap him or punch him?" Kendra asked.

"Just a slap. But it felt so damn good. I'd do it again. I'd do anything for my friends."

"Ditto!" I replied. But I wasn't sure I would want to face assault charges for anyone but Kendra. I didn't say that, though.

At the end of dinner, Liz had gone through two bottles of wine. I had no idea how she was still standing. At some point, she wasn't. She fell on the sidewalk outside the restaurant and started crying. We got her on her feet and handed her tissues.

"I can get her home," I offered. "It's on the way."

"Are you sure?" Kendra asked.

"Yeah, just help me get her in a cab?"

"Liz, honey, give me your address, okay?"

She complied but was still wiping her face. "I'm such a loser, making a mess of Kendra's dinner," she wailed, wiping her nose.

"It's fine, don't worry! I got you!"

Liz's apartment was in Gramercy Park, which wasn't a long walk. But I didn't want to risk her falling again, so I cabbed us there. The drive was short.

"D, you're so great, do you know that?"

"Thanks, girl." I laughed as I got her out of the cab and outside her building.

"I hate that Zabir. What he did to us is so messed up."

"Yes, it is. Now, do you need me to get you inside?"

"No, I'm okay. I love you!"

"I love you too." It was kind of funny seeing what kind of drunk girl Liz was. She was an I-love-you drunk, which was really the best kind. Though I suspected she was also a *woo* girl, as in the one who shouts "Woooo!" after a few drinks. And clearly, she was a sob-in-the-cab girl as well.

When I got home, I had texts from her, Kendra, and one from Zabir. I read his first, my heart pounding.

Your friend is crazy. you need to avoid her.

That was all it said. I didn't reply. I didn't know what to say.

———

The next morning I surprised Liz with bagels and coffee. I figured she would be hungover as hell. But when I tried to come in, the doorman informed me that no one by the name Liz Small lived there.

"She does, I dropped her off here myself?"

"Ma'am, I'm sorry, I don't know what to tell you."

Maybe I left her at the wrong building? I'd never been to her apartment. I texted her that I was outside and wanted to bring bagels. She didn't reply until later, so I ended up eating by myself in the park across the street.

She finally texted that I had the wrong address for her, she was another block over, but that she was at Pilates class. There went my attempt to surprise her.

I walked all the way back up to my apartment. It was one of those warm, beautiful days where you love the city more than life itself. I was thankful I was here and that I was alive. And I hoped I'd stay that way.

My sister called and texted me while I walked, but I wasn't ready to talk to her. I would, because I needed to know just what she and Zabir were up to. The more I thought about what had happened, the more I was convinced they were in cahoots. They had to be. It was the only thing that made sense. It made me wonder if my own sister wanted me dead.

Thirty-Four

Dunia, age five

I was playing with Baba. I was home after school, and Ammi was napping. I think Carol was busy, so it was just me and Baba. He didn't usually babysit me, but I guess today he did.

"Your sister is so mean to you. You should fight back," he said. He was mad at her because she wouldn't play with him.

"No, I can't. I have to respect my elders," I said. It was what my parents said to me.

"I am your elder."

"Let's just play." I didn't like when he got angry. I kept playing with my dolls, and he gave in and stopped talking about Nadia. But I saw him watching her at dinner. He acted like a child sometimes, not a grown-up. Maybe that's why he liked me.

That night, I remember sleepwalking. I remember getting up and standing by Nadia's bed. I did that a lot. I wasn't sure why. I felt like I had to watch her, even in my sleep.

But this time was different. I held my pillow in my hands. I could see this happening, but I couldn't stop it. No one ever believed me that I couldn't control what I did in my sleep. I watched as I put the pillow over her face and held it down. I didn't know why I was doing this, only that my dream said I had to. I had to do this.

Nadia didn't fight. She was asleep, and her breathing was coming more slowly.

"Dunia!" I looked up, confused. There stood my father. He looked angry. Scared. "What are you doing?"

I looked at the pillow in my hands, which he pulled away before we woke Nadia. She had slept through everything.

"What were you doing?" he asked again.

"I don't know?" I didn't. I didn't know. I was awake now. I only remembered I'd had to get out of bed. But that was it.

My mother came in, and when Abu told her what I had done, she screamed at me to get out. She called me a shaytan. A devil.

Abu took me over to Carol's and apologized for the late hour.

"Something's happened, can you watch her for tonight? I'm so sorry."

"Of course, I hope everyone's okay?"

I didn't hear what he said. I was standing there, holding Carol's hand, while sucking my thumb like I had when I was a baby.

"Let's get you inside. Want some hot cocoa?" Carol asked.

I nodded. But I didn't say anything. I couldn't tell her I'd done something bad. She'd never want me around then either.

———

Maybe my parents wouldn't want me to come back home. Maybe I'd live with Carol now. Or maybe they'd send me to Pakistan, where Rahmi Khala was. I could be in the hospital with her. I was bad; I had done a bad thing. I had to be punished.

But the next day I was brought home and taken to Abu's office, not my room. They'd moved my bed and my things into his office, and I was staying there now. Nadia had her own room. And more importantly, she had a lock on her door that hadn't been there before. To keep me out.

"You'll be a big girl with your own room!" Abu was saying, but I wasn't listening.

"I'm sorry I almost killed Nadia," I finally whispered. "I didn't mean to. I can't help it." The sleepwalking was too much. I wasn't just changing clothes and wandering the house. I was doing things.

Abu and Ammi decided to take me to all kinds of doctors then. So many. One tried to look at my brain with a giant loud machine that scared me. Another did a lot of talking and asked me questions. A third one wanted me to stay the night and let them watch me, but Ammi said no.

I was not normal. But the doctors said I was doing normal things and must have acted out a bad dream.

"Just keep an eye on her. She'll grow out of it."

What if I didn't? I wanted to ask that but was too scared.

Thirty-Five

Transcript: *The Disappearance of Dunia Ahmed* podcast

AMANDA ROBERTS: This podcast has been such a roller coaster. I dreamed about Dunia last night!

    DANIELLE MCGUIRE: Oh wow! Did she tell you where she was?

    AMANDA ROBERTS: I wish. She told me to go away. How funny is that? Anyway, I have so many more questions for Dunia's sister, Nadia, who has been gracious enough to come back on.

    NADIA CHAUDRY: Thanks for having me back on.

    DANIELLE MCGUIRE: Do you feel responsible for what happened to your sister?

    NADIA CHAUDRY: What? No! I had nothing to do with it, and I've put up reward money to find her.

    AMANDA ROBERTS: But it's sort of your fault she met Zabir, right?

    NADIA CHAUDRY: Zabir did not have anything to do with what happened to her. He was trying to help her. He's the sweetest, kindest person.

    DANIELLE MCGUIRE: I find it weird that you defend him but not your own sister.

    NADIA CHAUDRY: Okay, what's with the accusations?

    AMANDA ROBERTS: Dunia didn't like you. She told her friends that; she told Zabir to not bring you up; she wrote in her journal how much she didn't like you.

NADIA CHAUDRY: Wait, you have her journal?

DANIELLE MCGUIRE: Copies. The police have the actual one. We're very thorough. Tell us, Nadia, if you hadn't married into Zabir's family, do you think your sister would still be alive?

NADIA CHAUDRY: I—I don't know. I don't think anything I did had any bearing on my sister's life. We were fairly estranged.

AMANDA ROBERTS: For listeners who may have missed any of this story, Dunia's mother, it seems, blamed Dunia for her father's death. How is a five-year-old responsible for something like that?

NADIA CHAUDRY: You weren't there, you don't know—

DANIELLE MCGUIRE: Enlighten us, then. Why did your mother blame Dunia?

NADIA CHAUDRY: Because my father would never have been that stressed if it weren't for her. My parents fought all the time because of Dunia. Dunia would sleepwalk; she tried to kill me; she'd disappear—none of that was normal behavior.

AMANDA ROBERTS: It wasn't, but she was a child. Don't you think you, as her older sister, should have reached out to make amends?

NADIA CHAUDRY: I tried! I called her, I sent her gifts, I tried to get her to come out and visit with my family. I wanted her in my life. But it was too late. She didn't want a family—she wanted to be left alone.

AMANDA ROBERTS: I can't say I blame her.

Thirty-Six

I went to Kendra's on Sunday for brunch and beauty—Liz wasn't invited. Kendra wasn't mad at her about the other night. But we hadn't had much alone time since I'd met Liz. It was very much needed.

"Do we want to talk about dinner?" I asked, my mouth in a grimace.

"Liz was a mess. I don't know, she has some personal-life shit she won't talk about."

"Oh. I didn't know that." Liz hadn't mentioned anything to me, and here I was overwhelming her with my problems.

"Oh, try this, it's a new product that helps even skin tone." She was showing me her newest products for her upcoming Aphrodite launch, all while making us eggs. Get you a friend who can do both.

I would try anything she gave me, beauty or food. I was clueless about skin care. Mainly I did what Kendra recommended.

"So . . . how are you?" she asked.

"No one tried to murder me recently, so that's good!"

"Progress."

"Wait, I have something for you." I ran to my bag and pulled out a gift card to her favorite spa. "I figured you needed a little bit more after the other night."

"You didn't have to!"

"It's just some pampering. We all need it, right?"

"You're amazing. And I'm sorry if I've been so busy lately. Things are happening at work, and I haven't been fully around. I'll try to be here more for you."

"Tell me everything, and stop apologizing about it. I want to hear every detail about the launch." And I meant it. I wanted to get lost in Kendra's world for a bit. It was a far prettier place than my life.

She told me about what she needed to finish in time.

"I have to go to California tomorrow. There's an issue in production. I can't afford to have any mistakes. Everything must be perfect."

"It will be." I knew it would be. Everything Kendra did was thought out and executed to be the best.

"No mimosa for you, right?"

"Maybe just one."

We toasted to her success and me staying alive. It made me laugh. I know it's not normal to laugh at these things, but eventually, you have to or you'll go insane. Maybe I was already nuts.

I told her about Zabir and the papers he gave me. I hadn't had time to tell her on Friday because of Liz's antics.

"So he knew Skylar, but not well, and was trying to help him with, what, a ghost?"

"I think jinn? From his class."

"That just proves Skylar was nuts."

I nodded but didn't say more. She looked at me in the way she had, where she could read me without me opening my mouth. "Spill it."

"My family believed in that stuff."

"Okay, it's one thing to be a believer. I'm one. It's another to try to murder someone because you think you're being haunted."

"Fair point!" There was so much I wanted to tell her. But not now. The time was never right, but it was certainly not the moment. Not with her launch coming.

"Just to be safe, you should burn sage or rosemary."

"Maybe!" I should, but I knew I wouldn't.

———

Kendra's launch was all I looked forward to. I wanted it to be the best thing ever. But there wasn't anything for me to do to help except show up. And possibly keep an eye on Liz, who had seemed to vanish in the days leading up to it. Maybe she was embarrassed about the other night?

I'd text her I missed her, and she'd reply but not ask to hang out. I didn't push it. I knew how it was when you wanted to be alone.

The day of the launch Liz texted that she had been busy putting the final touches on things and that she couldn't wait to see me. That made me feel better, even if I wished she were meeting me beforehand so I had someone to go with.

I didn't know what to wear, so I settled on fake leather leggings and a cute (long-sleeved) top. It was my pretend-chic look. Anything looked better with leather leggings. It was a little chilly—the early October weather was finally turning. I did my makeup with Kendra's line. How better to support her than to wear her products?

I was satisfied with how I looked. I was no model, but the makeup made my skin glow, and I looked like a walking Instagram filter. I ordered an Uber (because the last thing I needed was to be stressed and anxious). The event started at seven, and it was already ten after.

The store was crowded. I'm sure it was always like that, being in Times Square and all. But in I went because I had to support Kendra. Any dread I felt being near people had to be pushed down and ignored.

"Dunia!" I heard my name and saw Liz waving to me. I waved back, took a couple of deep breaths, and made my way through the crowd.

"Hi! Wow, so many people!" I hugged her.

"Right? This is amazing. So proud of Kendra. Oh, there she is!"

Kendra was surrounded by a group of people, all clamoring for a moment with her. She had on a stunning magenta dress. She was doing a makeup tutorial and showing how well her products blended with different skin tones. I watched in awe. She was so good at it, you wouldn't know she went to pharmacy school instead of cosmetology school.

"She's beyond amazing," I said in awe.

"Let's go say hi to her!" Liz grabbed my arm and pulled me in that direction.

We walked over to the circle of well-wishers. I stood waiting because I didn't want to interrupt Kendra's moment. This *was* amazing. She'd had an idea and made it into a reality. I needed to do that. Be more like her. Stop letting things happen to me and instead make them happen. I just had to figure out how.

"Dunia!" Someone, not Liz, was calling my name. I slowly looked around. Nope, not one person I knew here. "You misheard, calm down," I said under my breath. Someone must have said something like my name.

"What's that?" Liz asked.

"Nothing, this is awesome. Should we just wait here or . . . ?"

"Yeah, it's all good." She grinned. She was excited. Her money and connections had helped make this happen, but it was Kendra's genius that drew this crowd. Kendra had made this happen.

"And if you want to add a contour, you can use our bronzer, which also has a bit of skin care in it. So everything you put on your face helps your skin, is healthy, clean, nontoxic, and animal friendly and vegan," Kendra was saying while using the bronzer on the face model. She saw me and smiled and waved. I waved back, excited to see her in action.

It was perfect. A perfect event for my perfect friend, and I wasn't envious, for once. I was just happy to be here. To see this. If Skylar had had his way, I wouldn't have been. I reached over to hold Liz's hand and squeezed.

"I'm really glad you're here," I said. And I meant it.

"Me too!" She squeezed back.

Everything was perfect. Just like Kendra had wanted it.

Until it wasn't.

It all happened so fast I couldn't stop it. There was no way. It was almost as if I were watching a movie and the main character was about to die. There was no way to save them, no matter how much you yelled at the screen.

"Dunia!" I heard a voice yell. Liz and I both jerked our heads in the direction it came from. She had heard it too. It wasn't in my head.

I saw a woman running my way. She was the one yelling my name. She was so fast it seemed like she was flying over the shelves, but that wasn't possible. In her wake, she left products and broken glass as she got nearer to me. All this happened in mere seconds. Liz grabbed my arm, holding me tightly. We couldn't do anything but watch. I couldn't move; I was transfixed by this flying woman. How was she able to do that? What was going on? My brain couldn't process this.

The woman landed on me. I saw it happen like I was outside of my own body. I went down. I fell right into the group of people around Kendra.

"Ooof!" I managed to grunt. I felt all the air pour out of me, like nothing could get me to stop exhaling. I'd never had the wind knocked out of me like this. It was not a pleasant experience. I was marveling at my inability to inhale, not understanding what had happened.

And then people started screaming. My head hit the ground, hard. My ankle felt strange, like it had twisted or sprained. I had a searing pain in my side, as if it were on fire. I couldn't move; the strange flying woman was on top of me. And her hands were now around my throat, squeezing any remaining breath out of me.

I heard things crashing. Something sounded broken—a mirror or glass. I couldn't move to see. I tried hitting the lady on top of me, to get her to loosen her grip. Fight dirty: that's what Terry had said. I tried to use my fingers to poke her eyes out. Her eyes were black. Was this real? Was I dreaming? Was I losing oxygen? I didn't know anymore. But I would fight, regardless.

Time stops when these sorts of things happen. I know, because I've become an expert at them. You can see things unfolding, but you can't do anything but witness them, as if you're outside of your body. Or maybe I had lost all my oxygen and my brain was shutting down.

The screaming had gotten louder. I closed my eyes. I was tired, I needed air, and my side was burning. If I gave up, gave in, would this all be over?

Someone pulled the hands off my throat, and I gasped for air. Giant lungfuls of it. I couldn't get enough. I inhaled until I coughed, and my side hurt even more.

"Dunia!" Kendra yelled. "Don't move!" Someone grabbed tissues and put them on my abdomen. I glanced down and saw that I'd been stabbed. Tackled, stabbed, and choked. All in one go.

My attacker was a woman. She was my age or younger, and she looked positively feral. She had on the telltale black smock that said she worked at Aphrodite. Or did, until this. She was being held back by security and was spitting as she yelled at me, her arms trying to break free.

"You have to die!" she screamed.

And then it all went blissfully quiet as I fainted. Or lost consciousness from a concussion and loss of blood and air. Either way, I didn't see the aftermath. That was probably a blessing.

———

When I was out, I dreamed of Baba. He told me I'd be okay. To not worry, everything was fine. I was safe.

"You just have to hold on for a little while longer," he said, his voice kind, his eyes full of love. "You'll be safe soon, I promise."

"Baba, I'm so tired. Can you make this all stop?"

———

I woke up in a hospital bed. The last place I wanted to be was in a hospital. My mouth was dry, my throat hurt, my head hurt. I couldn't move my torso at all. Everything hurt, to be honest. I wasn't sure how someone so small could cause this much damage. The woman who took me down couldn't have been much taller than my five foot two.

I tried to move my head, but the throbbing pain made me stop.

"You're going to not want to move for a while," a woman said. She must have been a nurse. "Do you know where you are?"

I opened my mouth to speak and could only rasp. "The hospital? That woman attacked me?"

"Good, no memory loss. The doctor is on his way to talk to you. In the meantime, you have a visitor."

I again tried to move my head and was hit with a blinding pain. Was this what migraines felt like?

"Dunia! I'm so glad you're okay!" Liz ran over to my bed. "Holy shit, that was the scariest thing I've ever seen in my entire life."

"How's Kendra?" I whispered.

"It's a mess. But she's dealing with it. Don't you even worry, okay? It will all be okay. I'm here to help take care of you. That woman was arrested."

I nodded. Liz's words had the reverse effect on me—I was now worried. Was Kendra upset? Why hadn't she come to see me? I needed to tell her I was sorry.

———

When the doctor came, he gave me something for my head that made me fall asleep. It was heaven. He said my ankle was sprained, my windpipe was bruised, and I'd been lucky to not have any major organ damage from the knife.

"Had it been the other side, she would have hit your liver." So, thank you, attacker lady, for not skewering my liver, I guess. I also had a full-on concussion. They were keeping me for a night or two.

The sleep I got from the drugs was deep and void of any dreams. Nothing I could recall, at least. And I didn't get out of my bed, which was promising. Even Sleep Me knew I needed the rest.

Detective Alvarez came the next day. She looked like shit. But then, so did I.

"You sure keep me busy." She cracked a smile.

"Sorry," I whispered. My voice would come back, the doctor had assured me.

"So, I got the rundown on what happened, but thought I'd ask you. Do you know her?" She had the booking photo of my assailant. I didn't know her at all. She looked ashamed. Good, she should be. Her name was Mary. Mary Ryans.

I shook my head, and then groaned. "Sorry, headache."

"It's fine. So from witnesses, we got that she screamed your name out of the blue and then tackled you. Is that right?"

"Yes." I had to keep my answers short; my throat hurt too much. Detective Alvarez handed me a cup of ice chips.

"They'll help." She smiled. "We have her in custody. She hasn't said a word. We're booking her and interviewing her again later today."

"She told me I had to die," I said.

Alvarez sighed. "I'll be honest with you. I have no idea what's going on. It's really bizarre that one person is attacked this often. At this point, I need to look even deeper into everyone around you. That may not be comfortable for you, but it's the best way forward."

I nodded, closing my eyes against the pain. "Anything to make this stop."

Thirty-Seven

Transcript: *The Disappearance of Dunia Ahmed* podcast

AMANDA ROBERTS: Listeners, buckle up because things are about to get weird. After Dunia is nearly killed by Skylar Jones, after she's almost run over by a mystery driver, she nearly dies at Aphrodite, of all places.

DANIELLE MCGUIRE: Can you imagine dying while beauty shopping? How tragic.

AMANDA ROBERTS: Right? God, so awful. We have Detective Alvarez here to fill us in on everything that happened at Aphrodite. Welcome back.

DETECTIVE ALVAREZ: The attack occurred October 3. Dunia was at the Times Square location of Aphrodite for her friend Kendra Wright's product launch.

AMANDA ROBERTS: And then all hell broke loose.

DETECTIVE ALVAREZ: While she's at the store, a woman by the name of Mary Ryans called her name. Witnesses said Ms. Ryans leaped over various displays in an attempt to get to Dunia. Once she landed on Dunia, she stabbed her in the abdomen and attempted to strangle Dunia.

AMANDA ROBERTS: That's such overkill for someone you don't know, don't you think? Like, an ex, sure, you'd want to strangle them. But a completely random person?

DETECTIVE ALVAREZ: It was a very violent act. I was shocked that Dunia survived it. She was taken to the hospital.

DANIELLE MCGUIRE: Can you tell us who Mary Ryans is and why she wanted to kill Dunia?

DETECTIVE ALVAREZ: We found no link between them. Mary was a student at Pratt; she worked at Aphrodite part time. We do know she had a large cash deposit in her account prior to the attack. She had absolutely no links to anyone Dunia knew—that we were aware of.

AMANDA ROBERTS: So someone paid her. Tell our listeners what happened to Mary.

DETECTIVE ALVAREZ: She killed herself in our interrogation room by shoving a pen into her carotid artery and choking on the blood. We could not stop or save her.

DANIELLE MCGUIRE: Holy cow.

AMANDA ROBERTS: Right? Do you think she was also haunted? Because I've watched the video of the attack at least fifty times, and I don't see how it was even possible for her to do that. Like, how? The video's on our website, by the way. You all need to watch it.

DETECTIVE ALVAREZ: You have video of the attack?

DANIELLE MCGUIRE: Yes—and there's video of her suicide. Just be warned, it's very NSFW. Unless you work with bodies or something.

DETECTIVE ALVAREZ: What!? How do you have that? You shouldn't have even seen that video.

AMANDA ROBERTS: We're very resourceful. The video shows Mary's final moments. I'm really enthralled by her face. Her eyes. They don't look human. Did you notice that?

DETECTIVE ALVAREZ: I am not answering that.

AMANDA ROBERTS: So the question now is, Who paid Mary Ryans? Cue up the suspenseful music, because things are about to get wild.

Thirty-Eight

Liz took me home the following day with doctor's orders to rest. She picked me up, carefully put me in an Uber, sat with me, and then helped me get into my apartment. I had a boot on my foot, and my throat had bruises all over it. I winced every time I moved. I had been given painkillers for everything.

She opened the door and helped me to the sofa. There was a bouquet of red roses on my coffee table.

"Did you bring those?" I croaked out.

"No, hold on." She read the card and made a face. "They're from David."

"David? How did he get in my apartment?"

"Maybe your doorman brought them up."

That made sense. I closed my eyes. Just the exertion of getting home and trying to talk was enough to make me need to sleep. I didn't have time to worry about David or anyone else.

"I'm going to go get you some fresh fruit and stuff, okay? Is there anything you want to eat?"

"No, I'm okay. Thank you." I meant it too. Liz was going above and beyond, and I didn't know how I'd ever repay her kindness.

"I'm just glad we didn't lose you."

I was on the sofa, foot propped up on my coffee table with an ice pack on top. Pillows kept me up in a lounging position so I wouldn't have to move. I closed my eyes. I was tired. So damn tired.

"Have you heard from Kendra?" I asked.

"Uh, listen, we need to talk about that, but when you're ready."

My eyes snapped open. She hated me. I ruined her big launch. "You can tell me." I was near tears, but I needed to hear it. I had to. I'd driven away my best friend.

Liz grimaced. "She needs time, okay? Just give her space and everything will be fine." I heard the doubt in her voice. I wasn't imagining it.

When Liz left to run errands, I picked up my phone and texted Kendra. I didn't even know what to say. Sorry I ruined your big moment please don't hate me forever. Actually, yeah, that seemed the best thing to say. I hit send.

Kendra didn't text me back.

———

Did you get my flowers?

You can at least reply.

Bitch.

David was texting up a storm from a new number—his previous one was blocked. I could always tell when he was wasted because he'd get belligerent so fast. And then he'd shift to remorse. I'd get apology texts later. I ignored them all. Whatever he'd hoped to accomplish with the flowers, I wasn't interested. I hadn't thrown them out for the simple reason that I physically couldn't manage it. So they sat on my coffee table, where I glared at them.

I made Liz go home with the promise I'd text her if I needed her. I wanted to be alone. I was exhausted. Not just tired, but soul-crushingly beat. I felt like giving up. You wanted to kill me? Come on over and do it. I wouldn't even fight it.

Not that I'd fought that crazy lady who jumped me. I was too shocked at the time to do anything. Terry at the self-defense class should add attacks from above to her repertoire. Because now I not only had to be aware of who was around me, I had to know if someone were flying above me. (Fine, she didn't fly, she leaped, but it looked like flying.)

I was dozing on the sofa when there was a knock at my door.

"Dammit. Hold on!" I tried to call out, but my voice wasn't fully back yet. I slowly got up, wincing with every movement. I shuffled to the door. This had better be good and worth my effort.

Zabir stood at the door with a bag in hand.

"I heard about what happened. Are you okay?"

"Here to finish me off?" I rasped. If ever I'd wanted to yell, it was now. But I couldn't.

"Don't be ridiculous. I brought you food. Let me put it in the kitchen." Like I could stop him. It was maddening to be this helpless. I couldn't fight anyone; I couldn't stop shit. I was a sitting duck no matter where I was or who I was with.

"Let's sit," he said, and helped me back to the sofa. "You look like shit."

"Thanks. So do you." He had a distinct bruise on his face. It was fading, but it was there.

"Yeah, courtesy of Liz. She waited outside my apartment and then jumped me."

I shook my head and then winced. "That's not what she said."

"I don't think she's playing with a full deck of cards. Hungry? I brought you soup, dumplings, and noodles. I wasn't sure what you'd be able to eat." He glanced at the roses. "Nice flowers."

"Throw them out," I said. "I don't want them."

He gave me a look but complied, taking the flowers to the trash room in the building hallway. I should have locked him out then, but honestly, that was so much effort. I didn't have that in me at the moment. And maybe I was enjoying someone caring for me like he did. Even if he was a liar.

He came back with bowls of food and sat next to me.

"Are you going to watch me eat?"

"I might. Are you up for telling me what happened?"

I shook my head again. Dammit! When would I stop doing that?

"Okay then, just eat. I'll find something for you to watch, and if you need anything, call me."

That was it. No begging for forgiveness, no telling me that meeting with Skylar and hiding it was a mistake. He came, he fed me, he left. Had I misjudged him?

The answer came not long after, when my sister called. Of course he'd told her what happened.

"What the hell did you get yourself into?" Nadia yelled.

"I can't talk," I whispered.

"What?"

"Can't talk." I hung up and texted her that I had no voice, I was alive, and I'd talk to her when I could.

If Zabir were truly on Team Dunia, he wouldn't have told my sister shit.

———

On the third day of convalescing, Liz and Detective Alvarez showed up. Separately, but they were both in my apartment at the same time. Detective Alvarez explained that Mary Ryans had killed herself.

The silence in the air was heavy. Thick. Something bad had happened. And then something even worse. I didn't know how to process this.

"What?" I finally rasped. "She's dead?"

"Yes."

"And she didn't say anything about why she did it?"

Alvarez took her phone out and showed us a photo of a piece of paper. It had blood on it. It read, *He said I had to die.*

"*He?* Who is *he?*" I demanded. "Is it David? Because I can't keep worrying someone is after me. He somehow got flowers inside my apartment." I'd emailed building management, and no one had fessed up to putting them inside.

"We've spoken with David. He didn't seem to know Mary. We've questioned him extensively. Dunia, I'm sorry we don't have more for you. We're going through all of Mary's things, talking to her friends and family. And so far, we have nothing. Except she had been a little withdrawn. But I promise you if we find a link to anyone, we will let you know." She hesitated before adding, "She wanted to tell you something. If you're up for watching it."

She held up her phone and played a video. Liz reached out and grabbed the phone so it was closer. It was Mary staring at the camera.

"Dunia, I'm so sorry. You have to stop this. I didn't want to do this, but he said I had to die." And then she picked up the pen. The video cut off after that.

I shuddered.

"No idea who 'he' is—besides your ex?" Alvarez asked.

"None. No clue." I was running out of people who could want me dead.

Another attack. Another dead body. I hadn't killed anyone, and yet I had a body count.

"I . . . need to sleep." It was all I could think to do. I wanted to be alone. To not have to think. I was exhausted; I needed rest.

Alvarez promised me she'd find out more and left. I didn't believe her. She still hadn't figured out why Skylar had tried to kill me. What made her think she'd know why Mary had?

Liz tried to get my mind off things. But that was impossible. She started asking me about family and whether I wanted to tell them what had happened.

"Do you want me to call your sister for you?"

"No."

"D, you've had major trauma. You should tell her."

"She already knows."

"Oh. Then I guess I'll go home. You'll call me if you need anything?"

"Of course," I lied. I didn't want to call anyone for anything. The only person I wanted to talk to was Kendra, and that was to beg her forgiveness. And she wanted nothing to do with me.

———

The calls had started soon after the last attack. The reporters asking me for a story. Camping outside my apartment like I was someone who mattered. I didn't want attention! I wanted them to leave me alone. If someone read a story about me, maybe they'd want to come after me next? It wasn't the most logical thought, but I held on to it like a talisman. No press. No attention. Stay home and hide.

I finally answered after my phone wouldn't stop ringing.

"Hi, this is Amanda Roberts with the *NY Post*—"

"I'm not interested. No comment."

"You don't want to tell the world what happened to you?" The world? Hell no!

"Absolutely not. I just want to be left alone! Please!" I hung up and hoped that would be the last I ever heard from her.

It wasn't. The paper ran stories about me being attacked, about how strange it was this kept happening to me, and implied I was to blame. I hated that reporter. I wish she knew how I felt.

Thirty-Nine

Zabir came over again. He must have been keeping tabs enough to know when Liz was around because so far he'd avoided her. Kendra hadn't reached out, and it was killing me. I didn't know how to fix it. Maybe that was why I let him in my apartment? I wanted fewer people mad at me—even though I was supposed to be mad at him.

He brought me food and didn't ask too many questions. He even had his laptop with him and was grading papers while I sat and stared at the TV. It was nice in a very surreal way. I shouldn't have felt so comfortable around him. He was hiding things from me. And yet, I liked having him around. But I had to know everything if this friendship was going to continue.

"What exactly do you want?" I asked. My voice was slowly coming back.

"To make sure you're okay." He shrugged. Simple.

"Why did you tell Nadia about this?"

"You can't be serious? You nearly died—again. Don't you think your family should know?" He stared at me.

"Not my family," I muttered. "I have questions for you."

He closed his laptop and turned to face me. "I'll answer them. Shoot."

"Why didn't you tell me or the cops about Skylar?"

"I was trying to figure out what was going on. He came to me because he thought something was haunting him, forcing him to do things."

"Yeah, it's called money. He was paid to attack me."

"Might have been. But I didn't know that at the time. It seemed like something else was at play, and I wanted to figure it out before telling you."

"Or the police."

He made a face. "Look, I bungled things, I admit it. But I've told them everything I know. Do you want to know what we talked about?"

"No, but I think I need to." I braced myself for what he would say. What had my would-be killer told Zabir? What had they talked about?

"We talked on the phone a few times, and then he came to my office. He didn't tell me what he was going to do. He just said he had a job to do, and he didn't want to do it. And that something was messing with him. Spiritually. Granted, he wasn't well. But the things he told me he saw and heard lined up with my area of study."

"Why did he want you, specifically?"

"He thought he had a jinn haunting him. I know, you don't believe. But I was trying to figure out if he was telling the truth."

I stared at him. A jinn? All this was because some lunatic thought a jinn was haunting him?

"Are you joking?" This wasn't funny if he was. "That's why you wanted to hang out, isn't it? Nadia told you, didn't she? You know, you didn't have to pretend to like me. You could have just asked me about it." The bitterness in my voice was thick; the accusation hung in the air. All this was because he wanted to know my secret.

Zabir looked at me like I had two heads. "Okay, now I'm in the dark. I don't know what you're talking about."

"Right, sure. Go on, tell me more about Skylar. Did he say *jinn*, or did you assume that's what it was?" Right now I hated Zabir. I was so mad at him for even bringing jinn up.

Zabir shook his head. "No, he said it was more than a ghost, it was something intelligent, which is what piqued my interest. There was something trying to stop him from doing a job. That every time he tried to do it, he got hurt, he saw things, he was legitimately terrified. I wanted to find out what was going on. And my curiosity was my mistake. And I should have made him tell me what the job was. I also wasn't entirely sure why he thought it was a jinn exactly? But from the things he told me . . ."

"Go on." I wrapped my arms around me gently so as to not tweak any wounds.

"He said there was a smoke monster following him. I know, it sounds absurd. But then he said he was certain it was from our culture because of how it looked when it came together. I wasn't entirely sure if he was insane or telling the truth. Or both, to be honest."

"He drew that smoke thing. But I still don't know why you didn't say anything afterward? Why hide all this?"

He sighed. "I messed up. I wasn't sure if my hunch was right. I thought, *Okay, maybe this is legit.* But then he attacked you, and I didn't know what to think. I came by the pharmacy that day to see if you were okay."

"So, you think he had a jinn." I couldn't let this go.

"Yes."

"And you swear on your mother that Nadia never told you anything?"

He held up his hand like a Boy Scout. "Absolutely swear. Why? What was it that's got you so upset?"

Maybe it was the painkillers or the feeling that I had nothing left to lose. But something made me want to tell him my secret. Perhaps if I told him, my personal load would be lifted. Or something. "I may regret telling you this, but please do not tell anyone. You have to promise."

"I promise." He looked absolutely puzzled.

I stared at him while I said it. I'd see it in his face, that moment when he'd begin to be scared of me. Fear me. I had to tell him. This secret I'd sworn to myself I'd never share again. That I'd take to the grave so no one would ever look at me the way my family had. But here I was spilling my guts.

"When I was little, my mother had me exorcised."

Forty

He blinked several times in a row. "Your mother had you exorcised?"

I nodded.

"I need to know everything. Right now."

"Nadia didn't tell you this?" I asked. I was certain she had, that this was what his interest in me was about. But he shook his head.

"No, and believe me, I'd remember if she had." I was surprised by that. I expected Nadia to warn everyone away from me.

I took a deep breath. "My mother thought I had a jinn haunting me. That was why I sleepwalked. And she swore that my dad died because of the jinn." Zabir's eyes never left my face. I continued. "She believed that whatever was haunting me and making me behave strangely had made my father keel over and die in front of me. So she had me exorcised when I was five. But the damage to our family was done. Dad was dead, she blamed me, and she would never be alone with me in a room after that." Even when I was an adult, she kept Nadia near when I was around.

"Okay, Nadia never told me that. Holy shit." He sat back. He was frowning, which I'd learned was his thinking face. "What if all of this is related? It can't all be a coincidence?"

"You mean Skylar's madness? I don't see how. That maniac at Aphrodite wasn't a jinn. She was just nuts. As was my mother. You don't exorcise kids just because they're different." I sounded so bitter even to my own ears. Would I ever be able to forgive her for what she'd done? I wasn't sure.

"Is that why you and Nadia aren't close?" he asked.

I nodded. "We used to be. But the sleepwalking was bad. I once almost smothered her with a pillow. And then after Abu died, she believed what my mother told her. And she stopped being my big sister and generally avoided me. My next-door neighbor—Carol—raised me mostly before she had to move away. Ammi wouldn't do a thing for me. Everyone avoided me. Can you imagine putting all that on a child?" I shook my head. I angrily wiped my eyes. I hated that I was crying in front of Zabir.

"I'm sorry." His voice was soft. "So when you were exorcised, what happened?"

"From what I remember, this man and his brother prayed over me. That was it. No vomiting, no speaking in tongues. I did pee the bed, though." I laughed at that. "But it was very anticlimactic, to be honest."

"And then were you fine? Per your mother, I mean."

"After the whole pray-over-Dunia thing? I quieted down, still sleep-walked here and there. I was mostly left alone. I wasn't allowed to go to any events or dinners with them; I had to stay with the neighbors. No one in the community wanted me around, as if I'd somehow do something to them. They all thought I somehow killed my dad." I shrugged, as if this were normal and no big deal. But it wasn't, and on the inside I was screaming. "I was sort of ignored my whole life. That's why I don't know that much about our culture. When I was twelve, Carol moved away, and I fended for myself. I lived with Nadia and my mom, but I was on my own. I don't think they even knew where I was half the time."

"Your mom should have done better."

"Yeah, well, she didn't. I mean, in hindsight, I sort of get it. She needed someone to blame for losing her husband. But I didn't give him a heart attack." I was five. I was a child. How could she have blamed me? How could anyone have?

"And then here I come talking about jinn, and you had all of this to deal with. I'm sorry. I didn't know. Are you feeling okay that you told me?"

I wasn't sure, which is what I told him. "I've never told anyone that. Not Kendra, not even my ex. Am I supposed to feel like a weight is lifted or something?"

He grinned. "Maybe you're transferring your burdens to me, and I'll gladly shoulder the load. I promise I won't repeat this story to anyone."

"Thank you. I'm not ready to have people see me in that light, you know?"

He sat silent for a moment. His face didn't look like he was scared. He looked . . . excited? His eyes were wide, like I'd told him the secret of life. He looked at me like he wanted to study me, like I was research. Another reaction I didn't want.

"Do you mind if I dig into this a little? In my books, I mean. I won't call Nadia. If it will help you get some sort of closure on your mother? I'd like to know what she thought was happening to you and if it's in any way related to Skylar."

"Suit yourself. But if you tell anyone what I've told you, I will murder you."

"I'm certain you will."

When he left that evening, I cursed myself for telling him. I didn't believe in jinn, and I didn't want to entertain any notions otherwise. The belief in the supernatural had ruined my family and my life.

———

That night I dreamed that the thing in my apartment was David and that he had to leave. I felt like he was there, watching me. I woke up to the sound of my door closing. Which wasn't out of the norm.

Sleepwalking and hypnagogic hallucinations went hand in hand. Sometimes, I swore I was awake, but then parts of my dreams would happen in front of my eyes. I couldn't trust what I saw or heard while sleeping. I couldn't trust my own brain. Add to that the drugs I needed to keep the pain at minimum, and nothing was quite what it seemed. There was no medical cure for sleepwalking, so I had learned to not trust my eyes and ears anymore.

When I woke up the next morning, I saw something on my cameras but wasn't sure what. A blur. If someone had been in my apartment, they'd avoided the cameras. I had to be imagining things, right?

Forty-One

Dunia, age five

Baba was sitting in my room. The one I'd been moved to after almost hurting Nadia. "It wasn't your fault. Try not to worry about it."

"But I do. I was being bad." There was nothing worse than being a bad kid, at least to me. Bad kids didn't deserve love. I needed to be like Nadia. She never got in trouble. "I'm going to be like Nadia."

Baba grimaced. "No, be yourself. She acts like I don't exist. In my day, we didn't treat elders like that." He always fumed about that sort of thing. Nadia didn't revere him. Mostly, he was mad because she didn't love him. Not like I did.

"Baba, will you help me be good?"

He scoffed. "Being good is overrated, beti."

"But then Ammi will love me."

His eyes flashed but he gave in. "If that's what you want. Fine."

"You don't like my idea?"

"I don't." He said it with no explanation.

"Why not?"

"Because your mother doesn't know everything."

"Yes, she does!" I yelled. I loved Baba, but Ammi was Ammi. And she could do no wrong. It was me who was wrong.

"Ask her, then. Ask what she did before you were born!" Baba was mad. He was furious in a way I'd never seen before.

"What did she do?" I asked in a quiet voice.

"Ask her what she did," he repeated.

So I did. I ran to her. She was watching her favorite soap opera—*General Hospital*.

"Ammi?"

"Yes, Dunia?"

"Baba said to ask you what you did before I was born."

She stared at me in confusion. "What?"

I shrugged. "He said to ask you what you did."

Her face went white. "Go to your room," she whispered. I stomped my feet as I went. How come she could keep things from me? It wasn't fair.

Later, I heard her talking to Abu.

"I need to take her to someone."

"Dunia is fine, the doctors said so. Why are you so focused on this?"

"She's not fine. She knows things she shouldn't know. She couldn't know."

I was sick of them talking about me.

"Let's play hide-and-seek," Baba suggested to distract me.

"Okay." It was better than hearing my parents say I was crazy. Baba was the best at hide-and-seek. He could hide in plain sight, and I'd never find him. But he always found me.

"Got you!" he said, finding me in the closet. I shrieked with laughter.

"No fair, you have better hiding spots than me!"

"Want to go to a good hiding spot?"

I nodded. Of course I did.

"Okay, but it's a secret place."

I was excited. I loved good secrets. Not bad ones that got me in trouble. Baba took me by the hand, and we walked to a garden he liked. I didn't know whose garden it was, but it didn't matter. It was beautiful.

"Where are we?"

"My favorite place," he said. "Do you like it here?"

"I love it!" He set me down so I could explore. "It smells so beautiful."

When we finished exploring, he said we had to go back. We walked back home. I hadn't noticed the time. We'd been playing for hours.

We walked into the house, and something was wrong. The police were in the living room, talking to my parents. Ammi was sobbing. Abu looked ashen. Nadia was standing there with a bewildered look on her face.

"Dunia?" Nadia said it first.

"Oh my God!" Ammi ran forward and hugged me. "Where have you been??"

"I was playing with Baba!" I wanted to tell them about the garden, but it was a secret, and they were all so mad and upset.

"You can't just leave like that! We thought something happened!"

"Oh. Sorry." I smiled at the police officer to show them I was sorry. I didn't mean to scare everyone. I'd just wanted to have some fun.

I hadn't realized I'd been gone for hours. It had seemed so much shorter to me. But I wasn't good at reading my watch yet. After that, Ammi started taking me to the Islamic center. To her, doctors and holy men were the only ones who could help me, and the doctors refused. Abu didn't object. I thought he would. I thought he'd fight for me. Only Baba did, but no one listened to him.

Forty-Two

I'd had to take leave at work for obvious reasons. I'd let Mandy know as soon as I was out of the hospital, but she wasn't returning my calls. I didn't know if I still had a job, and the stress of money was hanging over me. My savings would cover a few months, but that was it.

I needed to heal up fast, but so much was out of my control. I hated it.

Zabir knocked on my door.

"You look a little better!" he said. He was holding a bag of food. "I brought more snacks. Figured you could use some company."

"Thanks."

"I did some digging, and I have questions. But first, let me make some tea." He took a few minutes to make me tea and brought cookies with it.

"So, how are you?" He peered into my face, and I glanced away.

"I don't know. My side is killing me. My ankle hurts. And I think Kendra hates me for messing up her beauty launch."

"That was not your fault. She can be upset, but she shouldn't be mad." He tried to be kind, but we both knew it was my fault.

"You don't know how hard she worked on that launch. Ugh."

My hands shook as I held the tea, so he helped me put it on the coffee table.

"I'm fine," I said again.

"You're not. If you're not up for talking, that's absolutely fine," he said.

"No, I'm fine," I lied. "What questions did you have?"

"I wanted to ask you more about what you experienced. I'm trying to figure out if your mom just thought something was haunting you, or—"

"Or if I'm about to go all *Exorcist*?" I let out a harsh laugh. "Ask away." I sounded so angry. I was angry! My mother and her ideas. It was cultural a bit, sure. But she'd taken things to a whole new level. I used to wonder how much the inherited mental illnesses in my family had a role to play in things.

"What do you remember about things before she intervened?"

"Not too much?" I shrugged. "Ugh, I need to not move. I remember sleepwalking, and my dad used to tell me jinn stories at bedtime. They fought a lot about that."

"What were his stories?" His eyes lit up. An odd thought came to mind. My dad would have liked Zabir.

"Oh, you know, fairy tales about a princess and jinn. That sort of thing. Sometimes about churails? Is that a thing?"

He smothered a laugh. "Yes, it is. Sorry, I shouldn't laugh, but wow, you really don't know much about this, huh? It's cute." I didn't know much about my culture. I was the first to admit it. And I hated that. But I'd been rejected by it and now was trying to figure out who I was.

"Yeah, Carol's Urdu was lacking." I rolled my eyes. "Anyways, every time they fought, Baba would come and talk with me so I wouldn't get upset. He and Abu were the only ones who didn't think I was weird."

"And Baba is . . . ?"

"An uncle on Dad's side. He lived with us, or stayed with us for a while, before going back to Pakistan."

He nodded and took out his phone to write down notes. "When sleepwalking, what would you do?"

"Mostly mundane things. But I'd stand and watch Nadia a lot when we shared a room. I don't know why. That was unnerving for her, to say the least. And then after I tried to put a pillow over her, Ammi moved me to the study."

"Did you ever leave your house?"

"A few times, actually. Once the police found me in a park in the middle of the night. And then CPS started watching us, which upset Ammi so much. She was beyond mad at me."

"What made your mom think you had anything to do with your dad's heart attack?"

I blinked. I hadn't expected that question.

"I don't know, she was crazy. Can we move on?"

"Sure, sorry. Didn't mean to upset you. Can you tell me about the exorcism you had? What you remember?"

"I don't remember much. I've tried to block it all out. Ammi took me to some holy man, and he and his brother prayed over me. I remember wetting the bed. And then that was it."

"That was it? Was it all in one day?"

"Yeah, a few hours. There was no crazy head spinning, no puking. But after, Ammi seemed to tolerate me better. I think it was more for her benefit than mine."

"And did the sleepwalking end?"

"No. It quieted down, and then I grew out of it. But after Ammi died it's started up again."

There was a look in Zabir's eye like he'd found a clue and was about to run with it. "That's actually useful info."

"How? Oh wait, I have a question. Do you know what the secret kalma is?"

He frowned. "No, I've never heard of that."

"It was some prayer Ammi would say every day and night over me. Then she'd pretend to spit and clap her hands three times." He shook his head. "Nothing? Before she passed, I promised her I'd say it, but I can't remember it. And I have this weird guilt for not following through."

"Adding that to the things I need to research. And I'm assuming you can't ask Nadia about it?" I shot him a look that answered his question.

"What's the point of researching this? I mean, no offense, is this purely a curiosity thing? Because the people who tried to kill me were human. They were nuts, but they were people, not some supernatural entities. I know you think there was more to Skylar, but what if there wasn't? What if he was just an asshole who got paid to kill me?"

"You may be right. And I don't mean to make you feel like a research specimen. I have a theory that I'm working on, but I need to dig into it more before I tell you. Bear with me a little?"

"Like I have a choice. Wait, did Skylar ever mention his girlfriend?"

"I don't think so, but let me listen to the recording."

"You recorded him?" I'd missed that part. Had he told me that before? My head was not retaining information, or maybe I was just exhausted. But I made a note to possibly see a neurologist soon.

"Well, yeah, I wanted to make sure I had it down right. I'll relisten to it and come back. I think I know which direction to look in. And yes, I gave a copy to the police, before you ask."

"Suit yourself, but I only care about the girlfriend. No one's been able to find her." If he could help me find her or shed any light on who had hired Skylar, it could finally lead to something. Knowing who wanted me dead was necessary.

"If you need anything—"

"Yeah, I know, call you." I was supposed to holler for help, text people to do things for me. I hated it. I wanted to be self-sufficient. And frankly, my people meter was running low.

Forty-Three

Dunia, age five

Ammi was having one of her parties again. Desi dinner parties were big deals. The food, the house, your clothes—they all had to be perfect.

"Clean your room!" she yelled at us, her voice loud. She'd been cleaning all day, and cooking for a few more. Ammi took these things very seriously. She loved entertaining, showing off her home and perfect family. Well, Nadia and Abu were perfect. I wasn't.

People were always coming and going in our house. Aunties stopping by for chai. Full dinner parties of desi families. Days when I had to clean up my room, because Ammi loved giving people tours of the house. I'd grumble and put things under the bed or in the closet.

Ammi's parties were always loud, full of random people I had to call Auntie and Uncle (they weren't related to us), and sometimes, we had to do dances to entertain them. I never liked that part. We'd wear clothes my mother got us in Pakistan, or that distant relatives sent us, the smell of mothballs stuck in my nose.

My main job was playing with the kids. Sometimes I liked them, and we played with toys, and the older kids would be with Nadia. Ammi approved and would later tell us how proud of us she was. We were a good family, and the gossip wouldn't be about us. We were perfect. A husband who was a professor, a mother who could cook anything, and two adorable and obedient daughters.

Baba sometimes helped me entertain kids, but he often hung out with the adults. Or hid, because he didn't care for socializing. "I've done that enough in my time." He got away with it because you never told your elders what to do. Not even my parents could give him an order, and it was their house.

These functions—as Ammi called them—were everything. We'd go to parties; we'd host parties. Sometimes, the parties got loud, and the tabla came out. My mother would hit it with a spoon and sing her favorite song in Punjabi, "Kala Doria." I never knew the words. (She never taught us Punjabi—she saved that for adult talk.) But Ammi looked so happy and glamorous, her hair in an updo. She wore her best gold jewelry and a shalwar kameez that was full of embroidery. There was no such thing as too much at a desi party, even if it was just dinner.

This was when Ammi was happiest. Showing off her house, her family, being with other people who reminded her of home.

I ruined that.

This dinner we were hosting was for Ayesha Auntie, so I knew it was going to be a bad night. I'd have to spend time with Jamal. There were three or four aunties and their families over. Ayesha Auntie's sons were my responsibility. Adnan liked to play with all my toys, no matter how girlie they were. He was polite and sweet and told me we were now best friends.

"Okay," I said. I didn't have a best friend yet. Besides Baba, but I didn't think he counted. I needed a friend my age. "I like this doll the best because her hair is pretty," I said, holding up my newest Barbie. Her hair was only pretty because I hadn't ruined it yet. "You can play with her." I was being a good host. I held out the doll to Adnan.

"Who are you talking to?" Jamal asked. His voice sounded mean. He was going to make fun of me because that's what he did. And whenever I got upset, he'd run and tell a lie, that I hit him or something. The adults always believed him over me. I hated him as much as I'd ever hated anyone.

"Your brother." I rolled my eyes. It was a new thing I'd learned from Nadia.

"You're so annoying, Dunia. I'm calling you Duhnia. CILANTRO! You're a cilantro!" He laughed.

"Just ignore him," Adnan said.

"You're so much nicer than him," I said.

"Who is?" Jamal asked, this time coming closer to me. I didn't like him near me. I could feel myself tense. He was up to something.

"Your brother!" I yelled. He was always playing the ignore game. I felt bad for Adnan, having a brother like that. At least Nadia still played with me sometimes.

"I don't have a brother!"

"Why does he always play this game?" I asked Adnan.

He shrugged. "He thinks he's funny."

"Well, he's not. And I like you so much better."

"Want to hear a secret?" Adnan leaned in, grinning. "Jamal still wets the bed."

I giggled, laughing so hard I was nearly crying.

"What's so funny?" Jamal asked.

"You wet the bed! You're the baby, not me! Jamal wets the bed! Jamal wets the bed!" I sang it out like it was the funniest joke in the world. I'd never seen his face get so red. I thought he was going to cry. I was glad. He deserved this.

He left me and ran to get his mom.

"Ammi, Ammi!" he cried. "Dunia is talking to imaginary people!" I heard him shout it. I followed him, stomping my feet.

"I am not! I'm playing with Adnan."

"Beti, Adnan kon hai?" Jamal's dad asked. Who is Adnan? Uncle had a beard that I thought was funny looking. It wasn't as full as Baba's beard.

"His brother!" I shouted.

Auntie gasped. They all looked at me like I'd grown three heads.

"Adnan says Jamal wets the bed. And at night, he also sneaks into the kitchen to eat the gulab jaman." I was the tattler now. It felt so good to give it back to Jamal.

"Dunia is just joking," Ammi said. "Right?"

"I'm not! Adnan says Uncle is mean to Auntie and that they need to divorce. He says that Jamal is going to die for all the bad things he does!"

The silence that followed lasted for a long time.

And then Ayesha Auntie hurriedly said goodbye and got everyone's coats. Ammi's face was furious. "How could you ruin my party?" she yelled at me once everyone left.

"I wish they were dead," I said. "I wish Jamal and Ayesha Auntie were dead!" I ran to my room. I was going to be punished for this, I knew it. But I hated him. He was such a jerk.

Nadia came into my room to check on me.

"You shouldn't have done that," she said. "You ruined her party." She sat on my bed, trying to get me to come out.

"I didn't do anything. Jamal was being mean to me and Adnan."

"Dunia, there's no Adnan. You can stop pretending now." I didn't know why she was keeping up that joke. Adnan was as real as she was. So I stuck my tongue out at her.

Later that night, when I should have been in bed, I heard my parents talking. I got up and crept down the hallway.

"She's a pagal!" Ammi wailed.

"She's not. This is normal. Imaginary friends are very Amrikan of her. She probably saw someone on TV with one."

"This is exactly what happened with Rahmi. It started just like this. And you know how she ended up. This is my fault. I never should have—"

"Stop. You didn't do anything. Old superstitions and stories, that's all. You did nothing." My father said it firmly.

Ammi thought I was like Rahmi Khala. That meant they thought I was crazy. They were going to send me away. I went back to my bed, tears in my eyes. Baba was waiting for me.

He smoothed my hair. "Don't worry, I'll keep you safe."

———

We stopped being invited to things. Not all at once; it sort of tapered off. Baba told me not to worry about it and urged me to pretend I didn't see Adnan. That I had just been playing a prank. Which I did. I told that lie to my parents and crossed my fingers behind my back. I didn't want to be sent away like Rahmi Khala. I didn't want them to think I was a pagal.

"Ammi, I was just kidding about Adnan. I wanted to play a joke on Jamal." She nodded but didn't say anything. She'd stopped looking me in the eye. Adnan—Nadia told me—was Jamal's brother, but he'd died when he was born.

At first, we'd go to bigger functions. The kind not in anyone's house but in some sort of hall or hotel. And then the aunties asked Ammi to leave me at home with a sitter.

I was left with Carol, who was the best and so nice to me. The few times people came over for dinner, I had to ask Nadia who I could play with, in case any weren't real. She kept that secret. She didn't want to have a pagal for a sister either.

"There are three kids. Huma, Hena, and Bina. You can play with them," she'd whisper back. And I would. Anyone else I saw, I ignored until they stopped shouting at me for attention. "Just pretend you're normal," Nadia had advised. That's what I was doing.

Pretend you're normal.

Forty-Four

I got up to yet another knock at my door. I was getting tired of the doormen not calling before sending people up. I hated the constant surprise of not knowing who was on the other side of the door. Though to be fair, it was always Liz or Zabir, never Kendra. (Who had yet to speak to me. I kept texting her apologies that were ignored.)

I opened the door and was surprised to see David standing there. He was holding more flowers.

"Hey."

"You can't come in." My voice sounded hard, angry. Good, it should.

"Guess you're feeling better. These are for you." I didn't move to take them. He sighed. "Look, I'm trying to be nice, okay? You almost died. You can at least take my flowers."

"Will you leave if I do?"

"Sure."

I snatched the flowers and tried to shut the door, but his foot stopped me.

"You can't come in. Leave or I'll call the police."

"When did you become such a bitch?"

"When did you become a stalker? Get out!" I yelled it as loud as my voice would let me; my throat was still a bit tender. He blanched and took a step backward. It was all I needed to slam the door and lock it.

I called downstairs. "Why are you letting people up unannounced and who are banned from the building?"

The doorman was new and had no idea to not do that. I didn't want to cost him his job, but I was sick of this. "Make sure you announce every single visitor for me, got it? And no sending them up without my approval."

I sounded like a bitch. But I needed this to stop.

I called Detective Alvarez and let her know what had just happened, and then I threw the flowers in the trash.

———

Zabir left me a voice mail saying he'd found something and needed to talk to me. I didn't call him back. I just didn't see the point. Okay, he'd found something that would make his story fit. Great. It didn't mean that was reality.

But he came over anyway. This time, announced.

He had more food. Food over flowers, that was my rule. Snacks would always win me over.

"What do we have to eat today?"

"Ramen," he said, his eyes dancing. "I stopped at my favorite spot downtown." I watched him run around my kitchen like he lived here, like he knew where everything was. (At this point he did.)

I waited for the ramen to appear before me on the coffee table. If the price for this delivery was more silly jinn talk, then fine.

"So, I have a theory, and your prayer thing helped. I found it, by the way. It's not anything special, but some people have used it to keep away nazar. That's the evil eye."

"I know what it is. I have some sense of things," I snapped. I knew I was the least desi desi ever, but everyone knew what nazar was.

"Sorry, I don't mean to mansplain. But if anything doesn't make sense, let me know. Here." He handed me a printout with the prayer on it. It was phonetic, so I could stumble through the words. My tongue felt lazy; I hadn't had to say these sounds in decades. "Does that seem familiar?"

I tried to say the words, but I was useless. My Arabic lessons had ended a long time ago, and I was never good at it to begin with.

"What's the English translation?" I asked. That would have to do. I never promised my mom I'd say it in Arabic.

"'There is no power and strength without Allah.' The prophet said that in the Koran. Does it sound familiar?"

I made him say it in Arabic too. I nodded. "I think that's right."

"It took me a while to find it because it's a very common prayer and I was looking for something more elusive. It was right in front of me the whole time," Zabir explained. "The phook marring and clapping is more folkloric than religious, probably something your mom's family taught her. But the rest is nothing I would think of as a secret."

"Huh. I wonder why this was the prayer my mom wanted me to say?"

"Maybe because it in theory gives your fate over to God, as opposed to whatever she thought was trying to take over."

"Maybe. I wish I could just ask her."

"You could ask Nadia?"

"Nope. Not doing it. Look, I know you like her, but you don't know what it was like to have your big sister turn away from you. Like I was nothing. She used to defend me, and then she let people pile on me. And eventually, she joined in. I can't ever forgive that."

He held his hands up in surrender. "Okay, I get it. I won't bring her up again."

"So what's your theory?" I set my spoon down, ready.

"I don't think you had an actual exorcism."

"Oh. That's not what I expected you to say."

"By that I mean they didn't get rid of anything. They merely built a wall around it. And your mother was instrumental in keeping that wall up. It was tied to her."

"Oh," I repeated.

"You don't seem excited by this info?"

It was true, I wasn't. I couldn't match how he felt about this. "I mean, how is any of this affecting me? It's not. I still need to know why people keep trying to murder me."

He nodded. "You don't think that anything else could possibly be involved? Anything beyond human?"

"No. Not at all. And until you can prove otherwise . . ."

"Both the people who tried to kill you killed themselves."

"And?"

"Dunia, you're being obtuse."

"And you keep bringing up a past that's dead and buried. Show me proof that this is happening, that something is going on that's other-worldly." I hit my fist on the table, nearly spilling my ramen. "If you can't, it means this is just a theory." I wasn't trying to be difficult or a pain; I just refused to let what haunted me in childhood haunt me again. And I didn't mean jinn. I meant people's ideas of them, projected onto me. Which is what I explained to him yet again. "I appreciate you looking into this, but I don't believe in this, and I don't think I ever will."

"That's fair, and if I'd dealt with what you had, I might feel the same. But promise me if anything bizarre happens, anything unexplainable to you, you'll tell me? I'm not trying to fit a narrative; I only want to make sure you're safe."

"Sure."

"One more thing. I wanted you to have this." He handed me a small gift bag. "It's an evil eye tasbeeh."

I froze. It was nearly identical to the one my dad had. I asked him to get the wooden box from my bookshelf down.

"My dad had one, see?"

"Who broke it?"

"I think my ex."

"What an ass."

"Right? Anyways, thank you for this. I appreciate it." It was a sweet gesture. I was feeling overwhelmed, and the tears started up again. "Sorry, it just reminds me of my dad."

"Try keeping it near you while you sleep and see if it helps. But if you ever go near anyone devout, don't tell them about it. It's technically shirk to use it as a talisman."

Okay, that one I didn't know. "What's shirk?"

"Idolatry. Talismans are supposed to be forbidden, but I've found they're useful."

"Well, I'll keep this secret, then." Something at the back of my mind started to form. A memory. "Wait, I think you unlocked something. I remember my parents arguing about the tasbeeh my dad gave me. My mom called it shirk. Weird, I hadn't even thought of that in so long." Their fights and arguments over me had all seemed to blur into one unending fight where I was the root cause.

"Yeah, that would make sense. Was your dad's side of the family more mystical?"

"Like, Sufi?"

"Yes." He seemed relieved I knew what he was talking about.

"Actually, I think so. But I can't trust my memory of things. You'd have to check with Nadia about that." *But don't,* I wanted to add.

"Which is something else I wanted to ask you. I understand why you don't want her in your life. But she may have answers. Do I have permission to speak with her about this? Only this. I won't tell her anything about you except you're fine. I'll say I'm researching and you suggested I talk to her. What do you think?"

He seemed so hopeful I didn't want to let him down. I acquiesced but warned him she might not have much to tell him. She was a child then too. (That same logic didn't apply to forgiveness, however.)

"That's fair. Is there anything else you want me to ask her?"

"Yeah, why didn't she stick up for me. I was her little sister." I couldn't keep the bitterness out of my voice.

"I'll see what I can do."

My apartment door opening made us both jump for a moment. (And then I hated myself for jerking like that; my body couldn't handle it.) It was Liz, and I had been dreading this moment from the first time Zabir visited me. She stood there, her mouth open in shock.

"What is he doing here?"

"Did I give you keys?" I couldn't remember.

"I made copies while you were convalescing. Seriously, what is he doing here?"

"He's helping me with something."

"You need to leave," she said, pointing her finger at Zabir.

"Careful, I could press charges against you for attacking me outside my apartment," Zabir replied.

"Don't lie, you were outside my building. Like we can believe anything you say?" Liz shot back. Their stories weren't matching up. Who did I believe? The man who had withheld the truth about my killer from me or my friend who had been there for me since the day we met?

Zabir ignored her and looked at me. "You'll call me?" he asked, and I nodded. I watched him leave and then waited for Liz to calm down.

"I need to know why he was here," she said.

"You don't. It's about me, and I'm not ready to talk about it." I hadn't meant for it to come out that harshly, but I wasn't about to tell her details. "It has nothing to do with Skylar."

"D, I'm just worried about you. Too much has happened. Just promise me you'll be careful with him. I don't trust him."

"I promise. Maybe you two live near each other—that would really explain things."

"Ugh, I'd better move, then." She laughed, but it came out harshly. I was tired. I loved my friends, but I needed a break from all the drama.

"Can we not talk and just watch TV? Because I'm exhausted."

"Of course!"

I put on some syndicated crime show—I kept watching them to learn tricks. Like how to know if you're being followed, that sort of thing. Liz typed on her phone the entire time, before announcing she had to leave. She kissed my cheek and promised to come back soon.

I didn't ask her about Kendra. I was scared at what the answer would be.

Forty-Five

Dunia, age five

"Ammi says you're a pagal." Jamal said it like it was nothing. I was alone with him, except for Adnan, who always just watched everything. But I knew better than to speak to Adnan. He wasn't real; that's what everyone said.

"Well, your mom's wrong," I replied. Ammi told Ayesha Auntie everything, so I knew that's where Jamal had heard it.

"She says you're going to end up in a hospital, just like your khala." Jamal grinned when he said this. "You're a pagal!" He cackled. My aunt, Rahmi Khala, was a pagal. This much was true. But everything he said made me mad.

I hit him as hard as I could, right in the nose. There was a crunchy feeling and then blood. It felt good. And then the moment of fear hit me: I was in so much trouble.

He screamed so loudly. Ammi and Ayesha Auntie ran in. They saw his nose and the blood. I sat there, my hands in my lap.

"What did you do?" Ayesha Auntie yelled at me.

"Defended myself," I said.

"You—" She stepped toward me, but Ammi stopped her.

"I'll take care of this. Take him to the doctor."

I watched as Ayesha Auntie carried Jamal out, with Adnan in tow. And my mother didn't speak to me the rest of the day. She waited for Abu to get home.

"You're in big trouble," Nadia said. Baba agreed with her.

"Why did you hit him?" he asked.

"He called me a pagal. Said I'd end up in a hospital like Rahmi Khala!"

Nadia nodded; she knew I hated being called crazy. "But you shouldn't hit people."

"I know." I had messed up. I knew that. But he made me so angry.

When Abu came home, he came to my room after his tea. He sat down and looked at me. He didn't seem mad.

"Beti, sometimes when you're different, people treat you badly. But there's nothing wrong with you," he said.

"Yes, there is. Ammi said there was. Am I a pagal?" I asked him. He would know. He would never lie to me.

"No, you're not a pagal. You're just you. And I love you. But I don't want to hear of you hitting anyone." He leaned in to whisper. "That was a very good punch. Don't tell your mother."

I hugged him. He was my favorite parent. Ammi would never be happy with me. I knew that for sure.

That night, they fought so loudly, Nadia came into my room to hold me.

"I have no help here with her. None! I can't take it!" Ammi screamed. Nadia tried to cover my ears.

I felt bad. I had messed up.

"Don't listen," Nadia said. "You're not crazy, okay?"

"What if I am?"

"Then I'll stick with you forever, okay?" She hugged me closer.

"I hate Jamal and wish he'd die," I said, turning my face to the wall and closing my eyes.

———

We had a couple of weekends without Jamal and Ayesha Auntie over. That was a relief. Adnan told me they weren't coming back because they died, but I didn't tell anyone. Until I found Ammi crying so hard she scared me. She was on the floor, her back up against the wall. Her face was covered.

"Ammi, what happened?" I asked. Moms weren't supposed to cry. They were supposed to be happy.

She didn't answer me, and in a panic I called Abu at work. They'd taught us phone numbers and how to call if there were an emergency.

"Abu-ji, Ammi won't stop crying I don't know what's happening please come home!" I said in one breath when he answered. He promised he'd be there in minutes, and he was. He would save Ammi. He would make her happy again. Everything would be okay.

"What happened?" my father asked in English, kneeling down to be at eye level with Ammi. He moved her hands from her face. "Tell me, what happened?"

Her face was covered in tears, and I was terrified something awful had happened. Something so bad we'd never be the same.

"Ayesha and Jamal," she whispered. "They died in a car accident."

"I know," I said. They looked up at me in confusion. "Adnan told me they died."

Ammi's face looked mad. "You did this."

"That's enough," Abu said firmly. "Dunia, go play in your room."

I didn't hear the argument; I closed my door so I wouldn't.

"What happened?" Baba asked as I sat on my bed.

"Jamal and Ayesha Auntie are dead."

Baba sat next to me and stroked my hair gently.

"Ammi's very sad."

"She'll get over it," Baba said.

Abu knocked on my door and came in. "Your mother's okay now. She's going to take a nap."

"Okay."

"Why don't you come with me to pick up Nadia, and we can get some ice cream."

I brightened at that.

"Abu-ji, did I make them die?"

"Of course you didn't."

"But I'm not sad Jamal's dead either." I didn't add that they'd made me so mad, I'd wished they'd disappear.

He let out a breath. "Just don't repeat that to your mother, okay?"

Forty-Six

Transcript: *The Disappearance of Dunia Ahmed* podcast

AMANDA ROBERTS: So, I have to wonder what Dunia's mindset was at this point. She's now almost been murdered three times, if you count the hit-and-run, which we do. How was she not losing it?

DANIELLE MCGUIRE: Right? I'd be burning sage and paying witches to clear my vibes by now. Like, girl, you're in danger!

AMANDA ROBERTS: But from whom, and why? How frustrating it must have been for her. So we asked Kendra Wright to join us again to discuss. Kendra, how was Dunia after the Aphrodite attack.

KENDRA WRIGHT: I actually wouldn't know. We had some sort of mis-communication that—at the time—we weren't aware of.

DANIELLE MCGUIRE: What do you mean?

KENDRA WRIGHT: We each thought the other was mad at the other. We both texted and called, and neither of us got any messages. Our phones weren't blocked. It was only after—

AMANDA ROBERTS: Wait, wait—no spoilers!

KENDRA WRIGHT: Right. No spoilers. We learned there was a reason behind the phone sitch, but I guess I can't say more.

AMANDA ROBERTS: So you and your best friend just didn't speak after she nearly died at your launch event?

KENDRA WRIGHT: Not for about a week or so after. I showed up to her apartment because I couldn't take it anymore. I had to know if she was okay.

DANIELLE MCGUIRE: Did you go to the hospital?

KENDRA WRIGHT: I did. I went and was told my name wasn't on the approved list of visitors, and no one gave me info on how to get on that list.

DANIELLE MCGUIRE: Maybe she just didn't want to see you after that. I mean, she nearly died because of your event.

KENDRA WRIGHT: She nearly died because of an employee at the store. Not because of me.

AMANDA ROBERTS: Of course. We're not pointing fingers. You also suffered from the attack. How did it impact your launch and brand?

KENDRA WRIGHT: The immediate aftermath was that the press focused on the attack, which isn't something you want a new makeup company to be known for. But Aphrodite came through and helped me relaunch. They also put together a fund for Dunia's recovery.

AMANDA ROBERTS: That was nice of them—to not want to be sued. So when you did finally see Dunia, how was it?

KENDRA WRIGHT: I cried. We both did. She looked awful. Her neck was still bruised. She was limping. But she was alive, and that's what mattered. We decided once she was healed up enough, we'd go away so she could get a break.

DANIELLE MCGUIRE: And Zabir had been caring for her. Did you know the story there?

KENDRA WRIGHT: I knew what Dunia shared with us, but I think his tenacity won her over. Truthfully, I didn't trust him. I still don't. But she did. And she needed him. He and Liz were there when . . . when I wasn't. I'll never forgive myself for not going over to her apartment sooner. I really thought she needed space. I should have known.

AMANDA ROBERTS: Aww, that's so sweet. Now, you gave her a present that would shock most people, pun intended.

KENDRA WRIGHT: I got her a Taser. I got both of us one. Because if these attacks were going to keep happening, Dunia needed to protect herself.

DANIELLE MCGUIRE: I love that. So much that we've partnered with our favorite Taser maker, Shock Stopper. Use the promo code Dunia20 for a discount!

Forty-Seven

I managed to go outside one week after the Aphrodite mess. Sitting in my apartment was becoming suffocating. On the other hand, being outside meant being vulnerable: anyone could come at me. Until I knew who was after me, I couldn't relax.

But I really needed some air and bagels. I limped across the street, my hands shaking anytime anyone came too close to me. I wasn't ready to be out, but I was trying. I got my bagel and made my way back to my building.

"Looks like you're healing well." I glanced up to see Kendra standing outside my building. I had nearly snarled, thinking it was another person after me.

"Kendra! Oh my God."

"Let me help you with that." She grabbed the bag from me gently and took me to the elevator, and eventually my apartment. I had so much I wanted to say. So many things. Mainly how sorry I was. "I called up but you weren't home," she said.

"I needed a bagel."

We sat down. It was awkward, not like how we usually were.

"Ken—"

She held up her hand. "Me first. I'm so sorry for what happened. I didn't know who that woman was. Aphrodite had hired her recently, they didn't realize—"

"I'm so sorry too," I interrupted. "I feel horrible about ruining your launch. I don't know how to make it better, but tell me and I'll do it."

"You just need to get better. I know you texted that you wanted to be alone, but you can't push me away."

"I never texted you that." Had I? The blur from painkillers made it confusing. "I don't remember, at least. It's been a crazy week. I've been out of it."

"I know, and I'm here to support you. You didn't ruin things. Aphrodite was so horrified that their employee tried to kill you, we're getting a do-over. They're worried you're going to sue them."

Lawsuits hadn't even occurred to me. I guess that was one way to not worry about work.

"Oh. I hadn't even thought of that, to be honest. I just want to get better; the rest I don't know. If you're not mad, why haven't you returned my calls?"

She shot me a puzzled look. "I did call you. Why haven't you called me?"

"I did. I even sent flowers."

She shook her head. "I didn't get them. Or any calls or texts. What the hell." She pulled her phone out. "You're not blocked."

"Same on mine. I swear I sent you texts."

"That's bizarre. Let me look into it. But in the meantime, are you okay? What can I do to help?" Her being here and wanting to help, wanting to still be my friend, was enough to send me over the precarious edge. I started crying hysterically. All the built-up fear and anger and sadness over what had happened bubbled over. I couldn't stop.

"I'm s-s-sorry," I hiccuped. "It's just been the worst time of my life, and I don't know what the hell is going on. And I thought I lost you." The tears kept on coming. She got up to grab me a tissue.

"Hey, you're never going to lose me. I promise. It's okay. And we will get to the bottom of things. Tell me what you know when you're ready."

I nodded, relieved. I filled her in on how Liz took care of me. "I honestly owe her big time for this. She's gone above and beyond. And Zabir has been bringing food over."

She raised her eyebrow at his name. "I'm so glad she was here for you. I'm sorry I wasn't. I thought you didn't want to talk to me. I should have been more on top of things and come to see you." Kendra looked legitimately contrite.

"You were busy!" I knew that she was right, but I didn't want her to feel bad. I had my Kendra back; that was all that mattered. "You're family. You can't get rid of me that easily!" I laughed, wiping my face. "Anyways, I missed you. And before that shit happened, your launch looked amazing."

She grinned. "It did, didn't it? And because of you, I got mentioned in the papers. No such thing as bad press, right?" I snorted laughing. At least my trials and tribulations were useful.

She sat back while taking a deep breath. "I'm just glad you're okay. I tried to visit you in the hospital, but they had a list of people who could come. I guess because it was an attack? I don't know. But wait, Zabir. You're friends again?"

I nodded. "He's told me as much about Skylar as he knows. And it's been nice having someone around. I was going crazy being cooped up here. He's also researching stuff that may or may not be relevant."

"I'd go crazy, too, if I were you." I felt her stare at my neck, where the bruises had turned a gross yellow color. "Those from her?"

I nodded. "I really hope they find out who paid her. And her whole video interview was messed up. She kept saying 'he' was coming, and I have no idea who he is."

"Can your detective lady get her to tell us?"

I realized how much I hadn't actually told her. "She's dead. Mary, not the detective. During the interview, she plunged a pen into her throat."

Kendra blinked rapidly, staring at me as if I were speaking in tongues. "I'm sorry, did I mishear that?"

"No."

"So, two people try to kill you, and they each end up killing themselves?"

"Maybe the hit-and-run driver is also dead."

"We can hope. So what is Zabir researching?"

I felt my face burn. I'd never told her anything about what happened when I was five, beyond Abu dying. I wasn't sure I could tell her now. She'd look at me like I was nuts. But I needed her to know what was going on. "I never told you what happened when I was little." I took a deep breath and let loose on what my mother did and how Zabir thought this might all be related.

"But you don't believe that stuff? And how is it related? I don't get it."

"I don't know. Skylar came to him saying he was haunted by something, and Zabir thinks there's a connection. Things are so weird at this point, I want an explanation. I'm not saying he's the one who will find one, but I'll take whatever I can get."

"I can't believe your mom did that. Now I get why you don't want to talk to your sister."

I shrugged. "You know what they say. Sisters are the original frenemies."

"Who says that?" She laughed.

"Me."

"So, now what? Like, how are we moving forward?" Kendra liked having plans. She liked knowing her next step. So did I, except my next step was healing. And beyond that I had no idea.

"I stay in my apartment and let the police solve things. Or hope they do. And that's about it."

"No offense, but that would drive me nuts."

"It is! Maybe I need to go away or something."

"Oh, what about Liz's Catskills house? Once you're up for it?"

"I think that would be nice. I need a little more time to be in less pain. And then I can go. Would you be able to come?"

"Maybe? Like, I can come up for a weekend or something?"

"I'd like that." The more I thought about it, the more it seemed like a great idea. I just wanted to be able to walk without my foot hurting, even with the boot on. I only had to survive until then. Which wasn't as easy a feat as it sounded.

"I have a gift for you." She brought out a bag.

"More beauty?"

She shook her head, grinning. "Better." She watched me open it. "A Taser."

It was a pink stun gun, small enough to fit in my bag.

"Whoa. Are these even legal?"

"It is, don't worry. And if anyone tries anything, you just zap them! I got one for myself too."

It was the best gift I'd ever received. Maybe this would keep me alive? Who needed pepper spray when you had electric voltage in your hand. "You're amazing," I said. "I hope I never have to use this, but I am going everywhere with it."

"That's my girl!"

———

Liz agreed that we needed a getaway, but we decided to wait to go for as long as I needed. In the meantime, I tried calling Mandy at work to find out if I could put in for more leave. I wasn't in any shape to work, and I certainly couldn't be near people. I kept leaving messages. Nothing. I emailed the company's HR department for guidance, which maybe was a mistake. I knew doing that would piss Mandy off. She preferred to be in total control of us. But I needed to know if I still had a job or not.

Eventually, Mandy left a voice mail saying that this wasn't working out and they wished me well. I hated her. She didn't even say my name right in the message.

I called Alvarez next, just for an update. She had none. It was frustrating as hell. When would they figure out who was behind all this? I didn't know how to get them to work harder on this. Or why it took so long. I was stuck in limbo, in purgatory, not able to move. I don't recommend ever being in this position.

Forty-Eight

Dunia, age five

Ammi was taking me to the doctor, again. I hated going. They weren't normal doctors who checked me for owies. These ones asked me questions. Too many questions. I got tired of answering them.

"She sleepwalks a lot."

"That's normal, Mrs. Ahmed. Nothing to worry about."

"No, you don't understand." Ammi got up and quietly said, "She almost killed her sister in her sleep." I heard it even though I wasn't supposed to.

The doctor looked at me with interest. I stared at my feet.

"Interesting. Have you tried a psychiatrist? Because that may be what she needs."

"No! She doesn't need a psychiatrist." I was sent back to the waiting room while Ammi talked with the doctor. I was exhausted. My dreams last night had me running all over the place.

Ammi came out mad and grabbed my arm. In the car, after she buckled me in, she sat there in her seat and started crying.

"Ammi, why are you sad?"

"Kucch nhi," she said. It was nothing.

"Don't be sad, you're the best mom in the world!"

She smiled back at me and nodded, wiping her eyes. She was sad because of me. I was a bad kid for making my mom cry.

"Ammi, I promise to be better," I said as she unbuckled me and took me out of my seat.

"I know, beti. You're doing your best."

I spent the day trying to do things only good daughters would do. I cleaned my room. I put away my snacks and toys. I even brushed all my teeth without anyone asking me. I had to do a better job. I didn't want my mom to cry again.

I ate all my food and even helped clear the table.

"Dunia, you're being very helpful today," Abu said.

"I'm trying to be good."

Baba laughed. "You're already amazing, my love. Don't worry so much." But I did worry. Only bad girls made their moms cry.

Baba said he'd read to me tonight, but that meant he'd tell me a scary story—because he was the one who'd told them to Abu when he was a boy. I shook my head.

"No scary stories."

I was going to stay in bed no matter what. I was going to make Ammi happy. She'd never have to take me to another doctor again.

I tucked myself into bed so tightly, the blankets trapped me like a mummy. I wouldn't be able to get up even if I wanted to!

"Are you sure you're comfortable?" Abu asked as he came to say good night.

"Yes, very. Good night, Abu-ji!"

I dreamed I went to the playground. I wanted to play and have fun after my day of working and being good. I wasn't alone—Adnan was with me—and in my dream Baba watched us, so we were safe.

"What are you doing here?" a man asked me. I was on the swings, trying to go higher and higher.

"Playing."

"Isn't it kind of late for you to be here alone?"

"I'm not alone."

"Who's here with you?"

"Baba, and Adnan, but you can't see him, he's imaginary."

The man made the swing slow down and then stopped it. "Do you know where you live?"

I nodded. Of course I knew where I lived.

"Then let's get you home."

I woke up when this all happened, but sometimes when I woke up, my dream kept happening. So I saw Adnan play tricks on the man, try to trip him. Which made me giggle. The man looked at me warily.

He drove me home in a police car. I didn't realize he was the police at first, maybe because I was asleep. All I could think was that I had tried to be good and look what happened.

He walked with me to the door and rang the bell. I wanted to sneak into the house and back to bed before anyone realized I was gone. But the man ruined that.

Abu answered the door. He was tying the belt on his robe as he opened it.

"Dunia? What's going on?"

"Sir, did you know your daughter was out by herself?"

"I wasn't out—"

"Dunia, not now," Abu said. He looked so mad. "Officer, please come in." Abu sent me to my room, but I listened in from the hallway. "I'm sorry, she sleepwalks. We've been trying to keep her in her bed, but we're running out of ideas."

"Well, you need to do something because she could have been hurt or worse. I don't want to call children's services, but I have to. They'll be sending a social worker by to meet with you. Just explain to them what happened. They may have ideas on how to help."

After that night Abu put a lock on my door that opened from the outside. He said it was the only way to keep me safe. He meant the only way to keep me inside my room.

Forty-Nine

Transcript: *The Disappearance of Dunia Ahmed* **podcast**

AMANDA ROBERTS: We have breaking news on the case, everyone! So this is a special emergency edition of the podcast.

DANIELLE MCGUIRE: This is so exciting. Flash siren emoji, this is major.

AMANDA ROBERTS: So much. Detective Alvarez, please tell us what you've found.

DETECTIVE ALVAREZ: We got a tip recently about who paid Skylar Jones. It was an account not under the name of someone we already suspected. He'd used a family member's banking info and passed off money that way.

AMANDA ROBERTS: Who was it? I'm dying with excitement here.

DETECTIVE ALVAREZ: David Anderson is the one who paid Skylar Jones to murder Dunia.

AMANDA ROBERTS AND DANIELLE MCGUIRE: Oh my God.

AMANDA ROBERTS: So, was he responsible for everything?

DETECTIVE ALVAREZ: We can only definitively link him to Skylar. But this helps us understand how this started and who might be responsible for Dunia's disappearance.

AMANDA ROBERTS: I never believed he was a good guy. We both thought he was just awful.

DANIELLE MCGUIRE: The worst. So, is he arrested?

DETECTIVE ALVAREZ: Yes, and we're hoping the pressure of a prison sentence looming will get him to tell us more, which, yes, I will share with you what I'm able. I was skeptical of this podcast, but you guys got us a real useful tip.

AMANDA ROBERTS: Damn right we did! We have the best audience ever! Can you tell us who gave the tip so we can give them a shout-out?

DETECTIVE ALVAREZ: No, that's confidential for obvious reasons. We don't want anyone retaliating against them.

DANIELLE MCGUIRE: I bet a hundred bucks David knows where Dunia is right now.

Fifty

Dunia, age five

Ammi had gone to the mosque with Nadia. I was home with Abu. We were doing chores.

"Abu-ji, when you were little, who told you those scary stories?"

"Um, my father mostly. You met him when you were teeny tiny."

"I'm a big girl now." I smiled.

"Yes, you are."

I followed him around the house while he did chores Ammi asked him to do. I held tools or got him water. I was trying to be helpful.

He was fixing a light in my bedroom when Baba pretended to push him. I laughed.

"What's so funny?"

"Baba is trying to trip you!"

Abu sighed. "Dunia, come over here." He sat down on my bed with me. "You're a big girl, right?"

I nodded. "I'm five." I held up my fingers to show him.

"Right. And big girls don't need imaginary friends anymore, do they?"

"Like Adnan?"

"Yes, like Adnan. So maybe it's time you said goodbye to all your imaginary friends."

"But they're my friends."

"Yes, but big girls have to grow up and find real friends. Come on, I'll help you. Goodbye, Adnan! Can you say that?"

I nodded. "Goodbye, Adnan," I repeated.

"Good! Now say goodbye to—" He stopped speaking and looked at me. His face was funny.

"Abu? Are you okay?"

He tried to say something but couldn't. His face was sweaty.

"Abu?" I shook his arm. He fell back on my bed. "Daddy?" I kept shaking him, but he didn't move. I needed help. I got up and ran next door to Carol's house.

"Carol! Carol! Help me!" I yelled, ringing the bell.

"Dunia, what's wrong?"

"Something's wrong with my dad." She ran to my room and then called the police. She made me sit outside with her and not with Abu.

"Is he okay?" I asked. I wanted to see him.

"He's not okay. Let's wait for the doctors, okay?"

She held my hand, and we waited. When the ambulance came, she talked to them.

"Honey, where's your mom?" she asked me.

"At the mosque."

I watched them cover Abu with a sheet and wheel him out of our house. I wanted to go with him, but Carol wouldn't let me. She took me to her house and made me a grilled cheese sandwich while she made calls.

I didn't know what happened. I didn't know where they took my dad. But I never saw him again. Not after that.

———

When Ammi and Nadia came to get me, it was dark.

"We were at the hospital," Ammi said to Carol, who hugged her.

"Are you okay? Anything you need, just let me know."

"Can you . . . watch Dunia for a while? I need to figure things out."

"Of course."

I lived with Carol after that. Not all the time, but mostly. She took me to school; she picked me up. She made me dinner and played games with me. My mother and Nadia were busy.

"Where's my dad?" I asked after a couple of days. I liked Carol, but I missed Abu.

"Honey, sometimes, when people are sick, they go to sleep. And then they go to heaven. Do you know what heaven is?"

I nodded.

"Your father is in heaven. His heart stopped working."

"Will I see him again?"

"One day." She hugged me. "You poor girl." I didn't know why she said that.

———

Ammi was always gone. She had a job, thanks to Carol—she worked in an office now as a secretary. She said without Abu, she had to support us. Nadia stayed at friends' houses while I was at Carol's.

"Auntie Carol, can I stay with you forever?"

"Oh, I'd love that. But you have a mother who loves you very much."

I wanted to say that I didn't. That my mom didn't love me. But I didn't say anything. I did hear Carol tell my mom that she needed to be there for me, and then Ammi took me home.

She tucked me into my bed, her eyes trailing where Abu had lain down.

She didn't say good night. Or that she loved me. She just shut the door and locked it from the outside.

Fifty-One

It was another week before I was strong enough to go to Liz's house. I didn't want to make anyone take care of me, so I needed to be able to move around, even though I was in an ortho boot. I also had to get my stitches out, so that was fun. My side was killing me.

Zabir had given me updates but was still researching. I had no idea if his ideas would lead anywhere. And right now, my only focus was healing. Preferably not in my small apartment.

I packed a bag, which Liz carried for me. Kendra was going to come on the weekend. Liz and I would have a whole five days before then to hang out and relax.

"You'll love my place!" Liz said as we got into her car (a Jeep Cherokee).

"I'm sure I will! Thank you for doing this."

"Duh, I love visitors. It's hard to get anyone to leave the city, though."

Liz blasted an eighties playlist, and we sang along, and it was the most carefree I'd felt in forever. This was just what I needed.

"Liz, thank you. Seriously. I don't know where I'd be without you."

"I can't wait for you to see the house! You'll never want to leave."

———

It took three hours to get there, but the first glimpse of Liz's property told me it was worth it. She pulled onto a dirt road that led to a farmhouse. There was nothing but green for acres. No one around, just us and this house and grass and trees. It was stunning. I took big lungfuls of air.

"This is beautiful," I said. "I would never leave if I lived here."

"Thank you! I bought it years ago, and my ex helped me fix it up."

She helped unload everything, and in we went. I felt like a kid in a candy store, just taking it all in. This was Liz's secret hideout. It was a farmhouse and looked old and rustic from the outside. But everything was redone once you stepped through the doorway. It was modern and beautiful and looked like the sort of space that would be in those fancy magazines. It was all cream colored, and I was scared to mess things up. Spilling anything would be an absolute no-no.

"Your bedroom is upstairs, is that okay? Or will you sleepwalk? I can make a room down here if you need?" She was the consummate host.

"I'll be fine, don't even worry." I wasn't sure how true that was, but I was making it my mission to be an easy houseguest. That way I'd be invited back.

I followed her up the stairs. My room was gorgeous. It was done up in the same relaxing neutrals as the rest of the house. There were even plants in the room, which I was always amazed at. I could never keep anything alive for too long.

"Um, I think I'm moving in."

"I'd love it. You, me, and Kendra here!"

"Imagine the fun!"

She left me to rest while she ran to get groceries. I didn't know how I was going to repay all the kindness she'd shown me, but I'd have to find a way.

I texted Zabir and Kendra to let them know we'd arrived safely. Service was terrible, but I guessed that was the downside of getting out of the city. It took a few minutes to go through. I wasn't sure if the phone troubles Kendra and I had were fixed. I didn't know if she even got my text.

I unpacked but wasn't tired enough to rest. So I walked around the house. Partially exploring, partially being nosy. I wanted a glimpse into Liz's life that she hadn't shared with me yet. To know her better beyond her just being a great friend to me. And then I felt guilty for that. She'd done nothing but care for me. I shouldn't have been snooping. Maybe I needed air.

I sat outside facing nothing but trees. It was beautiful. I closed my eyes and breathed. After a while, I felt the hair on my neck stand up. I opened my eyes and looked around for anyone watching me. I shivered. It had to be my imagination. I kept watching, my eyes bouncing over each tree. The woods were on her property, but I wasn't sure if anyone was there. I peered closely, and I swore I saw black smoke rising up. Something nagged at me. Something Zabir said. Black smoke walking. I felt the overwhelming urge to run now.

I ran inside and locked the doors, feeling foolish for getting so scared over trees. If there was smoke, there'd be a fire. And there was nothing. I kept looking out the windows, but it was calm and beautiful, and nothing was burning.

"Get a grip," I muttered, and then laughed at myself for being so anxious, such a mess. If anyone at the pharmacy told me they were hallucinating, I'd be worried. But that concern didn't extend to myself. I chalked it up to PTSD. I'd been through so much; I was exhausted; my brain was going to play tricks on me.

It took a couple of hours for Liz to return. She set all her shopping bags on the kitchen counter.

"So sorry that took forever! Small towns are harder to find things in. I'm grilling tonight, so get ready for some yum food!"

I walked over and hugged her, unprompted. I didn't want her to know how shot my nerves were. That plant life scared me now. God, what would my friends think?

"What was that for?" she asked, her voice light.

"I just wanted to say thank you for being such a good friend. I don't know how I'd survive all this without you."

She hugged me back. "I'm just glad I finally got you here! I've wanted to lure you here since we met! This is my safe space, you know?"

"I can see that. It's beautiful." I wondered who watered the plants. Maybe she had a caretaker, because the entire house was spotless, not a speck of dust. Just another thing to be in awe of about her.

———

We spent the evening on the deck, where Liz grilled seafood and I made a salad. I was trying to be helpful. It was chilly out, but Liz had heat lamps on.

"I love being outside after being in the city," she said.

"Me too."

I sat and watched the trees. I kept my eyes open for anyone near, a glimpse of someone walking toward us. Or a smoke monster. (I wasn't sure I was serious about that, but I'd seen something.) Anything that said danger. I wished we had cameras up here. But we were alone and on ten acres. No one was coming. I was safe. For the first time since August, I was safe.

I took a deep breath, trying to relax. The quiet was broken by the sound of a bird, but not any bird. It was loud and sounded big.

"What the hell was that?"

"Oh, a neighbor down the road has peacocks. Just ignore them. They're pretty but annoying."

"Peacocks? Doesn't it get too cold for them?"

She shrugged. "I think they have a barn or something." I had never seen one in real life, so the thought thrilled me. Peacocks!

After dinner, we sat around talking until the bugs began gnawing at me.

"I'm a magnet for them. Can we go inside?"

"Sure! Also, I have a crazy idea. And you can say no, but also maybe humor me?" Liz said with a smile.

"Okay . . . ?"

We moved everything inside, and then Liz ran to a closet. "After everything, I thought it would be funny to do this." She held up a Ouija board. Was she joking?

"Oh God, nooooo. Tell me you're not serious." She couldn't be, right? I had never in my life wanted to use one. And after everything that had happened, the thought made me queasy.

"It'll be fun, I promise. Or are you scared? This is prime sleepover fun. Come on!" she cajoled, and I gave in. "At every slumber party we did this. You have to! You need the full experience." She was so excited, how could I say no?

"Fine. Let's do it."

"Yay!" She clapped her hands. And then ran to get some candles. "For mood."

I couldn't wait to tell Kendra about this. She'd probably laugh her ass off. Or tell me I was nuts for even saying yes. I was trying to be a good guest.

"Okay, let's do this. Put your fingers on the planchette," she said. I did as told. "Hello, spirit. Are you here?"

The planchette moved to *yes*. Liz's eyes got big.

I rolled my eyes.

We asked silly questions. "Are you a good spirit?" (Yes.) "Do we know you?" (Yes.)

"This totally feels like my teenage sleepovers," Liz said.

"I wasn't allowed to go to any."

"Why? Like, cultural stuff?"

"No, my mom was too worried I'd sleepwalk and cause problems, so she kept me home."

"Yikes. Your turn to ask a question." She nudged me.

"Um . . . okay. Is anyone trying to kill me?" (Yes.)

"It's a game. Don't take it seriously," Liz warned, concern on her face.

"Who is going to hurt me?" I asked. It started to spell out a name with the letter *B*, but Liz accidentally spilled her wine all over the board.

"Oh shit, I'm so clumsy! I'm sorry, hold on. Let me clean that up." She came back with a roll of paper towels. "Is the board ruined?"

"No, it'll dry out. Let's put it outside?"

"Good idea. Maybe let's finish our wine and call it a night. I'm beat."

Before bed, I pushed my bag in front of the bedroom door so I wouldn't leave. I didn't want to ruin our trip with my antics. But before I passed out, I heard the peacocks making a ruckus. I never knew they could be so loud.

I dreamed about the black smoke. It was coming toward me, threatening to engulf me. I woke up screaming, and Liz was banging on my door.

"Are you okay? Open the door!"

I was drenched in sweat. I let her in, pushing my bag out of the way.

"Sorry, I had a bad dream."

"You're all right?"

"I am, I'm sorry," I said again. I was sorry. I thought the bad dreams would stay back in my apartment. But you couldn't leave your brain behind.

———

I woke up before Liz, so I made coffee and toast and sat outside on the deck to enjoy the air. I could live like this. I really could. It was beautiful and quiet. I felt safe here. But if anyone with a name that began with *B* came by, I was going to yank my stun gun out. I kept my purse near just in case.

When Liz finally got up, she looked exhausted.

"Did you get back to sleep?" she asked, yawning.

"Yeah, so sorry to scare you like that." I was mortified about the night before. Flashbacks of David yelling at me for waking him played in my head.

"Don't worry, I'm here for you." She sat down and drank her coffee. "At least you didn't sleepwalk?"

I laughed. "I actually blocked my door so I wouldn't wander around and freak you out."

"Aw, that's kind of sweet." She laughed. "I'm going to go for a run to wake up. And then after we can go into town for some snacks and shopping?"

"Sounds perfect." In the meantime, I could relax and do nothing, my favorite thing. Doing nothing was just my speed right now. I couldn't have worked out even if I'd wanted to.

———

We had lunch at a small café, and Liz slid her bags under the table. She'd so far bought some glassware and a sweater. The stores were adorable, and I loved them. Maybe they needed a pharmacist here? Maybe I could move here?

"I could so live here. Move out here, relax, work in a local pharmacy. That would be amazing."

"I can put you in touch with my Realtor if you want?"

I shook my head. "I don't think I have the funds to buy anything. Maybe rent. I'm out of work officially—they fired me for taking too long to get better."

"None of that is your fault, though."

"I know, but it is what it is." I didn't mention the customer complaints I'd gotten.

"You should work for Kendra." It wasn't the first time the idea had been floated. And while that was a dream, I worried Kendra would realize what a mess I was. Even though she already knew. But what if it screwed up our friendship? I didn't want to risk that.

"Maybe." We ate our lunch. I felt anxious and didn't want to ruin things, but being in public was not something I was ever going to get used to. Not after Aphrodite.

"You okay?" she asked.

"Yeah, I can't help but feel like we're being watched. But I think that's just, you know, PTSD or something."

Liz glanced around cautiously. No one was looking our way. "I think we're okay. But if you want to go back to the house, we can."

"No! I'm fine. I need to get used to being in public, and this is easier than Manhattan."

We drank our lattes and ate salads, and I tried to keep the conversation going, but Liz was watching me to make sure I was fine.

"Let's do one more stop and then go home so you can relax?"

"Sure." Relief coursed through me. We'd be home soon. I'd be fine. I'd made it without freaking out.

We left to go to a candle-and-fragrance store. "It's the best place for candles," Liz declared. "Hey, look at this!" She held up a spray called Evil Eye. "You so need this!"

I protested. I didn't have the money to spend thirty bucks on a perfume for the house. But Liz insisted on buying it. "It will help us feel better." I bet Zabir would have laughed and called it shirk. Or maybe he'd be into it. It was hard to say with him.

On our way back to the car, I kept looking over my shoulder. I was relieved when we got home and nothing was amiss. I didn't know when—if ever—I'd feel safe being out in public. But at her house, I could relax. We locked the door and stayed inside, and Liz sprayed the whole house with the Evil Eye perfume. And then she went to take a nap.

Zabir texted asking how I was. I told him I was fine and that we'd played with a Ouija board.

You don't believe in jinn but you'll do a ouija board?

It was the full sleepover experience!

We need to talk when you have time. It's important.

I wasn't up for that. I knew he had spoken to Nadia. I needed a break from everything.

———

Liz made dinner again—I was no help. If I stood too long, my body started to ache. So we ate pasta and just kept it chill. I think we were both exhausted, me from my life, Liz from not sleeping well.

"Are you okay to have a glass of wine?" She held the bottle up.

"One won't hurt." I hoped.

"So, are you and Zabir dating again?" she asked as we ate.

I coughed. "Sorry, I wasn't expecting that. No, we are not. I accept his explanation for the Skylar stuff, but I don't know. I need to focus on me big time right now. But he's helping me with something." I didn't want to elaborate further.

"Good, because I'm still not over him lying about that fight we had. I mean, I would never just stalk and assault someone. And I don't like that he kept so much from you. And him being there when you almost got hit by a car is totally suspect."

"Hey, it's all good."

"Anyways, I think you can do better. I'll have to set you up with someone. When you're ready."

"Let's just see if I make it to next year."

She set her fork down. "D, that's not funny. You'll not only survive, you'll thrive."

I wanted to believe her. But the part of me that thought I'd have a great life no longer existed. I was merely trying to survive another day and find the person who was behind all this. If I thought about it, I would get frustrated at the lack of answers from the police. So I did my best to put it out of my mind. Which meant it was there in the back of my head, but I wasn't going to obsess. Not this week. I was here to relax and recuperate.

"I hope you're right," I replied. I changed the subject. "Your ex who helped you with the house, why did you break up?"

"He's the one who liked someone else. I thought we'd be together forever, but . . ."

"I'm sorry. I shouldn't have brought it up. But you'll find someone too. Maybe once I'm healed, we can go on double dates."

Liz laughed at that, which made me feel less guilty for bringing up her ex.

———

I was walking in the grass in my dream. The cold, wet ground felt amazing on my feet. I could feel the blades of grass between my toes. I was holding hands with someone. I turned to look. Zabir? No. No, it wasn't him. It was someone else.

"Baba?" He looked younger than I remembered.

"It's beautiful here, isn't it? Reminds me of that garden we used to go to."

"It is nice."

He held my hand as we walked.

"You're not safe here," he said.

"I am. This place is beautiful."

"Be careful," he warned.

And then, like in most dreams, I merely turned and went back to the house instead of asking him for details. Logic didn't count in dreamworld.

In the morning, I had flashes of my dream for a moment. A walk with Baba. That was nice. And then I realized my feet felt gross. Unclean. I threw the sheets off and looked down—my feet were covered in dried mud. I had sleepwalked, and worse, I'd tracked mud all through Liz's clean house and into my bed.

"Dammit!" I jumped into the shower and cleaned up, pulled the bedding off to wash it, and then found a mop and broom to clean the floors before Liz woke up. There was mud from the front door to my room. Creepy footprints that were leading to my room. My footprints. Yet again, I'd been humiliated by my own brain. My mental issues were affecting everyone and everything.

"Hey, what are you—whoa, what happened?" Liz stood near me near the front door, where the mud was worse.

"I guess I sleepwalked last night. I'm so sorry. I'm cleaning everything. And I'll pay to have your rugs cleaned."

"Don't worry about it, I have a cleaning woman."

"Let me at least get this mud out. I'll feel better."

"Suit yourself."

She was far too gracious about it, which only made me feel worse. I mopped for the better part of an hour, sweat pouring down my face from the exertion. My side was killing me—my ankle too. Walking on it without the ortho boot had been a bad idea; thanks, Sleep Me.

After I finished, I put the mop outside to dry. And I swore I saw Baba watching me from the trees. I blinked and he was gone.

Fifty-Two

Transcript: *The Disappearance of Dunia Ahmed* **podcast**

AMANDA ROBERTS: Dunia went on a small girls' trip with Liz, and Kendra eventually joined. And this, our dear listeners, is a pivotal moment in this saga. We had to know everything, so pleas12e welcome Liz Small back.

LIZ SMALL: Thank you for having me back. I really wanted to make sure Dunia had a relaxing time after everything she went through. And I love showing off my home in the Catskills. It's my safe, happy place.

DANIELLE MCGUIRE: Now, how was Dunia when you first got there?

LIZ SMALL: Tired, but who wouldn't be. She was very quiet, just sort of soaking it all in. She was obsessed with my neighbors' peacocks. They're very loud birds.

AMANDA ROBERTS: Now, can you clear something up for us? We heard you started using a Ouija board while Dunia was there? And if so, why?

LIZ SMALL: It's harmless. I don't know why people are so scared of it.

DANIELLE MCGUIRE: No, that stuff scares me. Do you use it often?

LIZ SMALL: I used to. I'd talk to my departed ones.

AMANDA ROBERTS: And did they talk back?

LIZ SMALL: Sure! It's basically like playing telephone. You're calling them. You're talking to them. It's just like them being alive.

AMANDA ROBERTS: . . . That's not what playing telephone, the game, is. But okay . . . so why did you want Dunia to use the board?

LIZ SMALL: Because her death baggage was a lot. Like, her parents, and then her . . . attackers. They all died around her, so I thought it would help her deal with all of that.

DANIELLE MCGUIRE: I'm sorry, I'm still stumbling over this. Your friend almost died several times, and you wanted her to use a Ouija board?

LIZ SMALL: I was helping her.

AMANDA ROBERTS: How was Dunia while she was there? Did she sleepwalk?

LIZ SMALL: Yeah. It was terrifying, to be honest. She woke me up screaming at the front door one night, and it scared the hell out of me.

AMANDA ROBERTS: We had to cut that particular interview short—we'll run more next episode. Because we have breaking news!

DANIELLE MCGUIRE: Right? It's so exciting. Detective Alvarez, please tell us what happened.

DETECTIVE ALVAREZ: As you know, we arrested David Anderson after linking him to the first attack on Dunia—

AMANDA ROBERTS: Thanks to tips from our listeners!

DETECTIVE ALVAREZ: Right. There's been a development. David Anderson killed himself in his cell.

AMANDA ROBERTS: What?

DANIELLE MCGUIRE: He's dead?

DETECTIVE ALVAREZ: He signed a confession and said he had no choice, that something wouldn't let him live if he didn't.

AMANDA ROBERTS: I have goose bumps. This is the third person to kill themselves, and all three tried to kill Dunia. That can't be a coincidence. Is she somehow getting people to kill themselves?

DETECTIVE ALVAREZ: At this point, it is a coincidence. No one broke in and forced him to do it, and no one murdered him. The idea of prison can be challenging for some people. This isn't something to blame on Dunia.

Fifty-Three

"Okay, tell me what's wrong," Liz demanded after the house was spotless. I'd been trying to hide my worries from her, but my brain had other plans.

"I'm fine!"

"You are not. Spill it."

"Just leaving the house last night freaked me out, that's all. I don't usually leave."

"And you're worried you'll do it again." I nodded; I was worried. "If it helps, I can stay up and see if you sleepwalk tonight?" she offered.

"You don't have to."

"It could be fun!" She laughed. "Like the ultimate sleepover game! What did you dream about? Maybe that's the key to all of this?"

"Just that I was walking in the woods with my uncle. Nothing too crazy. And he said to be careful. Then I was back in bed."

"Huh. That's so not what I expected. I thought you'd be acting out some crazy saga or something."

I laughed. "It could happen! But usually my dreams are so mundane."

I didn't want to tell her about the smoky thing I'd seen. That was what was really gnawing at me. Was I hallucinating? Was it real? I had no clue. Instead I texted Zabir about it. I was waiting to hear back just how insane I was. That was what this had to be, right? Some weird mash-up my brain was doing in an effort to be well? Right?

"Let's go walk the grounds. You have to see how wild and gorgeous it is. If you're up for it. Will your ankle be okay? If you're going to be walking in your sleep, I should probably show you how to get back to the house. I don't want you getting lost out there."

"Oh, I didn't even think of that! I'm game! I may be slow, though." I pointed to my ortho boot. What if the smoke thing was there? If Liz saw it, then it meant I wasn't insane. But if she did see it, were we both in serious trouble?

"We will promenade at a leisurely pace." She grinned. "And then I have to get some work done, if that's okay?"

"Oh God, yes, you absolutely do not need to entertain me. Sorry!" I had books I could read, or Netflix to watch.

"No, I'm happy to. Let's get out there!"

The greenery was like something else here. It was so lush and beautiful. No concrete everywhere, just wild and beautiful trees and plants. No wonder Sleep Me wanted to wander at night. There was even a pond with ducks. Liz laughed while I took photos.

"Ducks!"

"Wait till you see the peacocks."

I was so excited. We wandered through trees, and I had already lost any sense of direction. It was probably good she was showing me around. If Sleep Me got lost here, I wasn't sure she'd get me back to the house otherwise.

I was trying to gauge where we were, and couldn't. And my ankle was starting to hurt. Maybe I'd overdone it. I knew it was from last night, though.

"Where's the house from here?"

"Just down that way. You can't really see it, but it's there. I won't get you lost, don't worry."

She led me to her neighbor's property so I could see the peacocks.

"Oh, wow." One male and one female were wandering around. They were curious enough to come closer to us. I froze. No sudden movements. Liz just laughed.

"They're very friendly. And so loud."

"So loud!" I echoed. I wanted to pet one, but I didn't know the etiquette, so I just marveled at them instead.

"And over there is a barn I use for storage." She pointed to a building that wasn't near the house at all. "It's also great for workouts, to be honest. No one can hear me."

When we got back to the house, I was worn out from the walk. I napped while Liz did her work.

———

I was staring out the window in the living room. It was nearing dinnertime, and I swore someone was watching me. Standing in between the trees was something dark, but with eyes.

"What's up?" Liz asked, sending me jumping. "Whoa, what's going on?"

"Um, do you see someone over there?" My voice wavered. Either answer she gave me would be terrifying. Yes: then someone was watching us. No: then I was batshit crazy. A pagal.

"No? Maybe it's an animal. Some of the owls around here are super freaky."

Owls. Yes, that was what it had to be. An owl.

"You okay?" she asked for the thousandth time.

"Fine," I snapped. "Sorry, I'm feeling tense. I don't know how to not feel on guard all the time."

"It will take time. It's okay. And if you need me to help calm you down, I will."

If I told her I was seeing things, she'd want me to leave. On the flip side, I couldn't hide that from her. What kind of friend does that?

I sat down on the sofa. "I think I'm seeing things that aren't there."

"Hallucinations?"

"Maybe I should go home. I mean, I don't want to freak you out and—"

"Absolutely not! Kendra is coming soon, and together we'll take care of you. You've been through so much, you just need to relax. And you had a really bad hit to your head, so I would think hallucinations are normal."

I nodded. I didn't want to go home. I didn't want to be alone. "Okay, you're right. I need to pull myself together a bit. I've made a neurologist appointment for when we get back to the city."

"Good call, just to be safe."

Right then Zabir called. "Oh, I need to take this."

I went to my room to talk.

"Hey," I said, mustering up as much enthusiasm as I could.

"You sound like shit."

"I feel it."

"What's going on?" he prodded.

"I sleepwalked outside in the woods, and I swear I'm seeing things. I saw walking smoke. That's something you said, right? In your lecture? What is it?"

"Yes, but tell me more details."

I told him what I could remember, both the smoke thing and sleep-walking. "And I swore someone was watching me right now, but Liz said it was an owl. I know, I have a concussion, but still."

"It was Baba you were walking with? Listen, I don't think you're imagining things. I've been trying to reach you to talk to you. It's serious."

My stomach dropped. "Tell me." I sounded far braver than I was. I braced myself.

He let out a breath. "I talked to Nadia about the stuff you mentioned. And she told me something you need to know." Whatever Nadia told him couldn't be good. "Your uncle—Baba?"

"Yeah, what about him?"

"He wasn't your uncle." He waited for my reaction, but I didn't have one. "Nadia said you were the only one who could see him. You'd hang out with him for hours; you disappeared with him. That's what drove your mother to do an exorcism. Or an attempted one."

Baba wasn't real? "No, that's not possible. I have distinct memories of hanging out with him. Playing. He was real." He used to pick me up and throw me in the air. We'd play hide-and-seek. "There's no way he was another imaginary friend."

"I don't think he was imaginary," Zabir said, waiting for his words to sink in.

"You think Baba was a jinn. Oh, come on. He was real. He was there!"

"Nadia says otherwise, and I think you need to talk to her about it. Because there's a lot more to this. I think your mom knew something was up, and she tried to get rid of him. Didn't you say he went away after they prayed over you?"

"Yeah, but he went back to Pakistan."

"Dunia, no, he didn't." I could hear the pity in his voice. He believed in this tale, even if I didn't.

I didn't know what to say. My memories were so vivid, so real. Baba wasn't some specter that haunted me. He was tangible, as material as my own parents. "I saw him last night. When I was sleepwalking."

"Dunia, listen, I don't know who or what he is, but I don't think you should go with him if you see him again."

"Great, let me get Sleep Me on that." I scoffed. "How do you know Nadia's telling the truth?"

"What would she gain by lying?"

I didn't know. I didn't understand how someone who was so larger than life to me, flesh and blood, could be something else? It didn't make sense. None of this made sense. It was as if the reality I knew wasn't actually real.

"Are you okay?" he asked.

"I'm processing."

"Maybe call Nadia and talk to her about it. She remembers a lot." I didn't answer. I didn't know if I could handle talking to my sister. There was so much between us.

"I'm meeting with someone who knows how to contact jinn. I know, not your thing. But I think we need to know what's going on here," Zabir continued. "And I'm trying to figure out how to put a wall back up around him. Or whatever it was they did before. That prayer of your mom's factors in, but it's only one piece to this puzzle."

"Yeah, do whatever." I wanted this call to end. I wanted to never have to think about this stuff again. My life wasn't real; my memories couldn't be trusted. Who existed and who didn't? Was all this one giant hallucination? Maybe I'd been stuck in an asylum with Rahmi Khala this whole time.

"Dunia, be careful. And if you do see anyone outside, don't let them in."

We hung up, and I sat there, looking out the window. The sun had set. It was beautiful and eerie, the way woods and land are without humans. But right now, it felt a little sinister too.

"What did he want?" Liz asked. I whirled around to see her standing there.

"How long have you been there?" Had she heard me? Did she think I was a lunatic?

"Long enough. Who's Baba?"

"Honestly, I have no idea." That was the truth. Who or what was he?

"Why don't we make sure all the doors are locked, and in the morning, we can go see if it looks like anyone was around. How's that?" She said it like I was a scared child she had to placate.

I nodded, and we went back down to eat dinner. She insisted on wine to relax me. I didn't want to sleepwalk, but Liz promised to watch out for me.

I was looking forward to Kendra coming even more than before. If anyone were going to be logical about this stuff, it was her. She'd tell me if something was amiss with me. She'd be up front with me. I needed that. The medical part of me knew this was par for the course with concussions. But it would help if Kendra could tell me that.

After I finally fell asleep—I'd checked every door and window in the house and again put my bag in front of my bedroom door—I awoke with a start. Someone was screaming. It was me.

I was standing at the front door (so much for my fake booby trap to keep me in my room). It was open, and I was pointing out, screaming.

"You can't come in!" I shouted. I could see the walking smoke. It was moving and as real as Liz was.

Liz stood next to me. "Dunia, are you okay?"

I kept pointing. "Don't you see him?" Smoke and darkness moved outside. It was getting closer. It was coming for us. Didn't she see? He was going to take us.

"No, no one's out there. Let me just shut the door." She closed and bolted it.

I stood there confused. Unsure of what was happening. Was I awake? Was I still asleep? The two were so intertwined it was hard to tell.

"I think you're sleepwalking," she said gently.

I stared at her. Then I nodded. "Okay."

"Let's get you back to bed."

I complied and let her take me back upstairs. She tucked me in and closed the door. Once the door was shut, I ran to the window. I was awake now. I was sure of it. And standing there watching me was the smoke. Whatever it was. Walking smoke. I'd seen it before. Around David. In Skylar's drawings. And now here. It was coming for me.

Fifty-Four

Transcript: *The Disappearance of Dunia Ahmed* **podcast**

AMANDA ROBERTS: Liz, Dunia unraveled a bit at your house, according to your statements to the police.

LIZ SMALL: I have never seen anyone do that before. Like, she seemed awake until you talked to her. Then she was almost like a confused child. She kept insisting she was seeing something outside the windows. But I'd go look, and nothing was there.

DANIELLE MCGUIRE: So scary!

LIZ SMALL: One night I woke up to her screaming, and she was standing at the front door telling something it couldn't come in. It was bone chilling. I took video, if you want to see it.

AMANDA ROBERTS: Oh my God, yes we do.

LIZ SMALL: I'll have it sent to you. I didn't see anything that she was talking to, but I felt like I was in a horror movie. Now I kind of get how Dunia's mother felt. So freaky.

DANIELLE MCGUIRE: What were your thoughts at that moment? Because I'd be terrified.

LIZ SMALL: I was, but my main concern was Dunia. She was breaking apart. So fragile. Everything that had happened was destroying her mentally. So I wanted to make sure she had a good time.

AMANDA ROBERTS: But she didn't, because that was the start of the end for her. Or the start of her disappearance.

Fifty-Five

Dunia, age five

Ammi was crying. I saw her. I heard her. I went over to hug her.

"I miss Abu too," I said. I knew that's why she was sad.

"Dunia, would you do anything for us?" she asked. I nodded. "Good. Because I need you to be brave and good. Can you do that?"

I could and I would.

"Get dressed."

I went to dress myself. She didn't help me anymore. Sometimes the outfits I put together made Carol laugh. Sometimes they weren't clean. Ammi didn't mind how I looked anymore, now that Ayesha Auntie was gone.

Ammi took me to a house. I didn't know it. A man opened the door. He'd been to our house, but I'd stayed in my room. He had just looked around, nodding at the lock on my door.

"Who is this man, Ammi?"

"Shhh, just be quiet and do as he says."

I didn't know where Nadia was. I wished she'd been here, but she hadn't spoken to me since Abu went to heaven. I didn't make him go. I wanted him back. I wanted everything to go back to the way it was.

"Hello, Dunia," the man said, leaning down to smile at me. He wore an all-white shalwar kameez.

"Hi," I whispered.

"Do you know why you're here?"

I didn't. I shook my head.

"We're here to make you better. Your ammi says you've been sleep-walking and talking to imaginary friends."

I nodded. "I do that. I'm sorry, I've been trying to be good." I had been!

"You're very good, don't worry. Come with me. All you have to do is lie down. We'll do the rest." I looked at Ammi, who nodded at me. I didn't know what was happening, but if she wanted me to go with this man, I would.

The man's wife was there with another man. They were all in white. They made me change into a white shalwar also, and then had me lie down while they tied my feet and arms to the bed. I didn't like this game. It scared me.

"Ammi?"

She ignored me.

"Maimsaab, are you certain you want to do this?"

"I am. There's something I need to tell you." She whispered to him. Something about a bargain. A deal? And she said the word she hated more than anything. "Jinn."

"If she has anything attached to her, we'll take care of it," the man said. "You can wait outside."

And then he prayed over me. Him and his friend did, while his wife made sure I was comfortable. She gave me water. But she wouldn't untie me. I didn't know what they said because I didn't understand Arabic. Ammi kept trying to get us to learn.

It went on for hours. I peed the bed. I thought I'd be yelled at, but the nice wife lady just helped clean me up when it was over. She brought me water and some roti to eat. I was starving.

"Dunia, do you feel different?" the man asked.

"My arms and legs hurt."

"That's normal." He smiled. Then he took me to my mother. "She's free of anything not from God. But you know, if the story you've told me is true, you have a price to pay still. And nothing will save you from that."

"I know," Ammi said. "I'll do what's necessary."

I didn't know what she meant, but for the first time in a long time, Ammi hugged me.

Fifty-Six

"Good morning, sleep okay?" Liz asked. She was so cheerful, as if she didn't remember my somnambulism.

"Remind me of last night? It's a bit foggy." I wanted to know exactly what I did. What happened and what I remembered were two different things.

"Well, I woke up to you screaming at the front door, which was open. You were telling something it couldn't come in. I didn't see anything. And I got you back to bed, and that was that."

"Shit. I'm sorry." I was the worst houseguest on the planet.

"Stop apologizing. I kind of love how weird you are? Anyways, I filmed it if you want to see."

I nodded, swallowing to get the lump of fear out of my throat. She handed me her phone and pushed play.

"See, nothing was there. Just a bad dream."

I watched. I zoomed in when it was outside. I couldn't be sure but—"Look, right there. What do you see?"

"Um, some red lights."

"Eyes. Those are eyes."

"Let me see." She looked and shook her head. "Dunia, I don't know, I don't see it. And if there is something, it's an owl. Their eyes glow if you take photos of them at night."

I saw it. I knew it was there. But Liz's face told a different story. She had the same look on her face as my mother and Nadia. Pity with confusion. Annoyance. Fear. I was scaring my friend. I needed to pull it together. And her explanation made sense.

"You're right, sorry. I'm just—I think I'm tired, is all." I had to be better. Pretend to be normal, my mother's voice urged me in my head. Pretend.

———

Once Liz went to do work—after I assured her I was fine—I grabbed my phone and headed to the woods. If anything was there, I'd find it. Or signs of it. Footprints, something. I didn't have a plan beyond that, but at least I'd know whether I was sane.

I tried to remember my path from the other night, the one I took while asleep. I wandered around, peering into trees. I even went into the woods, hoping I'd see the owls Liz mentioned.

I clomped around, ignoring the pain from my ankle. I had to know. I had to know if I was crazy. But I didn't find anyone. No footprints, no glowing eyes. The only person disturbing things was me.

"You have absolutely lost your damn mind," I muttered.

When I got back, Liz decided we needed some R & R, and that meant beauty masks. She thought it would be a good way to calm my nerves. She was right, it was soothing. But every sound outside made me jump.

"Imagine anyone coming over right now? We'd scare them with our masks," I said.

"Good, that's what they get!"

"I just, I'm so glad we're friends," I said. "And that you put up with my crazy."

"As long as you put up with mine!"

"I'm doing masks, aren't I?"

Liz decided to nap. I went to my room to sleep, but I was too exhausted. Instead, I thought about what Zabir had said. Baba wasn't real. I'd either made him up—which seemed impossible to me—or he was some otherworldly being. Which wasn't possible. It just wasn't. Nadia had to be mistaken or lying. There was no way.

I sat up. I heard a voice talking. I crept out of my room, ready to scream. Maybe I was jumpy. But who wouldn't be?

The sound was coming from Liz's room. I put my ear to the door.

"I can't do it . . . you don't understand . . . this is all your fault."

Who was she talking to? I knocked on the door.

"Hey! What's up?" She popped her head out, smiling.

"Oh, just making sure you're okay? I heard voices?"

"Just me, watching some Netflix. Hey, let's go to town and pick up dinner."

"Sure."

I watched her run down the stairs, but something felt off. The voice I'd heard was hers. Who was she talking to, and why had she just lied to me? Had I really heard it, or was my brain playing tricks on me? I honestly could not answer that. Why was I doubting someone who had done nothing but help and support me? I was the worst friend ever.

I stayed in her car while she ran into the restaurant to pick up our order, and then we drove around for a little. It was soothing.

When we got back to the house, I looked around to see if anyone was there. Nothing. Just us.

"I'm starving," Liz said while serving everything, including more wine.

"Oh, I don't think I can drink. It makes me sleepwalk, and I don't want to risk it. I'm already doing crazy stuff."

"It's a glass? I was thinking after dinner you soak in my tub and relax. Maybe that will help."

"That's not a bad idea."

We ate pasta and salads, and then she drew my bath. She left my wineglass by the tub in case I changed my mind. It was decadent and relaxing. No one in my house ever did stuff like this. No soothing baths, no scented candles. No wine, that was for sure. It felt like a small act of rebellion to do these things.

I drank the glass even though I knew I shouldn't. I wanted something to take the edge off. Not for the first time I wished I'd gotten a Xanax prescription or something.

That night before bed, I said my mother's prayer. In English. I didn't think it would help, but I was grasping at straws. I didn't want to lose my mind. I wanted to live my life again.

I woke up in the woods. I was certain I was awake. It was dark out; the moon wasn't full, and the only light was from the stars. I shivered, rubbing my arms for warmth. What was I doing here? Was this real? I pinched my arm. Ow. I was awake.

I needed to figure out where I was. I had to get back before Liz knew I was gone. I stumbled over tree roots.

"Get up," a voice in my head said. It wasn't my voice.

"Keep walking."

I walked as straight a path as I could.

"You're fine, you are okay."

I swore it was Baba's voice. So melodious and amused and soft. But the idea that his voice was coming to me made me panic more than anything. Baba wasn't real. Was he . . . inside my head? Was it all some strange delusion?

I ran. I ran as fast as I could on my ankle. I was again barefoot. I was crying in fear when I finally saw Liz's house. I threw myself onto the deck and stayed there, not moving. If Baba was here, he'd find me. I didn't know what he'd do with me, but maybe he'd leave Liz alone. My thoughts didn't make sense, but at that moment, hiding on the deck was all I could do.

Fifty-Seven

Transcript: *The Disappearance of Dunia Ahmed* podcast

AMANDA ROBERTS: Kendra, you were going to join Dunia and Liz in the Catskills. Tell us what happened before you left.

KENDRA WRIGHT: I got a call from Liz that Dunia was acting strangely. That she was hallucinating and sleepwalking and kept leaving the house in her sleep. Liz sounded terrified.

DANIELLE MCGUIRE: What did you do then?

KENDRA WRIGHT: I called Zabir because I thought he could help.

AMANDA ROBERTS: And did he?

KENDRA WRIGHT: He said Dunia was in danger and that we had no idea what was going on. And then the next day we drove to Liz's house to try to help. And the rest is in the police report.

DANIELLE MCGUIRE: What did Zabir say was the danger?

KENDRA WRIGHT: I don't even know how to explain it. He said there was a jinn after Dunia. That all of this was related. That everyone who died who tried to hurt her was killed by the jinn. And he was worried for everyone's safety.

AMANDA ROBERTS: Oh God. That would explain David's death.

KENDRA WRIGHT: David's dead? When?

AMANDA ROBERTS: Not that long ago. We had the exclusive interview with Detective Alvarez about it. He killed himself in his jail cell.

KENDRA WRIGHT: I . . . don't even know what to say to that.

DANIELLE MCGUIRE: Was Dunia haunted? In your opinion?

KENDRA WRIGHT: I don't know. I saw things that didn't make sense.

AMANDA ROBERTS: What did you see?

KENDRA WRIGHT: A lot of lights. Like, so bright it hurt my eyes. And smoke. I don't know what it was. But something happened in the Catskills, and we were too late to stop it. We thought we were going to help Liz deal with Dunia, but then it all went to hell.

Fifty-Eight

Dunia, age five

Ammi was taking me shopping. She wasn't as mad at me, but she also didn't hug me anymore. She wanted me to have new clothes.

"Try this dress on," she ordered, handing me a red one. I did as she asked because she—and Nadia—was all I had left.

She bought the dress and made me wear it at the next desi function. It was for a wedding. Normally, we'd be in Pakistani clothes, but Ammi wanted all new clothes, and nothing else would arrive on time.

Nadia was supposed to stay with me, but she left me right away. I was alone. And terrified. A roomful of people was waiting for me to act out. Do something crazy.

I felt my eyes tear up as the voices around me got louder, and the lights swirled, and the smell of food overpowered me. I was going to make a scene. I knew it. I closed my eyes. And then I was on the ground. I blinked open, and the holy man's wife, the nice lady, was there. She was wiping my head with a damp cloth.

"You fainted." She smiled. "It's okay. You've been through a lot." She squeezed my hand. I liked her. She was so nice to me. I saw Ammi glare over at me. I had caused attention to come my way. Before I got up, the nice lady leaned over and whispered, "None of what happened is your fault. It's your mother's. Remember that."

I heard someone else tell my mother I shouldn't be there.

"No one wants her here. She's got too much nazar."

"You really should not have brought her here."

"Hey, don't play with her, okay? She's got nazar."

I looked up and saw Nadia watching. She didn't say anything. Didn't tell people to be quiet. Instead she turned away and went to play with her friends.

I sat away from everyone. I didn't even eat. I just waited for the night to be over. I wanted to go to Carol's house. At least she was nice to me; she wanted me there. She hadn't left me like everyone else.

My mom didn't come check on me. Neither did Nadia. Abu would have. But he was gone now. I was all alone.

Fifty-Nine

Liz decided we needed to do another Ouija board session to figure out what was happening with me. I hated the idea. I didn't want to do anything that was at all creepy. My brain was scaring me enough.

"Listen, if you're seeing things, then maybe we need to figure out if you're being haunted. We'll film it all. This is for science."

I rolled my eyes. "That isn't science."

"Do you have a better idea?"

I didn't. I had no ideas. Except to go into hiding where no one could find me and I could live my life out as a giant freak. But I kept that to myself. I watched her set up the board. I had to do this; it was the one thing she'd asked of me this entire trip.

"Is someone here with us?" she asked the board. (Yes.) "Are you haunting Dunia?" (Yes.)

"I don't like this," I said for the umpteenth time.

"The only way out is through, right? What is it you want from her?" This time the board spelled out a word. *H-E-R.*

"Who are you?" I asked. I watched as the plastic moved to spell out *B-A-B-A.*

"That name, you said it on the phone with Zabir," Liz said. "Who is it?"

"My uncle. But turns out I made him up. Or he was a jinn."

"Wow." She said that more for the camera than me. I didn't like being filmed. I didn't like doing the board. I didn't like any of this.

"I have a bad feeling. Can we stop?"

"No, let's keep going. Why do you want Dunia?" *M-I-N-E.*

"I'm done. No thanks. Sorry, this shit is crazy, and I don't know why you like it." I got up and went to my room. I hated Liz in that moment. It wasn't a kind feeling, but why would she poke the bear like this? I needed to calm down.

My phone rang, and it was Nadia.

"Great," I muttered. But I answered. I had to know if Zabir was telling me the truth. If she was.

"Dunia, where the hell have you been, and why is Zabir asking me about things?" Nadia demanded.

"Hi to you too."

"Sorry, hi. What is going on? Are you okay?"

"Yeah, I'm with friends in the Catskills. I needed a break from everything."

"What's the deal with the woman who jumped you?"

"She killed herself." I said it so matter of factly that it surprised me when Nadia gasped.

"It's Baba all over again," she muttered.

"Zabir told me what you said, and how is that true? Baba was our uncle. He lived with us." She had to be yanking his chain.

"No. He may have been in our house, but he was not our uncle."

"I remember him. He was so nice to me, especially when Ammi wasn't."

She paused. "I know, look, I get that it was hard for you. I'm sorry. I shouldn't have believed everything Ammi said. But she wasn't wrong. Baba was all over you, taking you places we couldn't find you. Don't you remember the kitchen messes that would happen? Ammi thought it was you until it happened one day while you were at Carol's. And then—"

"Go on," I urged. "I need to know this." I braced myself for whatever she was going to say.

"When we came home that day and Abu was . . . in your room and not moving, you just kept babbling about Baba going away and making him fall. Don't you remember?"

"No." I didn't. I'd spent the last couple of decades trying to block all this out. I closed my eyes. "I think I remember him joking. Like he was saying he was just going to make Baba leave if I kept misbehaving. And then he was half on my bed, half on the ground. I ran to Carol's, and then you guys came home. I don't know, parts of it are burned into my memory, but others I can't be sure happened, you know?" The memory of a five-year-old was not infallible.

She waited a moment. "And then Ammi took you to the holy man and had you exorcised because she thought Baba would kill all of us."

I didn't remember this. All the fear on my mother's face when she saw me was because of Baba?

"Was he real? I mean, did I imagine him or . . . ?" Was my crazy brain making things happen, or was I haunted?

"He was real. I remember things happening that shouldn't have been able to happen. Like things around the house would move, and it drove Ammi crazy. And you would talk to him endlessly."

I hadn't imagined him. I wasn't sure if that was good news. "If she got rid of him, why did she hate me so much afterward? I was just a kid." I was crying as I asked her.

"She didn't hate you, she was scared of you. And for you. And no one wanted you around when we went to dinners. She had to leave you with babysitters. She had no support system, no family to help us after Dad died. She needed our community for help. It was that or move us to Pakistan. She was in her twenties with two kids and no husband and possibly a jinn lurking. What would you have done in her place?"

I sat there letting her words soak in. My mother had been scared of me, for me. She hadn't hated me, she'd feared me. And I'd done nothing but hate her. She had done the best she could. And I'd never forgiven her for it. Not even as she was dying.

"Look, why don't you come here for a while. Just to visit. We could catch up, do some shopping, eat? My gulab jaman isn't as good as Ammi's, but it's not bad." Nadia sounded so hopeful. As if the past decades hadn't happened. As if we could pick right back up and be sisters. "And I've got a letter for you from Ammi, from before she died. I wanted to give it to you in person."

I closed my eyes to try to stop the tears that were flowing. "I need some more time to figure out what's going on." I had to process this. I had to understand who and what Baba was, and if he was dangerous to my loved ones. I didn't want anyone to get hurt or injured because I was near them. My entire worldview had just been flipped on its head.

"Okay. Is Zabir helping with this?"

"He thinks the exorcism wasn't complete. That it put a wall up around . . . Baba." That was so strange to say. "And that after Ammi died, the wall came down. And then all of these things started happening, and . . . I'm sorry, it's just not safe for you if I come. But once it is, I will. I promise. I started saying her prayer, but I don't think it's enough. I have to go. I'll call you again, soon. And, uh, thank you."

I wiped my face, then splashed water on it. I'd always had so much anger about my mom and my sister, and it turned out they were trying their best. I was the problem. Just like I was causing issues for Liz now. Maybe I needed to get away from everyone for their own safety.

———

It took me a while to pull myself together and go talk to Liz. I had to apologize. Though I thought it was over the top to keep busting out the Ouija board.

I went downstairs but couldn't find her. "Liz?"

Nothing.

I texted her.

In the barn working out, wanna come here?

I didn't want to go outside for fear of what I'd see. But I had to talk to Liz. I hiked over to her.

The door was closed, but it rolled open easily.

"Hey!" I said.

"Hi! Come in! This is my special place," she said proudly. It was part art studio, part workout area, part junk storage. I walked in circles taking it all in. The artwork was familiar, but I wasn't sure why. It was a nice space, if a bit raw still.

"Listen, I'm sorry I freaked out on you. Things have just been so jumbled in my head. I appreciate you so much and everything you've done for me."

"Awww, thank you." She was standing with a table behind her. "I'm sorry too."

"You have nothing to apologize for?"

"Oh, but I do." I heard a crack, saw lights in my head, and felt things move that shouldn't. And then I fell to the ground. Liz had hit me with a metal pipe. "I'm sorry I have to kill you."

Sixty

Transcript: *The Disappearance of Dunia Ahmed* **podcast**

AMANDA ROBERTS: Okay, so it seems like we're diving into things we admittedly know little about. The whole haunting-Dunia bit. So we asked Zabir to come talk to us about it so we can all figure this out together.

    DANIELLE MCGUIRE: Welcome, Zabir.

    AMANDA ROBERTS: What are your thoughts on Dunia's behavior? Was she haunted?

    ZABIR MIRZA: I don't know how to answer that in a sound bite. There are entities in our culture—and in African and Middle Eastern cultures—that Americans don't know much about. But nearly everyone I know from South Asia is a believer.

    AMANDA ROBERTS: This is what you call a jinn, right?

    ZABIR MIRZA: Right. And yes, I do think Dunia was haunted.

    DANIELLE MCGUIRE: I've heard of those. They're genies? I wouldn't mind one of those, to be honest!

    ZABIR MIRZA: They're not genies. I mean, yes, that's where the concept of genies came from, but there's no magic lamp. Jinn, in our folklore at least, are beings with free will. And they can say and do what they like. And Dunia's mother believed her daughter had one attached to her and that it was the reason Dunia's father died.

AMANDA ROBERTS: That's so heavy. What happened then?

ZABIR MIRZA: Her mother attempted to have her exorcised when she was five.

DANIELLE MCGUIRE: Holy shit. You said attempted—did it not work?

ZABIR MIRZA: I had a theory that the ritual performed was a temporary one. And that after Dunia's mother died, there was nothing stopping the jinn. If you look at Dunia's life then, the sleepwalking started up again right after her mother passed.

AMANDA ROBERTS: So because she was sleepwalking, you think she was haunted?

DANIELLE MCGUIRE: This is a little too woo for me.

AMANDA ROBERTS: Yeah. Say you're right. What was this being's involvement with her? I don't get it?

Zabir: I'd say I need permission for this story, but her mother is gone, and Dunia is . . . well, the story we pieced together—Nadia, Dunia, and I— was that her mother had made a deal with a jinn to have Dunia. She wasn't able to have more kids. And the catch was Dunia belonged to it, not her family. And once Skylar reached out to tell me about his hauntings, I started to think a jinn was around. At the time, I had no idea it had anything to do with Dunia.

AMANDA ROBERTS: So you think the jinn . . . killed Skylar?

ZABIR MIRZA: And Mary Ryans. And anyone who tried to hurt Dunia. I know it sounds far fetched, but I've seen this entity with my own eyes. I know it exists. And it very likely was with Dunia at Liz's house. This being, this entity, is very possessive over Dunia.

DANIELLE MCGUIRE: Was this thing a threat to Dunia?

ZABIR MIRZA: Very much. Because if she didn't want to go with it, then it could get mad and lash out. Hurt her. Hurt the people around her.

AMANDA ROBERTS: Can you recommend some books for us to read? Because this is a lot of info we had no clue about. We don't want to dismiss it just because it's foreign to us.

ZABIR MIRZA: Sure, I'll get you a list. I think part of what was happening was this entity coming for Dunia while at the same time she was dealing with human assailants. And frankly, that's a lot for one person to deal with.

AMANDA ROBERTS: She was so tortured. Ugh, I'm obsessed. And everyone, we'll post the list of reading materials, but make sure you also look at our shop. We have new "Find Dunia!" merch, from hats and tees to tote bags!

Sixty-One

Dunia, age five

After that day at the holy man's house, things got more normal. As normal as our house ever was. I stayed with Carol while Ammi worked and sometimes slept over. But I sleepwalked less.

Nadia still wouldn't talk to me. Ammi said she was just sad about Abu. But so was I.

Whenever Ammi had functions to go to, or anything with her friends, she took Nadia but left me with Carol. After that wedding, she said it was better. She said I scared everyone, so I had to stay back.

Carol made it fun, though. She taught me how to braid my hair, and we watched cartoons, and she helped me with my reading. She was my new best friend. I still missed Abu, though.

I started calling Carol Mom instead of Auntie. Because Carol was like my other mother. I loved her.

"Oh, honey, I don't think your mom would like you calling me that," she said. "Auntie is fine. But I love you like you were my own. You're a wonderful girl, you know that, right?"

I just nodded. No one wanted to be my parent. The only one who did had died.

One day Carol couldn't watch me, so Nadia had to stay with me.

"Nadi, do you hate me?" I asked her.

She looked at me. "I'm not sure. Mostly I don't want to be around you anymore."

It hurt. I ran to my room to cry. I wished Abu were with me. Or Baba, who'd also left me. I didn't know where. I asked Ammi, and she said he had to go back home. So he was in Pakistan while I was here, with no one who loved me.

I hadn't known what I did to deserve all this. Was I that bad? But I kept my head down and spent time with Carol and did my best to grow up like Abu wanted me to.

I was going to make him proud of me. I knew that. One day, I'd make him so proud he'd come down from heaven and tell me so. That was what I prayed for now. Not a kitten; I just wanted to make him happy.

I heard the lock on my door close, and I knew I was in for the night, even though I hadn't sleepwalked in a while. But it didn't matter. Ammi felt better when I was locked in. So I let her keep doing it.

Ammi was talking to Carol. We were next door, and she came to get me. They were having tea. Ammi was crying, and Carol was rubbing her back.

"It's okay, you'll be okay," Carol said.

"No, I won't. My entire community wants nothing to do with Dunia, and I need them to survive. I don't know what to do? How can I try to make it without help?"

"You have me. I'll help you. You can leave Dunia here for as long as you need, as often as you need. Do what you need to survive. It's not easy being a single parent. You need help."

I heard all this, and my heart hurt. I was making my mom so sad. I didn't know how to fix this. I didn't know how to make our lives better.

"I have to pretend I'm all better. Then everything will be fine," I whispered to myself.

Sixty-Two

I woke up to the sound of the peacocks yelling. The sound was so loud, so close by. I blinked. I was inside somewhere, lying on the ground. I could barely move my head. If I tried, I got searing pain flashing behind my eyes.

"You're up!" Liz said.

I groaned and tried to sit up but couldn't.

"What's happening?" It came out garbled.

"Shoot, sorry I hit you so hard. But listen, I tried drugging you, and you just take it all. You do weird shit, but that's it. I gave you so much Ambien, and you kept running around like a little mouse." She laughed before peering into my face. "Time to wake up."

I couldn't move anything more than my eyes. I looked at her with confusion.

"What's going on? Why . . . ?" My eyes were blurry. I looked at one of the paintings on the wall to focus. I knew that art. Was it . . . "Skylar," I whispered.

"His art. He was the one who helped me redo the house. It's why this had to happen here. You get it, right? Why I have to do this?" Liz said.

"Why?" I couldn't think straight. My thoughts were too jumbled.

"He's dead because of you. He only took that job because my family cut me off. He never wanted to hurt anyone. He had no choice."

I groaned again and tried to sit up. I fell over. I blinked at her. What was she even talking about? Was this some sleepover game I didn't know about?

"I want you to know that I really grew to care for you. I did. You're such a good friend. So I'm sorry, but he said I had to do this."

I tried to make my mouth move. I managed the shape of the word but not the word itself. I was going for "Who?" I whispered it. I couldn't get my brain to work.

"Skylar. He told me on the board. He said I had to finish what he started. He's here with us now, can't you tell?"

I stared at her. It was Liz, my Liz. But she'd completely lost her mind. It wasn't me who was crazy, it was her. "Liz, no one is here with us. Enough of this creepy stuff. Let's go to the house." I tried to get up, but the room kept spinning.

"D, you're the one being crazy. Don't you see? Once you die, everything is good again. I'll finish his job. And he can rest, then."

My brain wasn't processing. Bea? She was Bea? "You're Liz," I managed to say. Who was this woman standing above me with such a cold face? Not my friend. My friend was warm and loving. I couldn't grasp what she was saying. *Brain, work. Please work.*

By now I was an expert at being attacked. At being maimed. But I wasn't so good at the betrayal. Liz? My Liz? She wanted me dead? My friend who had gotten me through so much.

My lizard brain seemed to grasp things before my conscious one did. *Get up and run,* it whispered inside my head. My fingers could move; that was a start. I had to sit up. But before I could try, Liz took her foot and stepped on my fingers. I screamed from the pain as she ground her heel into my bones.

"Fingers are very painful to break, did you know that?" She grinned. It was an ugly smile, full of hatred and fury. I whimpered, and I hated myself for that. She stepped on my other hand next. "So they match!" This wasn't the Liz I knew and loved.

The pain made me retch. Once she stepped off my fingers, I managed to turn over and vomit. I couldn't get my brain to think at all. It was full of searing and blinding pain from where she had hit me. My previous concussion was worse now. Cataloging my injuries kept me calm somehow. For some reason the story of the churail with crooked fingers came to my mind.

"You're Bea," I said. Thinking was a struggle.

"Yes. He called me so many names. I wish you'd met him before all of this. You two would have loved each other." Who was this woman standing here, looking like Liz but not her? It couldn't be her? "Skylar told me to do this. He said I had to. I know we're besties, but true love conquers all."

I blinked. She was going to kill me. Liz—who had been there for me even as my life descended into madness—was going to kill me.

Liz was Skylar's girlfriend. The one the police couldn't find. My brain was catching up to reality, slowly. I closed my eyes and tried to move, but my fingers throbbed. I had to do something. I couldn't just lie here and die. I had to fight, if only my body would listen to me.

It took several tries, but I managed to sit upright without the room spinning. The pain from my fingers made me want to vomit again.

What was it that Terry had said? Fight dirty. Be loud. I had to do that. I had to try. My face was wet from tears. I was mad at myself for crying, but I was so tired and in so much pain.

"Why didn't you tell me who you were?" I asked, the words feeling foreign in my mouth.

"You're the reason he's dead."

She stepped closer to me.

"I didn't let him die! I had no idea. Honestly, if I had, I'd have done something to help!" I was desperate to get her to stop. I bent my legs and pushed up, my thighs straining as I tried to get up without using my broken fingers.

There were no bystanders here to help me. I was on my own. This was how I was finally going to die.

Liz was practically dancing in glee. The person I knew—my friend—was gone. This nutjob was in her place. I wanted this to be over. I was so tired. How much could one person endure?

"Can you just kill me and get it over with?" That made her laugh.

"No." It was simple and solemn. Not the bubbly Liz I knew.

If I died, this would be over. Maybe that was a good thing? But no, my need to survive reared up. I had to do something. I looked around for anything to fight her with. Not that my hands or limbs were really working.

"Fight her," a voice said to me. I knew that voice. I'd heard it in the forest, in my head. I listened to it. *Keep going.* I looked at my poor hands, the fingers bent and purple. I had to run. I had to get away from here. From this thing that looked like Liz but wasn't her. I refused to believe this was my friend. This was a monster I'd somehow summoned.

I stumbled to my feet, took a step forward, and fell.

It was then I realized she had a knife in her hand. A phone rang—my phone.

"Oh, hoping this will help you? It won't. It's creepy Zabir. That asshole. I was sure he knew who I was. That Skylar had told him about me. I tried to get you to stop seeing him, but no, poor Dunia needed help." She hit silence and grinned before smashing it on the floor. The screen—already broken—shattered. "Shall we do this already?"

She lunged at me. I should have sidestepped her, but my vertigo was so bad I couldn't do much. I needed to fight, but my body was giving up on me. I felt the searing pain I was now all too familiar with. She had plunged the knife deep into my abdomen. I couldn't breathe. I fell forward, landing on my hands. This was the cut that would kill me, I was sure of it.

"Aww, did Dunia get another owie?" She stepped toward me, ready to finish things off.

I knew that pulling out a knife meant blood loss. It meant death. But I had no choice. I had no other weapon. It was the only thing I could think to do. I yanked out the knife, grunting from the pain. My entire side was on fire. She'd torn where I'd been stitched. I would bleed out in minutes.

I waved the knife like a sword, slashing her on her arms and hands. "You bitch!"

She tried to take it from me while I stumbled. I was light headed; I was losing so much blood. I fell forward.

"You may kill me, but I won't go without a fight," I hissed. But it was a lie. I was already dying. I needed to get up before she finished the job, but part of me wondered what the point was.

I heard Liz scream, and I turned my head. She was being wrapped in something that looked like smoke. I blinked. Walking smoke. It was here. He was here.

"Not real," I muttered.

"I'm real," the smoke said back. I was losing blood. This couldn't be happening. "You need to run."

I had to move. I had to get help. I didn't know how, but I would have to save myself.

"You have to run. Go now. I can only hold her for so long." I'd have to marvel at that later. Right now, I needed to get moving. I grunted and stumbled out of the barn. I couldn't figure out which direction to go. My head was too foggy. I fell to the ground.

The peacocks made more noise. "Run to them," the voice said. I did as it commanded. I slowly managed to get to my feet, every inch of me in searing pain. I wanted to cry; I wanted to throw up. "Get moving."

I crawled as best I could toward the peacocks. I could hear them. I could get to them. I'd be safe. It took what felt like hours. I didn't know if that was how much time had passed. I didn't know anything, except that I was going to die if I didn't get to help. The peacocks had a human. They could help me.

The dirt and mud caked my hands. "Keep going, you're almost there." I grunted; I could do this. I was almost about to pass out when I saw it. A peacock. It was beautiful and blue and green. It stared at me with curiosity. It wasn't afraid. It was like a vision.

There was someone with it. I fell onto my back and stared up. I tried to get them in focus. Who was it? I had to know.

Finally, my eyes made them out. It couldn't be. It just couldn't.

"Baba?"

"She's over here!" someone yelled in the distance.

——

So much noise. I couldn't open my eyes. Baba was with me, holding my hand.

"Almost, beti. Almost," he said, squeezing my hand. I held on with all I had, but I knew it wasn't enough.

I was so tired.

"You can come with me now."

I shook my head, each movement making me want to throw up.

——

I heard yelling close by. Really close by. I tried to look, but I was so tired. My body was broken; the ground was wet under me from my blood. I heard a scream. Then I heard Kendra. I thought I did, at least. I might have imagined it. I had no idea what was real except death.

Kendra was next to me then. Her mouth was moving.

I just stared at her. Was she real? Was I already dead?

"Help me with her!" she said to someone. I saw Zabir's face looming. His lashes were so long. I wanted to tell him I wished we'd met at a better time. That we could have tried to be more than friends. But I couldn't say anything.

They had to half carry, half drag me to Kendra's car. She locked the doors and turned the car on. I expected Liz to pop up like a zombie, ready to finish things.

"Where's Baba?" I mumbled.

"I don't know, honey, but you're okay." Kendra kept saying that. "Stay with me. Come on."

"Dunia, stay awake, come on," Zabir said, holding my hand in the back seat. "Don't close your eyes."

I tried. I tried so hard. But I was so tired, my body so broken. I couldn't keep my eyes open. Everything went dark for the second time that night. It was the closest thing to heaven I'd ever known.

Sixty-Three

Transcript: *The Disappearance of Dunia Ahmed* podcast

AMANDA ROBERTS: Are you all ready for the bigger reveal? We now know David was behind the first attack. But here's the real kicker: Liz Small was trying to murder Dunia.

DANIELLE MCGUIRE: She was Bea! She was Skylar's girlfriend! And no one knew! We have another twofer episode. We're starting with Liz Small, who has been in a psychiatric facility since she was arrested for attempted murder. She's been conducting her interviews over the phone. Liz, how are you today?

LIZ SMALL: I'm okay.

AMANDA ROBERTS: So, let's start with the first question: Were you Skylar Jones's girlfriend?

LIZ SMALL: We were going to get married. After he finished with Dunia. We'd have enough.

DANIELLE MCGUIRE: We'll take that as a yes.

AMANDA ROBERTS: Why did you wait so long to go after Dunia? Why drag it out?

LIZ SMALL: She was my friend! I loved her.

AMANDA ROBERTS: You tried to kill her. Did you drug her? I read in a report that Dunia had high levels of sleeping pills in her system. Which would have made her sleepwalk more and maybe hallucinate.

DANIELLE MCGUIRE: That makes so much more sense than a haunting. Everything she saw was possibly a hallucination.

LIZ SMALL: I had to do it. I had to. She was why Skylar died. I didn't want any of this, but that moment, I had no choice. Skylar said I had to do it. Nobody but Dunia was supposed to die. This is all her fault.

AMANDA ROBERTS: I want to remind our listeners that Liz is under the care of psychiatrists right now. When you say Skylar said to, was it when you used the Ouija board?

LIZ SMALL: I love my board. They won't let me have one in here. Can you bring me one? Then you can talk to Skylar yourself.

DANIELLE MCGUIRE: Liz, what happened when you attacked Dunia? How did she get away?

LIZ SMALL: He came for her.

AMANDA ROBERTS: Skylar?

LIZ SMALL: No, the demon that she had. He came. He stopped me. He would have killed me, but he had to go to Dunia.

DANIELLE MCGUIRE: So you believe that her jinn stopped you from killing her.

LIZ SMALL: He's coming for us. For all of us. Until he finds her, we're all dead. He's coming! He's coming! He's going to kill us all! He's tried to get me, but I'm in here, I'm safe. But he'll kill us all. You're going to be next.

AMANDA ROBERTS: Whoa, okay, well, that was all we got out of that interview before her medical team intervened. So let's now shift gears and talk to Detective Alvarez. What the hell happened?

DETECTIVE ALVAREZ: This case was . . . I've never worked anything this insane before. Liz Small went by the name Bea while dating Skylar Jones. Her family had cut her off for dating him, and in an attempt to make money fast, he agreed to murder Dunia.

AMANDA ROBERTS: Big reveal time! Cue the flashing lights! Why didn't you look into her when this all started?

DETECTIVE ALVAREZ: Because Dunia hadn't met her when she was attacked. She wasn't on our radar at all. She was someone who came into her life after Skylar died. And to be honest, her family has enough connections that instead of being in prison, she's in a hospital.

AMANDA ROBERTS: So, because of David, Skylar died, and this set off a series of events that nearly killed Dunia? If Skylar hadn't died, Liz would never have tried to murder Dunia. Was she the one in the hit-and-run?

DETECTIVE ALVAREZ: We believe so. As you know, Liz's mental state is not conducive to getting the facts right now. We occasionally get some factual answers from her we can verify, but often we can't.

AMANDA ROBERTS: She's locked up in an institution and is unfit to stand trial. Why is she being treated so well?

DETECTIVE ALVAREZ: Her family has deep pockets, and connections. We've been digging through every bit of info, but it's not an easy feat when her family's lawyers have been fighting us tooth and nail. At this moment we know she paid Mary Ryans to attack Dunia at Aphrodite. We haven't linked her to the hit-and-run, but she's our main suspect. There were no prints on the stolen car when we found it.

AMANDA ROBERTS: Listeners, this tale has more twists and turns than a maze. And the story isn't over yet, oh no. Because Dunia is still missing, and no one has confessed to that crime yet. Not one person, is that right?

DETECTIVE ALVAREZ: No. I do think Liz knows where she is, but we can't get coherent statements out of her. At this point, it's anyone's guess what happened to Dunia or where she is. If it were me in her shoes, and so many people close to me had attempted to kill me, I'd possibly go into hiding.

DANIELLE MCGUIRE: You think she took off and pulled a disappearing act?

DETECTIVE ALVAREZ: It's possible. I see no evidence to the contrary at this point, knowing what we know. Unless Liz somehow got to her in the hospital, which doesn't seem possible to me.

DANIELLE MCGUIRE: I'm sorry, but I can't believe this is the end for Dunia. After everything, she just, what, vanishes? I need more answers. I need closure!

AMANDA ROBERTS: Maybe her jinn took her.

DANIELLE MCGUIRE: I have a question. Did Liz send her those creepy letters she'd get?

DETECTIVE ALVAREZ: No, and we didn't find out who did until we got access to the cameras that Liz installed in Dunia's apartment. The person who wrote those notes was Dunia, while asleep. I don't know what it means, I don't know if she realized it, but they were all from her.

AMANDA ROBERTS: Okay, whoa. Just whoa. I wonder what else Dunia did that she thought other people had done.

Sixty-Four

Dunia, age five

"Abu-ji, how did the jinn get the princess to stay with him?"

"He tricked her. She had to agree to it. See, jinn can't just hold you like that. They can take you, they can hurt you, but to keep you in their world? You have to be willing. Never agree to that." He was strangely serious. I didn't get it; usually he wasn't.

"Okay, I won't agree to it," I said, smiling. See? I was a good girl.

Sixty-Five

I didn't die. Not quite. I lost enough blood that they had to revive me a few times. I had so many transfusions. But technically, I was alive. They were sure I had a traumatic brain injury as well. And five broken fingers. Plus the stab wound. My catalog of injuries was growing.

I kept passing out and dreaming about Baba. In my dream he told me what Nadia and Zabir said was true. But that he was trying to help me. Save me. That I belonged to him; my mother had promised him that.

"I hurt the ones who hurt you," he said. As if it were that simple.

"But you killed Abu?"

"He tried to separate us. You're my family. We belong together. Anyone who gets in the way has to go."

I wanted to rage against him. But I didn't. He was Baba, one of the only kind beings in my life. He had loved me, and I loved him. Once.

"No more hurting people," I said.

"You don't get to tell me what to do. I'll kill anyone I have to." He leaned over me. "Anyone, including Nadia and Kendra. And that Zabir." He said his name as if it were distasteful.

"Leave them alone," I whispered.

"Only if you come with me."

I waved him away; it was the most I could do. I couldn't go with him. He was the reason I didn't have my father anymore. I couldn't forgive that.

Baba and I might have been family, but family sucked.

———

"There she is." The doctor flashed a light into each eye. "Your vitals are stable. You're going to be okay." I just stared, not sure what was happening anymore.

"Kendra," I croaked out.

"Your friend who brought you in? She's talking to the police. You need to rest now."

I blinked, and when I reopened my eyes, Zabir was there. It was like moments of lucidity followed by sweet darkness.

"You found me," I said.

"Of course I did. Are you okay?"

"Never better," I rasped.

"You scared me. I thought we lost you." He couldn't hold my hands because the fingers were wrapped.

"You need to let me die," I said. "It's the only way to keep Baba away. He told me he was coming. He was there. He stopped Liz. He's going to kill everyone. There was smoke."

The exertion of saying all that made me pass out. But I'd told him what he needed to know. The rest could wait until whatever afterlife awaited us.

In my dreams I saw my mother. She looked so sad. She reached for me.

"Ammi, I'm sorry. I didn't know what was happening."

"It's okay, just know I loved you. I tried to make things right. I tried. I didn't know how to fix my mistake."

I hugged her. I had missed her so much, even if I'd thought she'd hated me.

"Dunia, Baba isn't your friend. I know he seems like he is. Be careful. I'm sorry, I'm so sorry. This was my fault. I wanted another baby after Nadia, and I couldn't have one. And I went to a healer in Pakistan, and they said they could help me, but at a price. Baba was the price. He'll never stop coming for you. Do you understand? He will kill everyone you love. He'll make you all alone in this world. You have to stay away from him."

She told me everything, this dream mother. I didn't know if she was real or a figment of my imagination. But she told me all about what Baba threatened her with. How he showed her images of dead Nadia. How he taunted my mother. I wasn't the only one haunted, which I'd never realized. The tricks he played on her that I found funny as a child were horrifying as an adult.

"You have to do what I tell you. It's your only way."

And then she did something she hadn't done in so long. She stroked my hair. It was such a small thing, but her warm hand felt so real. My mother loved me; I knew this much.

———

When I woke up in the hospital, the lights were so bright I thought I'd died. But then I felt the pain. My fingers were throbbing; my side still burned. Tubes connected me to machines. I blinked. Zabir was sitting next to me, his head down.

I tried to speak, but my mouth was so dry. I rasped out, "Zabir?" He glanced up, and his face lit up.

"You're awake. Let me get the nurse—"

"Wait," I whispered. "I know what we need to do."

He waited for me to speak again.

"My mother told me everything," I said. He didn't question me. He didn't ask how that was possible. I was grateful for that. He believed me.

"She said to find the holy man who did the prayers. And that until you do, you have to keep Baba at bay. She said it was in your books. And I need a few things from you."

She'd told me to run. Run and hide while Zabir found what I needed to fight Baba. If I didn't, he'd go after everyone. But we could stop him. We could protect my loved ones.

I wasn't a victim. I was a survivor. And I would fight dirty.

When darkness hit, when fewer people were around, I changed into clean clothes Zabir had brought me. He helped unhook me from machines. I slowly walked out of the hospital. I wanted to stop and see if Kendra was around, but I knew if I saw her, I wouldn't be brave enough to do what needed to be done.

Baba had killed my dad. And Jamal and Ayesha Auntie. He'd gone after Skylar and that woman at Aphrodite. And Liz—who I wasn't sure was still alive. I felt nothing either way about her right now. Anyone could be next. I couldn't stay here. I had to leave. It was the only way to save the people I loved.

Sixty-Six

Transcript: *The Disappearance of Dunia Ahmed* **podcast**

AMANDA ROBERTS: Nadia, we wanted to reach out now that we have some closure on the attempted murders. How do you feel about things?

NADIA CHAUDRY: Like I want to find my sister.

DANIELLE MCGUIRE: We're with you. We want to find Dunia too.

NADIA CHAUDRY: If it's okay, I have a letter for her from my mom. I wanted to give it to Dunia in person, but . . .

AMANDA ROBERTS: Sure, please, go right ahead.

NADIA CHAUDRY: Thank you. "Dunia, my dear daughter. There was so much I wanted you to know, but I never knew how to say it. I love you more than I'll ever be able to put into words. I'm sorry I brought this into our lives. All I wanted was you, and then I couldn't keep you. I did what was necessary to keep you alive. To keep you safe. I hope one day you look back and realize you were loved, so deeply loved. I will never stop trying to help you, even in death."

AMANDA ROBERTS: Wow, that's beautiful—

DANIELLE MCGUIRE: That's it? I'm sorry, but no apologies? No "sorry I blamed your father's death on you, sorry I had you exorcised"? I cannot.

Nadia: Excuse me?

AMANDA ROBERTS: What Danielle means is that more needs to be said. And more evidence found so we find your sister. Which is why we're thrilled to share that our little podcast will now be a documentary on Netflix: *Finding Dunia*!

DANIELLE MCGUIRE: Knowing everything we know now, we're going to turn over every single angle until we find your sister. So get ready, everyone. It's streaming time!

AMANDA ROBERTS: I knew this case would launch us to stardom, but wow. Just wow. And we have another twofer, because Kendra Wright talked to us about that horrible trip to the Catskills. Welcome, Kendra.

KENDRA WRIGHT: I want to say for the record I had no idea who Liz Small was. She fooled all of us.

DANIELLE MCGUIRE: You said before you feel guilty for this.

KENDRA WRIGHT: I do. I wish I'd never introduced them.

AMANDA ROBERTS: But Liz sought you out because of Dunia. She would have found a way to her. Don't let it eat at you.

KENDRA WRIGHT: I realized after we got Dunia to the hospital that I didn't have the correct number for her in my phone. It was close, but not the same. I'm guessing it was the same on Dunia's phone.

DANIELLE MCGUIRE: You think Liz did that to separate you two?

KENDRA WRIGHT: I do. I keep playing everything over in my head trying to figure this out, figure out how we didn't know. Liz is just that good at hiding things.

AMANDA ROBERTS: She is. We'll be digging into that and more on our new Netflix show!

KENDRA WRIGHT: Or you could leave Dunia alone. I don't know. If she's alive, she doesn't want to be found.

DANIELLE MCGUIRE: How can you say that? She's your best friend! Don't you want answers?

KENDRA WRIGHT: I just want her to find some peace.

Sixty-Seven

Present day

From AP News:

Popular True Crime Podcaster Found Dead, Partner Missing

In a shocking twist to a story that had millions enthralled, podcaster Amanda Roberts was found dead on Tuesday. She was investigating the disappearance of Dunia Ahmed, who, after surviving several attempts on her life, vanished without a trace.

Her podcasting partner, Danielle McGuire, is missing and considered a person of interest. Liz Small, the daughter of venture capitalist Sam Small, told officials she knew who was behind it.

"He's coming for all of us if he can't have Dunia. You'll see, we're all going to die." It should be noted that Ms. Small is undergoing psychiatric treatment for her part in the attacks on Ms. Ahmed.

The cause of death has not been released, but sources close to the case say Roberts left a note saying she had to die for what she did to Dunia and that anyone standing in the way would go next. The podcast had recently been optioned by Netflix, but the deal is now on hold, per a Netflix spokesperson.

Police are asking for anyone's help in this case.

Sixty-Eight

They weren't going to find me.

I turned the podcast off. It was surreal to listen to your own life become entertainment fodder. I guessed that was the best anyone could hope for in this life. That people found you to be interesting enough to make a podcast about you. That your death was so interesting, white women wanted to make money off you.

I wasn't dead. I wasn't alive. I was here. Which was more than I could say for the women on that podcast. I knew Baba had gotten to them. He'd left a trail of human debris in his wake. It was a reminder that he was going to find me if I let him.

I'd run. I know, it was a coward's way out. But if almost everyone you loved and trusted tried to murder you, what would you do? If no one could find me, then I was safe. That included Baba.

How could anyone avoid something that wasn't human? The same way my mom had kept him at bay.

My mother had told me everything in my dreams, in the letter Nadia read. The price for me existing was Baba, and no way could I ever survive with him after everything. I wanted my life, not some prison with a jinn. Believe in them or don't: jinn didn't care. They were still here. With us. Haunting us. Hunting me. I hadn't believed, and he'd still come for me.

Zabir, that day in the hospital, had brought me my talisman and the prayer written out. He was trying to find a way to put that wall back up. My mother said the secret was hidden in one of his books. So far, he hadn't found it. But Zabir had found ways to trip Baba up. To temporarily hide me, and himself, Kendra, and Nadia, from Baba's sight. Everyone had to be hidden. I didn't trust the rituals to keep me safe, so I stayed physically hidden as well. Away from everyone. Because I trusted no one enough to be near them, except Zabir. Any person could try to kill me again.

Zabir kept looking for the holy men from my youth. I worried he wouldn't be careful, but he said we were okay for now. A Band-Aid fix, he called it. He didn't go into details, and truthfully, I didn't want to know. I just kept moving, kept hiding.

It might seem crazy to go on the run after all this, but if Baba killed Kendra or Nadia, or hurt them, I didn't know what I'd do. I couldn't risk their lives. I'd already done so much damage to them both. Was I insane? Perhaps. I'd had enough bumps to my brain to say my sanity wasn't what it once had been. But I had to save the people I loved. And that meant vanishing for everyone's safety.

And for my own sense of security, I had to stay away. Too many people had wanted me dead. I didn't know if anyone else did. The list of who I could trust was very short.

Zabir knew where I was. Or when I moved on to a new place. He helped me with money and supplies. He was the only one I felt safe talking to. If anyone came after him, human or otherwise, he could handle it. He had his protections in place.

"You look annoyed," he said.

"The podcast. It's ridiculous. Why'd you go on it?"

"Because it seemed suspicious if I didn't. But I got you this." He grinned at me. He was holding a tote bag with my face on it. It said, *Find Dunia!*

"Seriously?" I laughed. It was so absurd.

He was right, though. He had to act like he didn't know where I was. "How's Kendra?"

"I gave her your latest note."

I'd send her little missives now and then so she knew I was okay. I couldn't explain to her what had happened. I didn't want to risk Baba going after her just in case. So instead, Zabir mailed her my letters or postcards from random places. I missed her. I missed her so much it hurt almost as much as my injuries had. I wanted to tell her I was okay and where I was, but Zabir pointed out if she knew where I was and didn't tell the police, her entire brand would fall. People would hate her. I couldn't do that to Kendra. I didn't want to be found.

My sides still ached from the many times I'd been stabbed. Truthfully, once was enough. I don't recommend it. My fingers never healed right. They were crooked, just like in my dad's old stories. I had become the churail of legend, running around the world at night.

Liz was locked up, so at least she couldn't hurt anyone else. I wasn't mad at her. I should have been. I felt sorry for her. I hoped she got better, but I knew if she did, Baba would go after her. From what I read in the papers, she was in an institution, babbling on about Skylar and demons and Ouija boards. His death had made her snap. Or maybe she was always crazy.

"I've missed you," I said to Zabir. We couldn't see each other too frequently. And I emailed him from fake accounts, texted from burner phones. Like I was in witness protection. How did you hide from a force you couldn't see? I didn't know when or where Baba would show up. What the extent of his abilities were.

"I missed you. Are you okay?" He looked exhausted. This was taking a toll on him.

"You can stop if you need to." I stroked his face. "You don't have to keep helping me."

"I do. I need you to be safe. I'm sorry it's taking so long, but I found the wife of the man who prayed over you. Her husband and brother-in-law both died. She remembers you. She's letting me read her husband's journals. We're close, I know it. This will be over soon." I must have made a face. "Have I been wrong yet? No. We can do this."

"And then we can live happily ever after." I smiled. It was a fool's dream, but I still dreamed it. I needed something to hold on to. One day, I'd be free from this curse, this nazar, and I'd be able to be with Zabir and see Kendra, maybe even visit Nadia. I'd be able to live my life again.

"Yes, we will." His voice was hoarse. We sat there until he had to leave. "We will be okay. I swear it. I'll never stop until you can live safely."

"And then what? How do I go back to a normal life after this?"

"I don't know, but I'll be there to help you." He held my hand. "Two black sheep together."

"Two black sheep," I repeated. It was corny, but we had each other.

Part of me felt like giving in. I didn't tell him that. But then I got angry. My life had fallen apart because of Baba. Because of David. And Skylar and Liz. I was sick of others having a say in how my life was going. It was my turn to decide what happened next. And I was determined to get my life back.

In the hours alone, with no one to talk to, I spoke to my mother. I didn't know if she heard me. But I finally understood why she'd done what she had. She'd tried to save us; she'd had to make hard choices. I never got that before. It was like Zabir had said: he forgave his parents for being human.

Sometimes I still didn't know what was real anymore. I understood more than before, but I also needed to hold my sanity close. And my stun gun. But I knew Baba was real.

I touched my blue evil eye tasbeeh. It was the one my dad had given me. Zabir had it restrung. He thought it was a stronger talisman than his, and maybe he was right.

I believed in Zabir. If anyone could save me, if anyone could keep Baba at bay, it was him. And if he couldn't, well, I had me. I believed in me. And I would do anything to keep my people safe. I'd even fight dirty.

ACKNOWLEDGMENTS

When I was four years old, my whole family watched *The Exorcist.* The full pea-soup-vomit, crab-walking horror in full glory. Naturally, baby Amina was terrified. Especially when my older brother—Omar—said it was based on a true story. The terror! My father—when he found out I was afraid of demons—said to me, "Don't worry, I know how to do an exorcism." He was being dead serious.

My love for all things spooky and scary was born then, with help from my dad and his stories about jinn. Jinn were our childhood lullabies; they were our ghost stories; they were haunting our grandparents' homes. Jinn were my dad's playmates as kids; they were part of our family. This book is an homage to them and to my dad, who never once thought it was too much for a young child (I turned out fine! Fine!).

Thank you to my incredible editor Megha Parekh at Thomas & Mercer for helping shape this story. Without your insight and guidance, I don't know where I'd be! Thank you to the one and only Mindy Kaling for seeing something in Dunia's story that spoke to you. Major gratitude to the entire Thomas & Mercer team—truly the best in the business. Huge love to my agent Chris Bucci, who encourages me to be as weird as I want. And to Katrina Escudero, my fabulous TV and film manager, for being absolutely incredible.

Thank you to my friends in book world who encouraged me and read terrible drafts—you're the best, Alex Segura, Kellye Garrett, and

Elizabeth Little. Thank you to Chantelle Osman, Kelly Ford, Miranda Burgess, Alex Hestoft, Caroline Kepnes, and so many more. Major thanks to Rabia Chaudry for her *Hidden Djinn* podcast series, which drove me into a pile of books for research.

Thank you to my family for watching terrifying movies with me, even if they're too scared to nowadays. To my brother—thanks for scaring me often. To Star, thank you for being so supportive. My cousins Zahra, Usmaan, Subia, and Shahab for entertaining my jinn questions. And of course, to Bean, who I'm positive can see dead people and things.

And finally, thank you to our family jinn, wherever you may be.

ABOUT THE AUTHOR

Photo © 2018 Orlando Pelagio

Amina Akhtar is a novelist and former fashion editor. Her satirical first novel, *#FashionVictim*, drew critical acclaim. *Kismet*, her second book, was set in the stunning and creepy world of wellness.

Akhtar has worked at *Vogue*, *Elle*, the *New York Times*, and *New York Magazine*, where she was the founding editor of the women's blog *The Cut*. She currently lives not too far from the Sedona vortices.

Almost Surely Dead is Akhtar's third novel.